The Yoder Outsiders

By James D. Yoder

Illustrations by Darla Zook

Copyright © 2006 by James D. Yoder

ISBN 0-7414-3026-6

Previously published by Faith and Life Press, Newton, Kansas, 1988.

Published by:

PUBLISHING.COM

1094 New DeHaven Street, Suite 100
West Conshohocken, PA 19428-2713
Info@buybooksontheweb.com
www.buybooksontheweb.com
Toll-free (877) BUY BOOK
Local Phone (610) 941-9999
Fax (610) 941-9959

Printed in the United States of America

Printed on Recycled Paper

Published March 2006

Dedicated to
Michael Lynn Yoder
and to the memory of
Angela Maria

May we be faithful and worthy to be called thy people. Send down thy power and make us thine.

-Noah Troyer, the Sleeping Preacher

1.

Great Uncle, the Sleeping Preacher

It was a late August afternoon in 1880. A south breeze stirred the leaves and rattled the dry cornstalks, bringing relief from the heat of midday. Seven-year-old Louella Yoder looked across the Iowa landscape from her own front porch. Here and there, the houses rose up perpendicular to the earth. Stark and plain, they dotted the hills and valleys of the Amish districts of Sharon and Lower Deercreek. As the sun, like a burnished wheel, swept toward the horizon, dust and haze softened the writhing contours of the summer landscape. White clouds melted at the edges in the blue sky and became tattered in the wind as it swept over the yellow-gold wheat stubble in the fields. There had been just enough rain to bring about a shimmering green over the pastures, farmyards, and roadsides.

Louella's heart beat with excitement as she thought ahead to the evening gathering where Uncle Noah Troyer would preach. Though she often grew weary of long Amish sermons, this evening's meeting would be different. Already she felt anxious and even a bit fearful.

Louella's father, Daniel, a deacon in the church, would often stand to read the German Bible or lead in prayer. But tonight, if it happened, and everybody hoped it would, Uncle Noah would surprise, startle, and admonish them, for he was known as the Celebrated Amishman or Sleeping Preacher. People hoped God would direct his actions. Surely, he would fall into his trance and again bring a special message to the Amish families who had settled here. Anyway, that's why the people had planned to gather.

Frank and John, Louella's brothers, climbed the limestone steps that led to the porch. Five-year-old Frank, who had reddish-blond hair, a deep summer tan and blue-green eyes, reached back to help three-year-old John up the steps.

"Flower, flower," said Baby John as he dragged a bright red, withered zinnia pulled from his mother's garden, stalk and all. "Mother might scold the boys," thought Louella, "but maybe not." The zinnias grew thick and heavy through two long rows of the carefully weeded, though somewhat depleted, August garden.

The fringed newspaper nailed to the top of the screen door swished to keep the flies away as they pulled it open and entered the huge country kitchen to be near their mama.

"*Daenke!*"

Fannie Yoder beamed, wiping the sweat from her forehead with her arm. Taking the wilted flower, she hastily broke off most of the stalk and placed the bedraggled zinnia in a green Ball jar that contained young, green cuttings. Other farmer's wives might be short with their children as supper time neared, but not Fannie Yoder. Ach, no! Though bearing children was painful, they were a delight ever afterward.

She swooped down, gracefully for a woman of her bulk, and planted kisses on the fat cheeks of both her sons.

Fannie had taken time to freshen up before getting over involved with making supper. She had changed from her drab and stained garden dress to a clean blue-gray homespun, severe in its plainness, with only metal hooks and eyes to close it at the waist and neck. With her jet-black hair neatly parted in the middle and drawn back into a tight bun, covered by her Amish prayer veil, ironed, neatly pleated, and tied under her chin, she was willing and ready to serve her family and her God. For that indeed was what she would be doing this evening. She and Daniel had talked about it far into the night while the bullfrogs croaked out in the pond and an occasional coyote howled at the moon.

"It just don't seem proper," said Fannie to her thirty-five-year-old farmer-deacon husband as they lay side by side on the wheat-straw mattress held high off the floor by the sturdy walnut bedstead. Fannie meant her brother Noah and the strange illness that seemed to have swept over him lately, especially this August. Daniel turned to her as the wind stirred through the south bedroom window, drifted over their bed and out the curtainless north window. He was a good man, her Daniel. His most redeeming quality was his kindness. Both the German Amish people and the outsiders, whom they sometimes called the English, loved Daniel. He was a skilled and nimble carpenter whose hands had helped raise half-a-dozen heavy-beamed barns from their stone foundations. People at the meeting every other Sunday were deeply moved by his soft-toned voice as he read from the German Scriptures, "Who shall ascend unto the hill of the Lord? Or who shall stand in his holy place? He that hath clean hands and a pure heart, who hath not lifted up his voice unto vanity nor sworn deceitfully. He shall receive the blessing of the Lord."

Daniel, too, was more than a little troubled by his brother-in-law Noah who, since last summer, seemed possessed by God. Or was it the devil?

"He'll be all right, Fannie," said Daniel as he patted the hand of his big-boned thirty-two-year-old wife whom he adored. They would pray about this strange matter. Yes, they would pray, both Daniel and his happy-dispositioned wife, who loved him and his three children. He pondered in his mind, searching.

"It does say, though, in Second Corinthians, 11: 14 'for Satan himself is transformed into an angel of light.' "

But, they both knew that, though strange as it was, Brother Noah was not devil possessed. Maybe the English doctor from Iowa City could be called in to help if Noah became worse in his affliction. Once the doctor had come to witness the strange event. To determine if the Sleeping Preacher was really in an unconscious state, he ran a silver pin, an inch-and-a-half deep, into his leg. Sleeping Noah had not flinched!

God seemed to be blessing Louella's Uncle Noah and his trim wife, Fran. Even the booklet, *Sermons Delivered by Noah Troyer, the Noted Amishman, While in an Unconscious State,* gave testimony to his faithfulness to the Lord and to the Amish church. The author of the booklet had written, "While he has never been a well man, he has always been ready for work and able to do as much as the average farmer. His present prosperous financial condition fully attests that he has been a sober, industrious man, and a successful tiller of the soil."

Deacon Yoder and his family sat around the round oak table as they ate their evening meal, served a bit early tonight. They needed extra time to take the long wooden benches out of the barn and place them in rows, two groups of benches, paralleling each other with an aisle between. The men and boys would sit on the right side, the women and girls on the left. After eating their supper of cold potato salad, boiled ham with garden lima beans, pickles, freshly baked bread, and crumb pie, Louella and Fannie would come out into the glowing August eventide and help him carry and place the benches.

They were quiet, hardly speaking at all, as they lined up the handmade benches east of the locust grove, so that the long shadows cast by the graceful, lacy trees would cool the air for the service. Looking down the road toward Joetown, to the west, Louella could already see tiny black objects moving and swaying on the road, amidst a trailing cloud of dust merging into the evening shade. Glancing to the right, far on the hillside where the fences were crowned with the deep-pink wild roses that she loved so much, she noticed three more horse-drawn buggies slowly sliding into the shadows in the small vale, lost for a moment from view.

Soon thirteen black buggies with teams of horses of various shades, browns, reds, and black were tied to the fence posts in the barn lot. The horses were stomping and giving out an occasional snort while at the same time brushing away the annoying flies.

The congregation was gathering. It would be slightly different tonight, however. Two of the English would be here. They were sent by the *Iowa City Republican* to sit in their Amish service and take down Uncle Noah's sermon, in rapid, odd-looking script, that is, if the Spirit saw fit to move Uncle Noah to preach.

During this harvest season, he had spoken every night for the past eleven evenings. Poor Aunt Fran was showing signs of weariness from worry and wonder over her husband's strange behavior and words. Like Mary, "she pondered them in her heart." First, he began to complain of severe headaches. This was followed by cramping and bloating of his stomach. Sometimes even his face became swollen and puffy. Unconsciousness rapidly came over him as he would lie on either his bed or the couch in the room. Who was she, Fran Troyer, that she should have to bear the burden of a husband with so wondrous an affliction. Already some of the Amish youth were acting strange around her sons. Who knew, maybe they would soon be shunned.

After falling into the deep sleep, Noah would reverently get up off of his couch or bed, then kneeling alongside, offer to God, in a voice of praise and supplication, a prayer of such beauty that she and the witnesses would be moved to tears. But it was wearing on her. Fran's hair was already touched with gray at the sides and front, which softened her face, above her severely styled plain dress.

After the prayer to God the Heavenly Father would come the long and loud sermon. Even though Noah would be speaking only to his family, wife and six children, and an occasional Amish neighbor family or two, who came so that she would not have to sit alone chilled by the strange ways of God moving among men, he would preach with a loud voice the sure decrees he heard from his God.

But, the behavior that worried them all the most was that he would depart from using German, the tongue they spoke in the daily visiting and exchanges with each other in their work and worship. The reporters had written of him: "He is a German by birth, had but limited education, uses the German language in his family, reads a German Bible, never attended any church other than the Amish church where all the services are in German-and yet his sermons are, as a rule, in English."

Maybe the Spirit of God was moving among these Amish Mennonites, jarring them by this strange visitation through their Brother Noah, trying to teach them that they must adapt and change in this rich land on the frontier.

Already they had endured too many strained and anguished moments over the growing need to modify their stern and orthodox rules. It usually fell two ways, the old against the young. Resist the new wherein evil may be lurking.

In a little more than two hours it would be dark. Streaks of red, mauve, and burnished gold intertwined with a bank of shadowcasting clouds on the western horizon, providing the perfect setting for their evening worship here by the locust trees. A few cicadas began their metallic, scraping songs. Louella sat with her Aunt Fran and cousin Sarah. Her father was standing to lead the assembled group, almost two hundred Amish folk, with a sprinkling, here and there of their English neighbors, including the two English reporters.

Uncle Noah, wearing his black, homespun and homemade wool plain suit with its high fitted collar, was reclining on the couch they had placed by the bishop and deacons on the men's side at the front right. His hands were folded over his chest. His head reclined to the left, eyes closed. He had already fallen into a deep sleep.

Because of the anxiousness and nervousness brought about by this peculiar situation, Brother Daniel began to lead the group of worshipers in one of their old songs of faith, sung from memory from the *Ausbund.* The song came from the hand of Felix Manz, the first martyr among their forebears who was drowned near the head of the Lake of Zurich in January of 1527 for refusing to give up his faith.

Daniel's voice led, mild-toned and steady: *I sing with exultation, all my heart delights in God, who brings salvation, frees from death' s dread might. I praise thee, Christ of heaven, who ever shall endure, who takes away my sorrow, keeps me safe and secure.*

Three more verses were sung in their German tongue, men, women, children, all singing in plainsong, a mode so old and yet so beautiful that the mood was set for silence, for wonder, and for worship.

While they were singing the last verse of the hymn, the Sleeping Preacher uttered a low moan. Eyes still closed, he sat up, drew his legs to the side of the couch. Then, reverently kneeling with his head bowed and hands extended heavenward, he began to pray. He prayed in English, loud and clear. Silence swept over the assembly.

They strained both to see and to hear God speaking to them through this sleeping, unconscious man.

Reverently, he prayed: "Lord God Almighty, our Heavenly Father, in our weakness we come to thee. Thou hast promised to be a present help to those who come to thee. I am weak and speak only as the Lord Almighty gives me power."

Baby John began to whimper softly, as he sensed the charged air of the meeting. Louella drew him to her lap, buried his head under her chin to comfort him. His whimpering stopped.

"Lord have mercy upon those who are going on in their sinful work," intoned the stricken man.

"May we be faithful and be worthy to be called thy people. Send down thy power and make us thine. The Lord taught his servants to pray: 'Our Father which art in heaven, hallowed be thy name, thy kingdom come, thy will be done on earth as it is in heaven, give us this day our daily bread and forgive us our debts as we forgive our debtors, and lead us not into temptation, but deliver us from evil, for thine is the kingdom and power and glory forever, Amen.' "

Slowly but surely, the Sleeping Preacher eased up from his praying position to stand before the gathered brothers and sisters. His arms swept toward them, opening to a gracious, imploring gesture.

"Dear friends," he began the sermon, unaware of what he was doing. "Can't you see the great work of the Almighty in the creation of the world? How all things were created in the power of God? God is the great power. He created the earth, the heavens and things therein. He did all this powerful work in six days and rested upon the seventh. He commanded us to keep it holy but we are standing against his commandments in many ways. We are not all right."

Sounds of nervous clearing of throats were heard near the front of the men's side. Were they going to be called to repentance? By and large they were wholesome folk, though occasionally a brother was aided through the chilling blasts of winter by the warming nip of schnapps. All the folk knew that Grandma Annie Swartzentruber made the best dandelion wine, even outdoing the Lutherans. Now was this strange, God-possessed preacher going to castigate them?

The mystic Amishman, deep in his trance, lifted his muscular arms imploringly, pleaded to his audience for their response of obedience. "Our Savior Jesus gave us commandments that are for our salvation. Open your hearts to his voice so that we may be with him forever."

The entire audience was swept into the trance by the seeming miraculous power overshadowing them.

Little Frank Yoder edged closer to his father, who sat expectantly, awaiting the word of God from this prophet brother-in-law. A locust zoomed from one tree to another. One could hear the tinkle of cowbells and the low bleating of sheep in the south pasture. The wind of God swept over the crowd and through their brother Noah as his sermon unfolded from unconscious depths. With eager ears, they received the message of healing and salvation, as Noah's gentle voice focused upon the young Christ in the temple. They were beckoned to "be found in the temple, seeking the understanding of the Lord and his righteousness."

A farm wagon, drawn by heavy, prancing, bronze-colored horses lumbered by. Above the banks of the dirt road, the straw hat and shoulders of the Lutheran farmer and the backs of his horses were visible. The man turned, looked back upon the gathering, wondering as he heard the strange intonations of the Sleeping Preacher.

"When Christ was asked, who was the greatest in the kingdom of heaven, he called a little child before him and said: 'Except you become as a little child you can in no wise enter the kingdom of heaven.' If we continue our quarreling, we cannot be right. We must come under his commandments. If we do not, we are not on that road. And if we are not on that road, we can never be in that heavenly home."

Indeed, there had been some quarreling among them. At least, some differences regarding their customs and codes of dress. Little did these listeners know that soon there would be a break. A swarm would leave the Old Order to form the Union and later East Union Church.

Preacher Noah still had not opened his eyes. The reporters on the front bench were taking down his words with great speed. They were astonished at what appeared to indeed be a miracle among the Amish. Turning to one side of the group and with graceful gestures, the preacher continued.

"The time is coming when God will appear in the clouds and his angel will call with a loud voice. When Christ with Mary and Martha came to the grave of Lazarus, he called in a loud voice and Lazarus came forth. So he will call with a loud voice for all of us and if we are not known to him, he will say, 'Depart from me.' You may think me rough, dear friends. Yes, there may not be one person within the sound of my voice. I know not. It matters not. I speak as God gives me power, and I cannot help it."

With tears streaming down his ruddy cheeks into his graying

beard, Noah lifted his arms again in his passion for their souls.

"Dear young people, dear young souls, I have a great love for you. Come and live as did your Savior. Dear old people, some of you may be very near the grave. Let not your hearts be fearful or troubled, for the grave will open the door to your heavenly home. Where do you stand?"

The rosy-mauve glow of twilight had softly crept over the crowd. Soon it would be dark. The earth smells of the barnyard mixed with the fragrance of the roses on the fence reminded them of their ties to heaven and earth. Among the young people, there was a sudden palpitation of hearts, quickened by the preacher's words, his encouragement, the love in his voice as he called them to Christ.

He was drawing to a close. Soon the divine revelation through their brother would be over.

"I cannot be with you always, dear friends. I may appear again soon. I do the will of God, not my will. He taught us to pray." With pleading voice, the mystic Amishman led them through the perfect prayer Jesus taught his disciples to pray.

His hands fell to his sides from their gesture of imploring and supplication. Limply, he sagged toward the ground, only to be intercepted by Daniel Yoder and Eli Zook. Carefully, they laid the unconscious man on the couch. Sweat covered his brow. Slight convulsions swept across his body. Six strong Amish farmers carried him on the couch, as if he were in an open coffin, toward the house where he would be put to bed in his sister Fannie's home.

When he awakened the next morning, he did not know that any persons, strangers or brethren, had been present during the evening, or that he had spoken.

Daniel pondered the preacher's message. Indeed, they had been given food for their souls and minds, even though it had been spoken in the language of the outsiders. They had been exhorted to love one another and to love and serve Christ, as he, their brother Noah loved and served Christ among them. They had been told to cease from quarreling, that the love in their hearts and the love of Christ could draw both the young and the old together in unity. Maybe, with this kind of love between them, they need not fear the changes sweeping across the country in the 1880s. God would be with them and show them how to adjust. They would still follow a straight and narrow path.

Fannie Yoder had raced ahead to light the kerosene lamp. She emerged through the screen door, holding it firmly against the wall with her back, raising the lamp to light the way for the men carrying the prostrate preacher.

A chill swept over Louella at all these strange doings. She placed her small hand into the palm of her father's calloused one, the hand of a carpenter and farmer. She felt safe, then, and protected. He was singing softly, I *praise thee, Christ of heaven, who ever shall endure, who takes away my sorrow, keeps me safe and secure.*

Soft sounds of wheels turning in barnyard dust and mulch mixed with the murmurings of the departing kin. The heavy velvet of the August night was broken, softened as a cloud slipped past the full moon. The earth was mystic with luminescent light.

2.

To Sugar Creek Meetinghouse
and Back

During that year, Louella's Uncle Noah Troyer preached in his trance state 133 times. Indeed, he was becoming celebrated. Louella sensed from her father's face that there was fly in the ointment. Or was it the buttermilk? Louella never could remember. Anyway, she had seen her father's worried expression as he had ridden over to Fry town to purchase a few needed staples. It had been a quick trip on the back of Bob, that gentle roan, whose soft, velvet nose she petted whenever she fed him an apple. Returning with the flour and the cornmeal, Daniel's face appeared somber.

"Diener Versammlung" will meet tomorrow," he said, announcing the conference of the ministers, scarcely looking at Fannie as he carried the heavy sack of flour across to the pine-board flour bin on the south side of the kitchen.

"Diener Versammlung?"

Fannie turned, wiping her hands on the lower half of her apron.

Her dark eyes stared out from her round face, reflecting a trace of anxiousness.

"About Brother Noah?"

"Probably. At least, that will be a part of it."

Daniel seated himself on the bentwood kitchen chair they'd brought out all the way from West Liberty, Ohio. He knew that as a deacon, some of the focus would be on him. He felt hollow and uncomfortable.

Give our hearts and minds perception
Far above the earth and sky,
So we can clearly grasp your Word
That we may be devoted
And always live in righteousness;
Forever to the scriptures true,
And not to be misguided.

-Ausbund, 131

Fannie's eyes strained. The discipline of the church was severe. It could lead to the ban and to shunning, social separation. They lived in a community where religious orthodoxy reigned, and its knife cut clean and sharp. Such strictness could lead to repentance and confession, and it could bring grief and brokenness. Only those who lived in a community such as the Old Order Amish could even begin to know the power and strength of the discipline of the church.

"*Gottes Will.*" Fannie's voice broke. Tears sliced down her hot face.

"Noah is becoming a spectacle. The *Iowa Republican* calls him the Celebrated Amishman." Daniel pulled off his worn work boots. Shame swept through him, shame for his brother-in-law, whom he loved and for whom he prayed. To know that Noah's name was spread in the papers of the outsiders filled him with sadness.

"It's because he's not ordained," Daniel said, removing a cocklebur that had stuck to his sock.

Only the ordained were allowed to give sermons, and each night, Noah Troyer was preaching to crowds, sometimes a hundred or more. By now the elders in Amish churches throughout the Midwest had been told of the strange conduct of the sleeping preacher. Fannie had saved a clipping from the *Herald of Truth* about the growing controversy over her brother. She had underlined one of the paragraphs written by John P. King, who noted with firmness that one must not be hasty in judging Noah Troyer or concluding that his strange preaching trances were from the devil. Fannie read once more the quote she'd underlined. "How can we reconcile the fact that he rebukes and reproves all manner of evil and beseeches all sinners to turn from their evil ways?"

Yes, Brother King had defended her brother, but Fannie knew the controversy was spreading.

"It's not just Noah's preaching," Daniel said, his voice trailing off wearily.

"What else? It wasn't like this back in Ohio. Here the *Audnug* is so different," said Fannie, referring to the set of rules which ordered the life of every person in the Amish community. "*Audnug* here is so strict."

Her eyes came to rest on her cupboard shelves. Her dishes

looked clean, orderly, and even pretty. She had arranged them on the oak boards lined with new shelf paper with notched edges.

A fleeting feeling of embarrassment, even a tinge of shame, swept through her as she'd remembered Bishop Swartzentruber's sermon at Amish service four weeks ago. Notched shelf paper along with fancy dishes had been mentioned as unnecessary worldly advances. And right there in the oak cupboard in her very own kitchen were the shelves draped with the suspect covering. "For shame!" Why it must have been that Suzie Miller who gossiped about it to the bishop's wife. And Suzie, forgetful and foolish as one of the virgins who carried no extra oil, just last week had to walk all the way over to the Swartzentrubers to get a starter when she'd let her yeast run out. "Foolish, foolish! Es *ist eine schand!*"

Anyway, Louella had liked the paper. They'd picked it out in the general store in Kalona, washed the shelves with soap and water, then lined them with the new paper with the white lacy edges. Why, in Ohio, this would never have happened. "Notched shelf paper! *Unvorstendich!*" Her thoughts became almost audible as Fannie turned back to her tired husband.

"Then the bishop spoke to you today?"

"Yes, in Fry town, just before I got the flour. We talked outside on the porch. I'm to be there."

Fannie knew now that the focus was on more than her shelf paper and flowered dishes. It would be more like the spotlight of an October moon upon a circle of dancing rabbits. Now they were all involved; both she and Daniel, the John Gingerichs, Jacob Bollers, John Troyers, Noah and Fran Troyer, and Joseph Yoders. She searched her mind as she tried to remember who all had gathered at their house when they'd asked Brother Milo Miller from Ohio to preach for them. Considered too worldly by the Sharon bishops, Brother Miller had been denied the opportunity to bring the Lord's message in their community.

Fannie Yoder struggled with the two parts of herself. Like Daniel, she respected the voice of the church. They had a long-held custom and practice of holding in deep regard those ministers and bishops who had charge for their souls. They knew Hebrews 13:17, and could quickly recite it in the language of their Amish people. "Obey them that have the rule over you, and submit yourselves: for they watch for your souls, as they that must give account, that they may do it with joy, and not with grief."

Feeling torn and anxious, Daniel and Fannie realized that they were fast becoming part of what might be considered grief.

More and more it seemed that the little dry ditch was becoming a creek, rippling along, beginning to tear away the soil from its banks. Would it widen and deepen? All this over what would be considered matters of no consequence back in Ohio.

As is the custom and with the full biblical instruction of the first Christians, "greet ye one another with the holy kiss," the bishops, deacons, and ministers carried out fully this exhortation as they gathered. Gray beards, shiny, young, black beards, chestnut beards, and white beards mingled as they extended to each other their right hand and brought together ruddy cheeks and lined farmer's faces in this kiss. Some looked down as they did this act with Daniel. But all of the duties of the church and the rites of Christians must be carried out. And, after all, this was the kiss of peace.

Old Order Amish and Conservative Mennonite groups often found themselves boxed in by their attempts to keep their orthodoxy. Even though the principle behind many points of controversy was important, or pointed to an issue of eternal value, applying a principle was usually confined to a small area with little latitude.

Being simple folk of the land and committed to a historic and persecuted faith, they knew only one way to deal with differing opinion: black and white, good and evil, *Audnug* or no *Audnug.* Couldn't these clustering Yoders, Troyers, Gingerichs, Bollers understand the finality of traditions and *Audnug?*

So gentle Daniel, who could state his belief or position, but would not argue or assert himself, had hitched Old Sandy to his Amish buggy and rode over to Bishop Swartzentrubers for the *Diener Versammlung.* A cold, late March wind laced the air with a chill. Daniel hunched forward in the buggy seat as he turned into the lane. It was colder than he'd realized. He should have worn his heavy woolen coat with its shoulder cape.

The gray, chilly day itself seemed to set the mood of the meeting.

The faces of the Sharon bishops looked stern, fully

undergirded by their staunch beliefs and attitudes regarding changes in their community. Seated by the stove, Daniel lost his anxiousness. An inner peace filled him and began to lighten his blue eyes. His ruddy cheeks above his beard reflected the stark light from the uncurtained window. Fannie had been right. The focus was not on the whimsical shelf paper but upon the dire threat brought to their religious order by the visiting ministers. These ministers were simply unclean. They could not enter this community with their innovations and advances and be given a voice before the congregation. Other flocks might hear them, but not this one with the beautiful name Sharon.

The meeting went on. Faces that were solemn at the beginning grew more solemn. Some of the ministers were shedding tears, weeping over the inevitable conclusion. The fire in the potbellied stove glowed in the waning light. Soon their cattle and other evening chores would call them. They must finish.

Standing with dignity and eyes gleaming with the unqualified note of an authority, Bishop John K. Yoder, in his frock coat, cleared his throat to speak the conclusion of their labors together. He had been called in as an outside consulting bishop.

Bishop Yoder shifted his eyes to Daniel. Though stem, his look was also one of concern. He cleared his throat again.

"This group who does not in all respects practice *Audnug* of this community should seek their spiritual house in the Henry County Amish Mennonite Church."

Deacon Daniel Yoder, with his dreamy, impractical ways, and the unordained, "celebrated-clown," mystic preacher Noah Troyer and their following must go. It was finished: finished among people who more than sincerely believed that "What is agreed among men on earth is agreed upon in heaven."

They understood it as *Gottes Will.*

"Ach du Zieber!" thought Daniel as he began to comprehend what this edict would involve. "Seek their spiritual home in the Henry County Amish Church?" Why, the Henry County Amish Church by Sugar Creek was more than thirty miles away! *"Es ist sehrecklich,"* a frightful thought to Daniel, worrying now over how to break this news to Fannie on that cold and dismal evening. Already the sun was sinking and red streaks marked the

clouds in the chilly Iowa sky, traces of cold snow glistened on the still frozen black earth. He must not let the shadow and cold overtake him inside. Their labors were concluded. Though tired from the strain, Bishop Swartzentruber felt a relief. This group nearing secession was given proper instruction, he had kept his vows to preach the gospel and to keep his flock unspotted from the world. It is better to lance a boil than to allow it to fester and burst. Was it not written in the Gospels that one cannot sew new patches on old garments? How can *Audnug* be sincerely kept with such unorthodoxy being spread by these visiting ministers and innovators whom the Daniel Yoders and the Troyers had harbored, let alone the new Sunday school.

Daniel did not tell Fannie until all the children had been put to bed. Little John had cried with his sore throat, so Fannie sat by his bed, making sure that he was covered with a thick comforter. She hummed in her low soothing voice, as she patted him until sleep carried the small boy into his rest for the night. Louella and Frank were already fast asleep.

Fannie and Daniel knelt with their arms propped and hands clasped above the straw mattress of their bed. They were not aware of the rough boards beneath their knees. Fannie, silent in her meditation, followed Daniel's voice as he prayed. Words came so sincerely from his lips, and tonight she felt the tears fall as she listened to the sad gentleness of his voice.

When the lamp was blown out and they were covered from the cold of the night, and when the summer's straw in their mattress had stopped crackling and rustling, he told her.

"To the Sugar Creek Church in Henry County!" she cried out in her German-accented contralto voice. "Why we will have to drive all the way through Johnson and Washington counties before we get to Henry County. *Ach du Zieber!*"

But as Frederich Nietzsche reminds us, "Words and deeds require time before they are heard and understood." It took the Daniel Yoders a few days before they fully comprehended the meanings of the ministers' meeting. Fannie was an organizer and a hardworking Amish woman. She would not throw up her hands in dismay at a time when Daniel and her family needed her more than ever. She did not, however, tell her tired husband that night that their fourth child was growing within her womb.

So, now on a warm Saturday morning in May, Louella, wearing her dark blue dress, head covered with her organdy covering and the strings neatly tied under her chin, rode beside her gentle father Daniel as they, the Noah Troyers, the John Troyers and the Jacob Bollers and John Gingeriches began the long journey toward the Sugar Creek Amish meetinghouse in Henry County. Within an hour they had ridden past the oak and hickory timbers that were of such value to the early settlers in the Sharon district. Tall prairie grass sweeping in wavelets in the wind rose ahead. To the left, plowed fields awaited the planting of the corn. Fences lined the right-hand side of the road. Louella began to count the golden breasted meadowlarks upon the posts as they lifted their heads heavenward with the joy of their spring songs. Soon the wild roses, already heavy with their new greenery, would be radiant in their pink splendor.

Leaning into her father's side, she was comforted by his warm presence. Her mother and the two small boys had stayed behind. Old Sandy and Bob clumped along the dusty country road as the buggies swayed and rolled. Louella thought of her mother as she remembered the large hickory basket in the back of the buggy, covered with an old blanket to keep the hot sun's rays from heating it. In it was a whole smoke-cured ham. Fannie had willingly sent it along so that they would be well provided for as far as earthly food was concerned. The basket waxed heavy with jars of red beets, sweet and sour pickles, and two of her loaves of brown-crusted bread. Their basket lunch would be shared on a common table as they reached their destination for the evening, the home of the John Conrads by Mill Creek in Washington County. Louella and Daniel and the other outcasts from their Sharon Community would eat, rest, and spend the night at the Conrad farm, then pursue their journey on to the Sugar Creek Church Sunday morning.

By five o'clock the small entourage of buggies had reached their destination. Ahead lay the gray wooden bridge over Mill Creek. Stands of hackberry, oak, and hickory softened the scene. The light green willows drooped their velvet fronds over the rippling shadows on the soft dirt of the bank and road.

Moses and Samuel Conrad, sons of their hosts, sat on the banisters of the wooden bridge in happy anticipation of the event. Their bare toes curled in the sunlight.

Sarah, their sister, almost the same age as Louella, jumped up from the swing, hanging from a giant oak near the windmill. She ran, covering strings untied and flying, as she waved to the Yoder buggy as it pulled into the drive.

The horses, Sandy and Bob, were tired. They had done their work well for the day, and the laborer is worthy of his hire. Daniel would take care of his horses first, water them, then feed and allow them a welcome rest.

Spaced by intervals of fifteen to twenty minutes, the other buggies arrived, carrying the Bollers, Troyers, and Gingeriches.

Anticipation and a feeling of loneliness about this venture were both present. They all felt it. But this was life. One may not put it in a formal philosophy, but it was very human and very real, that life was changing and transitory. The New Testament said it well, that we are indeed pilgrims and strangers here. This group of pilgrims was now called upon to live at the frontier of their religious discovery and life. But they were not dispirited or downcast. They were people on a journey. Their Anabaptist faith was dear to them. They would not hesitate when life called them to enter lonely places, including the risk of the new.

Farm smells rose from the warm ground at eventide. The sweat of the horses, the drift from the pigpen on the south side of the towering red barn, the radiating sweetness of the grass and leaves caught and mixed with the scent from a clump of lilacs. When the kitchen door opened and Sister Annie Conrad strode out to welcome them, the rich smells of her freshly baked loaves of bread mingled with the odors of the evening. Mouths began to water, dry throats were more than ready for the water from the cold, deep well.

Then came the usual evening chores carried out by the members of the Conrad family, self-sufficient and organized. Tonight, they accepted the help offered from the friendly folk of like faith. Children of the same culture mingle with surprising rapidity. Louella was glad to show her kitchen skills, as she and Sarah Conrad and Dorcas Boller set the table with knives, forks, spoons, and water glasses. The extended table stretched almost from wall to wall in the spacious country kitchen.

Gradually the atmosphere began to change, from the somber formality at the beginning, to the aliveness and quickening brought about by these late-frontier pioneer people of similar culture, tongue, and background. It became a religious air. Even the names reflected this. Daniel, Moses, Seth, Samuel, John, Noah, and Dorcas; Mary, Sarah, Anna, Ruth, and Martha. The evening took its own form, as the informality increased. First, the men and boys sat at the long table. Their eyes glistened and smiles touched the edges of their lips. An air of peace descended. They must pray first. Bishop Conrad, host at the table, prayed with fervor and diligence. Though his eyes were closed, his head was lifted to offer his prayer of both thanksgiving and supplication for the extended mercies of God in their lives. His deep bass voice lifted the words heavenward.

"0 Lord God, Heavenly Father,. bless us and these gifts which we shall accept from thy tender goodness. Give us food and drink also for our souls unto life eternal, and make us partakers of thy heavenly table through Jesus Christ. Amen." A chorus of voices joined in thankfulness and supplication, as the gathered evening pilgrims, child and adult alike, male and female, spoke the Lord's Prayer together.

Then they were ready. Appetites were not spared. Bread, rolls and cool butter, pulled from the cold well, journeyed around the table first, hand to hand, up and down from man to small male child. Nine-year-old Laban Conrad held a giant slice of his mother's bread as he spread the butter with a case knife. His dark eyes stared through the space by his father's shoulder.

Louella, catching his glances, dared to offer him a smile. Laban turned to his father to ask for the jam for his bread.

Next came platters of meat: Fannie Yoder's ham, sliced thick and generously heaped, plus chunks of dark brown savory beef, canned just this season by Sister Conrad herself. The rich brown gravy would come later after the mashed potatoes. Mary Gingerich's fried chicken followed fast. Louella hoped the wishbone would not be taken when it came her turn to sit at the table with all of the gathered sisters and other girls. She could hope. Who knew? Maybe she could ask Laban Conrad to hold the wishbone with her, break it, and make a wish.

Green beans with bacon, shelled limas with butter, a salad made out of the fresh spring lettuce and radishes of the garden and tossed with chopped, hard-boiled eggs came next. Happy sounds of eating filled the air. Dishes were scraped empty and

refilled by the quick hand of a waiting Amish woman. The
heavy treading sounded, back and forth, back and forth, across
the wide boards of the kitchen floor. History cannot record all,
but there were other dishes and salads too. The only ripple at all
was when Jonathan Hooley tipped the dish filled with the red
beets in his anticipation to fork the biggest one and three or four
rolled out on the floor.

It was not a question of "will there be any pie?" They all
understood and knew that there would be pie. Slices of raisin,
mince, cherry, and gooseberry vanished with hearty appetite and
spirit. Some even had room for Maude Miller's frosted spice
cake and white-bearded Grandfather Conrad himself even took a
piece of the three-layered, black walnut cake before it made a
complete turn around the corner. This was their supper. The
sisters and girls would take their turns next. This was their
custom and order, properly understood. Their eating would be
with no less spirit, no less clank of the fork and spoon upon the
plate.

The coals died down in the giant black kitchen range. The
coal oil lamps were lit. Sister Conrad kept her lamps ready and
the wicks trimmed. She despised a smoking lamp and blackened
chimney. Following the washing of the dishes, the women and
girls settled in the chairs, circled in the spacious dining room,
six or seven sat in the overflow in the space between the dining
room and living room, still within the circle.

They did not so much feel the weight of the day, these
tanned, strong, hardworking women. Their feet may have been
aching, their backs weary, but the spirit transcended. The
evening mellowed in the golden light. Eyes brightened as they
began to share stories and family talk.

Louella shivered as Dorcas Miller had to retell the chilling
story of how Lydia Hershberger, an early settler in the Iowa
community of Amish, had circled out to her spring garden one
day, only to step across a gigantic rattlesnake . Lydia had not
screamed or fled in panic, but like Jael in the Bible who'd kept a
calm and serene outward face while planning to do a gruesome
task, simply lifted her hoe heavenward, then chopping down
with a mighty swing, severed its ugly head. They all knew the
rest. Sister Lydia then gathered it up with her hoe, wanting to
keep it awhile to show her husband Joseph when he came in

from the daily plowing. She moved its scaly body into her half-bushel basket. It circled and circled, as she coiled its large thick carcass. The rattlesnake filled her basket to the top.

Louella shuddered again. She liked the story, even though she never wanted to step across a rattlesnake, or any other snake, for that matter, herself.

Outside on the fine wide-planked porch, the men and boys had gathered. They too were rising above the strain of their daily toil, and from the glare of the sun, dust of the road, and the ache of their joints. Time stood still, it was as if the evening lasted much longer than its hour or two. When people truly gather, let down the bars, time changes, lengthening and deepening. In such moments, people experience the deeper meanings of the human experience.

Listening to the warm rumble of conversation of the men outside, Louella could hear her father's voice as he began to tell the story of her great, great, great, great-grandfather, Strong Jacob Yoder, who'd settled with his widowed mother and her eight sons in Pennsylvania in 1742. Strong Jacob's father had died on the ship on the journey across from Canton Bern, Switzerland. Louella loved the stories of the powerful Amishman, how Strong Jacob was hauling his wheat to market. A tremendous rain had flooded the creeks and he came to a bridge that had washed out. However, there was a good foot-log stretching over the stream. Strong Jacob simply unhitched his four horses and made them swim to the farther bank; then he carried the wheat across in sacks. Taking the wagon apart, he carried it across, dragging the bottom over the footbridge and reassembled the whole works on the other side. Strong Jacob whistled as he went on his way as though nothing unusual had happened.

Resting, story telling, eating the food their own hands had raised and prepared, they did not leave out the offering of their souls and spirits to God. They were on a journey; this was a transition time. Tomorrow opened a new horizon, new worship, even in a white meetinghouse. Brother Conrad, host for the evening, called upon Brother Daniel Yoder to come and stand in the doorway separating the men and women and lead in evening hymn. Daniel stood, cleared his throat, hummed his pitch, then began, as the gathered pilgrims followed.

Then came rest for the evening. They had faith that on the Sabbath tomorrow the sun would rise, bless them with its light. The larks would offer the first morning prayers, but they would soon follow, dressed in their somber gray and black, beards combed, faces ruddy and clean, eyes gleaming with anticipation, clutching their *Ausbunds* and Bibles in their hands as they set out for the Sugar Creek Amish meetinghouse.

But the Henry County Sugar Creek Church venture seemed to be a trial experience only. Some of these pilgrims from Johnson County actually became communicant members of this more liberal congregation with its white meetinghouse and its alert and brighteyed European minister, Sebastian Gerig. But they could not endure for long the thirty-mile journey from their Sharon community to Sugar Creek. Such a biweekly sojourn, the slow transportation, the blasting cold of the winters, the need to stay near home for the heavy farming season, all led to the end of this venture, probably lasting not more that two years at the most.

But the Sharon dissidents were filled with courage and an undaunted spirit. They simply invited the talented, up-and-coming Bishop Sebastian from Henry County to come over to them in Sharon and continue the services there.

We are told in the historical accounts, "Gerig, lover of peace that he was, did not do this willingly, realizing that it would cause ill feelings. "

So it did. This, coupled with Noah Troyer's strange trance preaching was more than the Amish bishops of Sharon District could bear.

The records say, "Finally a committee of arbitration was chosen, composed of preachers from the Sharon church and from the Sugar Creek church. It was decided that the Henry County preachers could hold one more communion service for this group, and after that, they were to hold no more services for them. The Troyer followers were to go back to the Old Order church, and the preachers in the Old Order group were to cooperate with the ministers of the Sugar Creek church.

But stern Bishop Swartzentruber of the Sharon community learned of an incident occurring in the Sugar Creek church, he set his heels and would not budge. He voted a dissenting no. He'd learned that Sugar Creek minister Joseph Schlegel had walked to his church dressed in a short coat instead of the customary frock coat and with the legs of his trousers tucked inside his boots. Preaching for the gathered worshipers in this dress, he dared to break the Amish Mennonite custom that ministers wear frock coats during religious services.

So the record adds, "Now when the ones who had been dissatisfied before-the families of Deacon Daniel Yoder, John Troyer, Noah Troyer, Jacob Boller, John Gingerich, and others-saw Swartzentruber's attitude, they continued their separate meeting, holding services in their homes. For church services, they had Scripture reading and prayer, and when visiting preachers came, they preached for them. Others joined this group, and soon their number was too large for worship in a dwelling house. The Prairie Dale schoolhouse, north of Kalona, was then used for a meeting place. It was in this school house in 1883 that their first Sunday school was organized. "

No doubt, Daniel Yoder, Louella's father, had been a leader in the group. Having been ordained and still holding the office of deacon, his word carried much weight. But one more event occurred that may have led to the Daniel Yoder family's eventual move to Garden City, Missouri.

In 1884, a new family came to the Sharon community from Elkhart County, Indiana, none other than Daniel's sister-in-law and Fannie's sister, Mary, and her husband Christian Warey, already an ordained preacher. Now Preacher Warey rode into this conservative community sporting a folding-top buggy and wearing a raincoat, two conveniences that were not tolerated by the Sharon group. So, Louella's Uncle Chris and Aunt Mary Warey were asked to join their new group.

Soon they'd outgrown the Prairie Dale Schoolhouse, and began building the Union Mennonite Church. We do not know what happened to Daniel. Was he overshadowed by his talented brother-in-law? Gentle though Daniel was, did he not, however, feel some pangs of jealousy? some tinge of being crowded over to the side? Why had he not been chosen as minister? Wasn't he next in line? Anyway, God moves in mysterious ways. Daniel simply was not chosen to advance in the Union Church. The lot was cast. He was not numbered among the selected ones. Maybe this, the hard times, his growing family, and the cheaper land in Missouri congealed until Daniel and Fannie looked southward to

Garden City, Missouri, where already they had relatives waiting, and a spanking new church, the Bethel Church, was being built three miles northwest of Garden City. Surely a man of Daniel's loving ways, singing voice, and knowledge of the Scriptures would be of further service to the Lord and his fellow brothers and sisters in the church.

The Mennonite Community

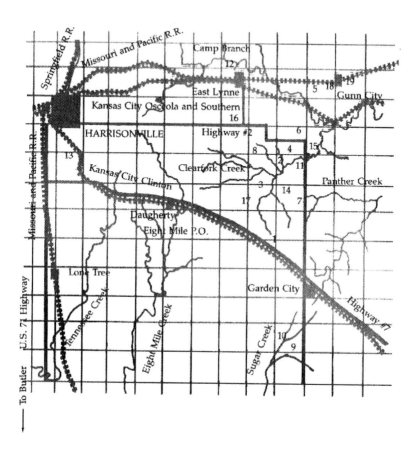

1. Bethel Church
2. Sycamore Grove Church
3. Old Amish Clearfork Church
4. Smith School
5. Miss Eller's house
6. Barb Yoder farm
7. Clearfork School
8. Clearfork Creek
9. Daniel and Fannie Yoder place
10. Sugar Creek School
11. The King place
12. Camp Branch Creek
13. Leakyroof Railroad
14. Roy Yoder place
15. Bishop Hershberger's farm
16. Preacher Manassah's farm
17. Number Nine School
18. Gunn City Methodist Church
19. Gunn City School

We confess that all penitent believers who through faith, the new birth, and the renewal of the Holy Ghost, have become united with God, and whose names are recorded in heaven, must, on such scriptural confession of their faith, and renewal of life, according to the command and doctrine of Christ ... be baptized with water, in the ever adorable name of the Father, and of the Son, and of the Holy Ghost.

- From the Dordrecht Confession, 1632

3.

The Baptism

Louella Yoder, now an olive-skinned, black-haired, blue-eyed German young woman, sat on the wooden back steps of the stark two-story white frame house just three miles west of Garden City, Missouri. Down the road a couple of miles rose the roof of the new Bethel Mennonite Church, nestled in a grove of elm and catalpa trees.

Louella dug at the sticky black mud clinging to her shoes. She gouged furiously with a broken stick, scraping and shaking her heavy foot. Would she ever get it off her shoes?

Her mind wandered, caught up in a memory of their train ride to Missouri in the middle of winter. The Rock Island train had swayed from side to side across the snow-covered landscape, as if to comfort them, uprooted pilgrims, seeking transplant in Missouri soil.

She hung her head, the muddy stick dropped to the rain-soaked ground without a sound. Gray evening settled.

Louella, though, was beginning to like Missouri and call it home.

Even the mud was little different from that of Iowa. She missed Aunt Mary and Uncle Chris Warey, however. Her reverie, bordering on the edge of sadness, was interrupted by her mother's rich German voice.

"Louella, Louella, where's Dora?"

Their family now had seven children. Louella had just turned fifteen, Frank was lanky and lean at twelve, and ten-year-old John who'd survived the whooping cough that very winter, kept them in stitches with his maverick ways.

Wispy-haired, blue-eyed Dora was eight, and Ida, pudgy and heavy at five challenged them all. A toddler, Ollie in his flannel dress volunteered daily to mop the floor as he waddled and rolled from corner to corner with his equally flannel-dressed baby brother, Aaron who had just turned two years old.

Crops grew well, the children flourished, and Louella and her singing father Daniel learned new songs.

The church they now attended did not hold to the old ways of the Amish. Louella and Frank especially liked their worship services where both the singing of hymns and the preaching were in English. This Bethel church was a branch off of the old Clearfork Amish Mennonite Church over north toward the cemetery. A division had occurred among the brethren and sisters there. Those who had insisted upon maintaining the more severe styles of dress and the German language withdrew. Forming their own church in a grove of sycamore trees, about a mile down the country road, they named it Sycamore Grove.

Louella liked Bethel church, and loved the sound of the name. In Hebrew it meant house of God. Joy swept over her as she sat by her mother, Dora, and little Ida, singing the newer gospel songs of the evangelical movement.

Her father, Daniel, was no longer a deacon. He had been ordained a preacher in the most agonizingly long service on the hottest day of the summer. But the heat hadn't mattered that much at all. A calm joy had filled all their hearts.

That fall, during a series of revival meetings, Louella and six other young people of the congregation had *come out* (a phrase often used among Old Mennonite groups to refer to accepting Christ or being saved).

They had planned to be baptized in the late spring or early summer, whenever the ever changing weather would be hot enough to warm the water of Clearfork Creek which flowed through the shady grove near the bend and bridge.

Most of the mud was scraped from her shoes. Louella rubbed them briskly with a wet burlap sack, opened the door, and stepped into the warm kitchen. Her mother, apron tied around her waist, was using a small poker to stir up the fire in the Home Comfort kitchen range. She added a short piece of split wood to the crackling fire, pushed the wire-bound cast-iron handle into the notch in the round lid, then slid it into its place in the top of the stove.

Fannie had changed some since the move from Iowa. She was heavier, but always being a stocky woman, she carried her weight well. No longer did she wear the white, severe organdy covering of the Amish. Her hair, black and shiny, had not even a trace of gray. She still wore it parted in the middle and swept back into the bun. Of course, on Sundays, during worship, and some of the time at her own table she did wear the covering. The modified design, however, permitted rounded corners, untied strings at the sides of her neck, and a material of mesh or netting, rather than the organdy. Black wool stockings and black shoes warmed her feet and legs. She wore a simple pink and gray gingham dress, made with roomy wide sleeves, tight fitting at the neck. It sported a row of tiny pink buttons down the front. On Sundays, now that Daniel was a preacher, she would change into a plain dress with the cape, designed to slip over the head and neck and fasten at the waistband. This was the customary plain dress, especially worn among ministers' wives of the Mennonites. On the ride to church in their buggy, and whenever she did get to Garden City through this Missouri mud to do some shopping, her head and brow were protected by the black bonnet. She tied its wide ribbons firmly under her fat chin.

Fannie was smiling and humming to herself as she rolled out the pie crust. Hearing Louella, she turned: "Ach! You're home. I thought it was yer' Pa scraping mud out there."

"Oh, Ma! Are we going to have gooseberry pie?," asked Louella, placing her one-gallon lard bucket lunch pail, weathered bluish gray with age, on the cupboard near the dry sink.

"Yes, hurry along, Louella, and bring a jar of gooseberries from the cellar," Fannie replied, tossing the rolling pin into the open flour bin. The cellar was the common raised earth-domed root cellar, found on many a farm homestead, which served as a cool dry storage place for baskets of apples, pears, long bins of potatoes and onions, plus rows of canned fruits and vegetables.

Louella leaped through the back door, stepped carefully on the flagstones raised above the dark Missouri mud to the root cellar. In the gloom her eyes searched for the berries. Finding them, she took the six steps to the earth and sky above in two eager strides, letting the heavy door slam behind her. Back in the kitchen she wiped the dust from the blue-green jar with a damp rag and tugged at the rubber seal, to open it.

"Where are the children?" said her mother. Taking the opened gooseberries, she emptied them into a saucepan as she prepared the filling for her pie. She referred to her two daughters and their older brothers as the children. Louella was no longer a child. She was thought of as a young woman. She would get her diploma from the eighth grade at Sugar Creek School and no one knew better than Fannie that Louella could work circles around many women her own age.

"Dora and Ida are comin,' Ma. The boys rode the pony to fetch the cows." Louella remembered she'd forgotten to bring in the boys' lunch pails. She'd have to do that yet, open them to air out overnight, smooth out the waxed paper that kept their sandwiches from drying out. They would use the waxed paper again.

"Dora moseys so."

That was certainly true. The child was simply fascinated by all growing things. As she poked along, dragging in the mud, she studied each living thing, animal or plant. Late last fall she brought home a caterpillar in her lunch pail.

Looking out the window, Louella caught a glimpse of her father as he came out of the milk house with a lantern in his hand. Soon it would be dark on this misty, cold evening. He would light the lantern in the barn so that he and the boys could finish feeding the calves and the milking.

The wind died down following the evening chores. The glow of the lamps warmed them as they ate their supper with relish. Young Frank emptied the dish of the last of the canned beef in its rich gravy over his remaining potatoes. Dora reached for the gooseberry pie. Daniel buttered another piece of homemade bread. His thinning hair and thickened middle were in keeping with his forty-two years. He loved the earth, he loved his family, but he also loved his food. Fannie wondered though how successful they'd be on this farm. Sometimes he seemed to drift, look away. He was thinking. He was a serious man, but, pshaw, you could plow out a whole row of corn with your mind on next Sunday's sermon. Fannie was of a more practical bent.

Even though they might not be the most successful farmers in this new settlement, Daniel's carpentry skills had already distinguished him among his Mennonite brothers. The proof lay in the three red barns he helped build in the community. Each one had the earth graded in a slope to the hayloft on the second level with an impressive overhang on the back. She was proud of him.

Wiping his graying beard on the back of his hand, he looked at her with his kind blue eyes. Bowing his head, he spoke a final prayer of thanksgiving before they rose from the table.

Dora, Ida, and Louella all shared the same upstairs bedroom, the one with the window facing Sugar Creek School. Louella, lying under a warm comforter, pondered, as she looked at the ceiling. Ida and Dora turned, getting settled in their bed across the room. The straw mattress rustled as they settled in.

Louella was thinking of her coming baptism, of the meaning of that holy and sacred event. It wouldn't be long until the ice melted and frogs croaked in the creeks and ponds. Wild ducks and geese would wing their way northward in the spring sky. Cattails would push out of the ditches and shallow places. The days would grow languid and hot. Flowers would open, lilacs, poppies, and sweet peas would pour out their lavish aromas. Black and yellow swallowtail butterflies would cling to the lilacs.

Louella pictured Jesus himself going into the water. "And Jesus, when he was baptized, went straightway out of the water, and 10, the heavens were opened unto him, and he saw the Spirit of God descending like a dove, and lighting upon him."

She too would go into the water. She and the six others. Would Bishop Kauffman take them one by one, or would they go in twos or threes? It would be a comfort if Anna Yahn could go in with her. She would not be alone. The Spirit of God would be with her to anoint her soul as she received the waters of baptism. The angels would be there too. Oh, she wouldn't be able to see them, but they would hover there just the same above the trees. Would they know the same songs the gathered congregation would sing?

Her mind drifted on as she grew drowsy. The congregation would stand on the north bank of Clearfork Creek, their feet in the tall grass and sweet Williams. Lifting their voices in perfect harmony, they would sing "O happy day that fixed my choice, on thee, my Savior and my God." Then she and the six converts would march through as the crowd parted to make way, like Moses and the children of Israel coming through the Red Sea. But no! The north bank of the creek dropped straight down eight or ten feet into deep, dark water. That would never do. No. They would surely find some rocks, some gravel to protect their feet from the mud on the south side. It sloped gently there. Yes, there they would gracefully enter the water as the assembled crowd hummed a tune.

Oh, so many questions about baptism remained unanswered.

Should she take off her shoes? Mama had ordered her Sunday shoes from Sears and Roebuck. She would not spoil them, even for so holy a day. But her work shoes, what would Jesus think? And the overlooking angels? Shouldn't she wear her best for Jesus? The more Louella thought about it the more apprehensive she became. Would her dress billow up like Violet Schantz's did last June when she fell into the pond? Air caught beneath her skirts, her dress billowed up as Violet floated and eased across. It was a pity that she didn't enjoy the ride, but she couldn't for the shame and humiliation of it.

Just before Louella fell asleep, she thought of one of the other converts who would go into the water with her, Amos Miller. She was glad to see Amos get redemption. Maybe what'd happened one afternoon at school had jarred him loose from his foolish ways. Amos, fun loving and a merry prankster at heart, had found great pleasure in annoying Louella, who sat in the desk directly in front of him. When Amos's mind wandered from his geography lesson, his attention turned to Louella. Sometimes he tied her two pigtails together, or pinned a foolish note on them. But the day he stuck the end of her pigtail in the inkwell, she stood up, right in school during the ciphering match, turned facing him, raised her slate above her head. "This'll teach you, Amos Miller!" she exclaimed. Then with all her force she brought the slate down on his head. Poor Amos. He hardly knew what hit him. There was a resounding crack as the slate shattered. This was followed by a thud as Amos sailed out of his seat onto the oiled plank floor. The scholars roared and hooted at the stunned Amos, sitting there slightly grinning and wobbly, with Louella's slate-frame hanging around his neck.

She'd been disciplined by Mr. Heidelberg, the teacher, though.

But pshaw! What was washing blackboards and sweeping the schoolroom floor for two weeks after school compared to the glory she'd received from putting Amos Miller in his place?

Anyhow, she thought, the way she felt right now, she'd even smile at Amos and point for him to go ahead of her at the baptism, if he wished. They were among the redeemed now, and this would be fully witnessed when they were in the holy waters of their cleansing.

Finally, June the tenth came, the day for the solemn service. God was with them. The day was matchless in beauty. Fluffy clouds billowed against the blue sky. The giant sycamores spread their white branches heavenward, offering a cool shade below. The water ran deep and black-looking below the bank, but on the south side among the gravel and stones, it rippled clear. Yellow-breasted meadowlarks sat on the barbed-wire fence, pouring out their songs into the air. Sweet Williams and May apple blossoms waved in the wind, filling the air with their heady aroma.

Rows of buggies were in line by the pasture fence near the shady retreat by the creek. Then the procession began to this Eden-like glen for the baptism. Leading the way were the two bishops, black coated and sober, Bibles under their arms. Next came the two ministers of the congregation and her father, Daniel, followed by the two deacons.

Louella and her three girlfriends were all dressed in long-sleeved blue dresses. They had agreed upon blue for their baptismal dresses, simple and plain, high-necked, with no ornamentation. On their heads were their carefully pressed white prayer coverings, the narrow ribbons falling down around their shoulders. They moved gracefully, willingly, and submissively. Amos Miller and two other teenaged young men followed them, all wearing white broadcloth shirts, buttoned at the necks and sleeves. The shirts were neatly tucked into their black trousers. These seven converts were followed by the members of the congregation.

The beauty and the solemnity of the occasion now had moved Louella almost to tears, especially as they began to sing in moving four-part harmony that ancient hymn written by Felix Manz. *I will sing with exultation, all my heart delights in God, who brings salvation, frees from death's dread might.*

Yes, it was a song often sung in Amish and Mennonite circles, a song born from the baptism of persecution by drowning, fire, and the sword.

By the time the final verse was sung, the congregation was spread in a crescent under the shade of the giant trees. The bishops, ministers, and deacons, backs to the sloping creek bank, faced the seven applicants for baptism and the gathered worshipers.

Bishop Kauffman lifted his shoulders, threw back his handsome, bearded face, and began to read from the ancient manual the rite of baptism according to the Anabaptist faith.

"Go ye therefore, and teach all nations, baptizing them in the name of the Father, and of the Son, and of the Holy Ghost: teaching them to observe all things whatsoever I have commanded you."

Only the call of the cardinals and the baby cry of eight-month-old Dorcas Troyer was heard above the sound of the reading. Mother Troyer held her baby closer.

The bishop continued. A look of joy reflected from his suntanned face as his blue eyes swept over the youthful applicants for baptism. He had been pleased with their honest study of their Anabaptist doctrines and teachings.

"They have been instructed in the doctrines of the gospel and in the ordinances and requirements of the church, and have given evidence that they are prompted in their purpose by the Spirit of God, that they are willing to forsake sin and the world, to consecrate themselves to the service of God, and from henceforth to be the disciples and followers of Christ."

Spring pollen in the air caused Amos Miller to sneeze violently.

He tried to look solemn and penitential as he brought his white sleeve across and under his nose.

Finishing the reading, the bishop, now beginning to perspire, turned his blue eyes to the waiting applicants and said, "And now if it is still your desire to be baptized and to be received into the church fellowship, you will follow me into the water."

Removing his coat, he placed it upon the fallen log. Next, he stepped out of his shoes, slid off his stockings and began to roll up his trousers to the knees. The boys, waiting to be baptized, watched the bishop and followed his example. The girls, however, simply removed their shoes. They would go into the water in their stocking feet, with all propriety and modesty.

Carefully, lest he fall on the slippery bank, the bishop eased down the sloping bank. A frog, disturbed by the footsteps, croaked and hopped into the pool ahead. Then came the converts, Louella, Dorcas, and Sadie. Poor Sadie, who was afraid of the water and petrified by snakes, was shaking. Was she laughing or about to cry? The girls held their skirts about them as they knelt in two feet of water just off the sandbar. The bishop, in deeper water, towered before them, stern and sober. The three boys knelt in a row to the right of the girls. Louella looked at Sadie who was still trembling, her face blanched.

She whispered a prayer, "Dear God, let there be no snakes." The water was colder than any of them had expected. The gravel was only a thin layer. Their knees began to break through into the rich ooze of the creek bottom. Suddenly, there was a strange sound among the boys. Louella couldn't tell for certain if it was a sneeze, a cough, or a snicker. They were all nervous as they waited expectantly.

The bishop cleared his throat and began his questions. "Do you believe in the one true, eternal, and almighty God, who is the Creator and Preserver of all visible and invisible things?" He then looked directly at each convert as they, one by one, replied as they had been instructed and as they truly believed in their hearts, "I do."

Next they responded to the question about their belief in Jesus Christ as the only begotten Son of God, the only Savior, and the one about the Holy Ghost who is an abiding Comforter, sanctifying the hearts of all people.

"Are you truly sorry for your past sins, and are you willing to renounce Satan, the world, and all works of darkness and your own carnal will and sinful desires?"

They were sinking deeper into the mud as their voices rose with consternation and courage, "I do."

"Do you promise by the grace of God and the aid of his Holy Spirit to submit yourself to Christ and his work, and faithfully to abide in the same until death?"

A chill swept over Louella, but she answered forcefully, "I do."

The others followed her example.

The bishop began to pray for God's blessing upon them that they might have grace to remain steadfast and be faithful to the end in the promises they had made.

After his Amen, the bishop, wading through the water a few steps until he stood directly in front of Louella, reached out and placed his hands upon her head and said, "Upon the confession of thy faith, which thou hast made before God and these witnesses .... " In mid-sentence, he removed his hands from her head, bent over and with cupped hands, scooped up the now rather troubled water and parting his rough farmer's hands, allowed it to pour over her waiting head. "I baptize thee with water, in the name of the Father, and of the Son, and of the Holy Ghost."

The cold water, no longer clear, drenched her covering and hair, and was dripping down over her shoulders. She shivered again.

When he had finished with the anointing of water upon all seven heads, the bishop waded back to Louella.

"In the name of Christ and his church, I give you my hand. Arise!

And as Christ was raised up by the glory of the Father, even so, thou also shalt walk in newness of life, and as long as thou art faithful and abidest in the doctrine of his word, thou art his disciple indeed, and shalt be acknowledged as a member of the body of Christ and a sister in the church. The Lord bless thee and keep thee."

Water streaming from her dress, which now clung to her body, Louella turned, waded up the sloping bank where the bishop's wife, warm and smiling, came forward to embrace her, and give her the holy kiss of peace as Christians are exhorted to do in First Corinthians 16:20, "Greet ye one another with a holy kiss."

The congregation watched as the bishop greeted each of the standing, dripping boys with the same salutation, the holy kiss of peace.

They gathered in front of the waiting worshipers, the boys staring ahead solemnly, heads slightly bowed, Louella and her two girlfriends, standing close together, supporting each other. The clear tenor voice of the chorister rose in the warm, sweet air as members of the congregation joined him in singing the old hymn for baptism Louella had thought about. O *happy day, that fixed my choice on thee, my Savior and my God! Well may this glowing heart rejoice, and tell its raptures all abroad.*

The holy observance was over. Louella was now a sister in the church.

O merciful Father, we humbly beseech thee to keep us from the
death of sin, and enable us to walk in the life of righteousness,
that when we depart this life, we may rest in him who is the
resurrection and the life.

4.

The Funeral

"I can't remember such an evening," Louella groaned, pushing
her rocking chair back onto the screened porch.

" 'Twas like this in Iowa back in eighty-seven. Every seven
years God throws in a clinker just to keep us humble," her mother
Fannie replied, dragging her straight-backed chair behind her.

They'd tried it outside under the cedar tree, but the parched,
cracked earth radiated the absorbed heat of the day until they were
drenched with sweat. No whippoorwills called this night.
Turtledoves had long ceased their plaintive prayers before the
summer rains. A single locust gave an occasional halfhearted
chirp in response to a bullfrog, whose world grew smaller daily.
This was the night of no song.

Suddenly, a drift of hot wind rattled the leaves of the brown,
dried-up corn that had grown so green with promise last spring.
Fannie didn't like the smell of dried-up corn. That meant frugality
and hard times ahead. "Poor Daniel, he works so hard plowing
these clods," she thought to herself.

Voices drifted around the corner of the porch, carried by the
hot evening wind. Men's voices rose and fell in the slow rhythm of
dialogue between a father and his son. Daniel and John were
talking.

"I'm gonna' take a job in the city, Pa," said the stocky dark-skinned seventeen-year-old boy.

By now Daniel knew that his son John had a nature different from the quiet Quaker ways so desired and sought by serious members of their community. John took dangerous risks, racing his horse and buggy recklessly at times. Even so, Daniel wanted to encourage his teenage son to stay near in the safety of the community. However, Daniel could not deny the wanderlust in John's eyes.

On the porch, Fannie picked up a basin of knotty, small apples and began to peel them. She'd removed her white prayer covering and rolled up the long sleeves of her calico dress. Through the screen, Louella and her mother warily scanned the brassy moon in the sky which seemed to carry on where the sun had left off. It offered no solace. They saw it clearly, for the morning glories, that usually shielded the porch, wilted and gave up grasping for a hold on the screen. No four-o' -clocks graced the air with their heavy odor. Fannie wouldn't spare water from the cistern to water them even for the luxury of their perfume.

If only a cloud would brush across the moon, giving some hope in this night, some token that soon the drought would break. They sat in silence, Fannie, stiff in her straight-backed chair, worried over the water supply and no crops. She began to rock, fanning herself with a cardboard fan.

Suddenly her voice sang out in an old German hymn: *Lobe den Herren, den mächtigen König der Ehren! Meine geliebete Seele, das ist mein Begehren. (Praise to the Lord, the Almighty, the King of Creation!* O *my soul, praise Him, for He is thy health and salvation)!*

John's deep bass voice drifted around the corner.

"Pa, I'm goin' to Kansas City. Pete Hankins showed me an ad out of the *Kansas City Star.* They're hirin' men for street building and concrete work," said John, steadily, but determined for both adventure and spending money for his pocket.

Daniel did not stand in his son's way. His own experience with moving and the need for change allowed him to send his son off with a kindly smile and whispered blessing for success and an urging to "Come home as often as you can." Already Daniel sensed that John would soon leave the Mennonite community.

It was late September before the rains blew over the land to drench and bless the earth. John returned. He'd traveled the distance from the city on the Kansas City, Clinton, and Springfield Railway, a train that had humorously been nicknamed "the Leakyroof."

Dora and Louella stood in his bedroom door and oohed and aahed as he unpacked his canvas valise, unfolding and placing a store-bought, blue tweed suit on a wooden hanger. He'd already tossed a dandy bowler hat upon his bed. His manner was more daring, reckless, and spirited than ever. They loved their dark-skinned brother, even though he appeared more *fancy,* to use the jargon of the community.

Fannie Yoder had prepared her usual bountiful supper for her brood, smiling and glad that they all were once again at her table. She had thick slices of ham on a platter and heaps of fried chicken on another. Though the crops had been slim and the harvest next to nothing because of the drought, she had joy in her heart. After all, there'd be other seasons, and now the rains had come. Her heart rejoiced as she cut the pies, one apple, the other gooseberry.

Frank kept them all in stitches as he told the story of how they had smoked out their teacher, cranky old Adam Fullhart. The old grouch never came out for recess or noon-hour play, except maybe for a furtive sneak to the outhouse, then back in again. Seemed as if he actually was afraid to get close to his students.

One cold spring day, he'd loaded the school furnace with the soft, dusty coal. He closed the iron door, hoping it wouldn't belch and blow open, as it sometimes did, pouring a rotten smell throughout the room. He'd seated himself at his teacher's desk and commenced to grade a stack of folded papers. Suddenly he looked up. The room was filling with smoke. The dead, rotten coal smell filled the room. Black smoke was creeping out around the cast-iron furnace door and now was seeping through cracks in the stovepipe joints. Suddenly there was a boom! The furnace door blew open. Old man Fullhart gasped and choked, struggling to breathe. Hastily, he moved down the aisle to slam the furnace door shut. No sooner did he close it than it belched open again. "Merciful heavens!" His glasses dropped to the floor. Stricken and afraid, he ran for the door, mouth agape. Turning the latch he pushed, pushed again, straining with all his might upon the door, stuck as securely as a bank's safe.

Outside, gasping, laughing and shoving, the Bolling brothers and skinny Hank Troyer heaved their shoulders against the door.

On top of the roof, Fenwick Price and Solomon Hershberger held a flat board tightly over the. chimney.

They'd finally let the crotchety old man out before he'd choke to death, though. But, oh, did they catch it. We reap what we sow. The five snickering boys involved in the ordeal were soundly thrashed. Two of the boys, Hank Troyer and Sol Hershberger, actually cried out, tears running down their cheeks at the forceful, rhythmic slashes from the long hickory stick in the teacher's hand. Lowering their pants when they got home that night, they found strange red streaks they didn't tell their folks about. Their folks had found out anyway. News like that travels faster than crabgrass after a summer rain.

The Yoders roared with laughter at the funny episode. Daniel sternly reminded his own sons that he'd expect a much better example from them than such foolishness as smoking out the teacher. No one, though, seemed to feel too sorry for old man Fullhart, maybe the smoke would season him some. Could teach him a lesson, you know.

"Tell about the apple. Tell about the apple," cried little towheaded Aaron, waving his spoon in his excitement.

But, no, Frank would not tell the apple story here at the supper table. Heaven forbid! Judging from his father's reaction the last time it was told in the family circle, he knew if he repeated it again, it would have to be out in the hedgerows or in the open field with his comrades.

It seems Fenwick Price, again goaded on by Sol Hershberger, often went too far in teasing poor bumbling Lootie Hankins, a gangly sixteen-year-old who seemed so absent-minded that he even needed help to find his pockets. Frequently, and with furtive skill, when the boys were eating their school lunches under the hackberry tree, Sol would sneak out a hand and substitute a rock, or a clod of dirt for an item out of Lootie's lard-pail lunch bucket. One day, Sol sneaked a large, handsome red Delicious apple from the pail, the very one Lootie'd been polishing on his sleeve when the teacher wasn't looking. Hastily, while Fenwick kept Lootie occupied by drawing patterns in the dirt, Sol took out the long sharp blade of his knife, cut the apple in half, gouged out most of the center. Next he reached for a piece of horse manure lying just across the fence. Filling the center of the apple, he slapped it together, fastening the beautiful red apple with a nail. Poor Lootie.

His world fell apart when he sunk a tooth into his prized Delicious apple.

Following supper, John retired early to his room to read. Suddenly he'd felt a bit dizzy. Too much food and excitement, he thought. By nine o'clock he adjusted his lamp, turning down the wick a bit so it wouldn't smoke the chimney. "Why do I feel so hot?" Perspiration broke out on his forehead.-His hair felt damp. He decided that he'd read the Zane Grey Western that he'd packed in his valise, bringing it all the way from Kansas City. Frivolous reading like this wasn't condoned in this community, he knew.

However, he had a flair for the exotic and unusual. In an hour or two, John's head was aching so badly that he put his book away. Sitting on the edge of the bed for a moment, he steadied himself, then decided to go down to the kitchen and get himself a cold glass of water. That might make him fell better.

Instead of getting a glass out of the cupboard, however, he, out of force of habit, simply grasped the dipper off its hook, dipped it in the water bucket, tipped back his head and drank the cool water. He took another dipperful. Wiping his mouth with the back of his hand, he hung the dipper back on its nail. His hand shook as he groped for the nail.

Staggering upstairs through the dark hall, he decided, dizzy as he was, he'd better go to bed. He stripped off his clothes, throwing them on a straight-backed chair. His shirt was already drenched with sweat. Climbing into his bed in his underwear, he felt a welcome relief for his tired body. He just simply could not hold himself up any longer.

By three o'clock that morning, John was murmuring and crying out in his sleep. Awakened by his garbled murmurings, Louella got up, crossed the hall, and knocked on his door. He didn't answer. His groaning continued. She darted back into her room, threw a shawl around her and headed for the stairs, taking them two at a time, even in the dark. She knocked rapidly at her parents' bedroom door. She knocked again, louder. "Pa, Mama!" she called in a nervous voice. Her mother answered first.

"What is it? Is that you, Louella?"

"Yes, Mama. I think John's sick. Or somethin' terrible has happened. He's making noises or talking in his sleep."

Daniel quickly lit the lamp by the bedside. He slipped into his work pants, sliding the suspenders over his shoulders. The shirt would have to wait. Fannie ran to the wardrobe, grabbed a house duster that she wore only occasionally. The two heavy middle-aged parents lumbered up the stairs, fear and consternation on their faces.

Hearing the moans, Daniel didn't wait to knock. Fannie followed him, carrying the lamp. She held it up.

John lay on his back, tossing from side to side. His exposed skin and face were as red as a Polish sausage. His hair hung in wet threads, black with perspiration. The sheet was drenched.

Placing her hand on his forehead, Fannie exclaimed. "Go for the doctor; he's delirious with fever!" Daniel looked at the stricken young man. One glance confirmed that indeed his fun-loving son was very ill. Taking the lamp and placing it on the nightstand, he put his arm around Fannie. Her eyes were wide with worry. "Don't worry, Fannie, you an' Louella sit by the bed while I saddle Old Major and go get Doc Halstead."

By the time the doctor arrived, John's raging fever reached 105.

Fannie was bathing his arms and face with a cold cloth. Fear clutched at her heart. "What dreadful pestilence was this that had struck in their home?"

Louella sat by his bed as the doctor gathered Daniel and Fannie in the kitchen below. A pained expression crept over the tired doctor's wrinkled face. "What is it, pneumonia?" asked Daniel, worry in his eyes.

"No, not pneumonia. Lungs seem clear. I'm worried though." He turned to Fannie. "You must keep bathing him with cool water. That'll help keep his temperature down. Give him these tablets every four hours. I'll ride back here tonight after I close my office."

"Maybe you won't need to do that," said Daniel, hoping that indeed John would be better and that the doctor would be spared the inconvenience.

"No, I believe I'd better plan on coming," replied the doctor, closing his small bag. He strode out the door towards the yard, concern showing openly on his face. So Fannie bathed her son, now a young man in body. Louella sat by John holding the cloth on his forehead in the afternoon so that her mother could wash herself and lie down to rest.

By evening her feverish brother had awakened, but he was so

drained and fatigued from the fever that he could not even raise his head.

"What's happening?" he whispered.

"Shhh. You must rest," said his sister, changing the cloth on his forehead.

When Dr. Halstead examined his young patient that evening, he saw odd-looking red spots on his stomach. He smoothed the sheet back over his patient and patted him on the hand.

In the kitchen below, Dr. Halstead told the anxious parents and gathered children. "I'm sure it's typhoid fever."

The words fell like lead dropping to the floor. A loud groan swept through the small crowd. They all knew that those dreadful words almost always meant certain death.

The next day Dr. Adam Greenbaum from the County Health Department rode to Garden City on the Leakyroof train. He hired a buggy from the livery stable for the rest of the journey out to the Daniel Yoder home. Outside their front door he tacked a square pasteboard sign with black lettering. "QUARANTINED TYPHOID FEVER" It was the sign of death.

Each member of the Yoder family took their turn doing hospital chores for their stricken brother and son. But it was Fannie who bore the heaviest burden, kept vigil by him the longest hours, for he was her son whom she loved. She wept silently into the night as she prayed by his bedside.

John slowly recovered. God had answered their prayers. Even the folks of the congregation had special prayers for John. They'd brought gifts of food to their home, leaving their gifts by the yard fence where the Yoders could pick them up, as they could not enter the quarantine house.

In three weeks, John was able to come downstairs. He looked pale and gaunt, having lost thirty-two pounds. His hearty constitution and the prayers of his parents and friends had pulled him through.

In four weeks plus one day, Fannie Yoder came down with a headache during the middle of the Sunday service. She could scarcely wait for Daniel to bring the buggy to the steps of the church after the service. She wanted to get home. The girls would have to get the Sunday dinner. She wanted only to lie down for awhile. "Oh, no, could it be that I'm pregnant again?" she thought. But Fannie Yoder wasn't with child again as she had been for so many years. The ugly germs that had ravaged her son John now settled upon her, to smite her, to bring her low.

There was weeping and sorrow in the Yoder home because of their stricken mother. Daniel wandered in the yard, walking around and around, half out of his mind. His lips did not cease to entreat God to spare his wife. No words were uglier to his children, faces wide-eyed and fear-ridden, than *typhoid fever*.

Louella and Dora did the nursing for their mother. On the seventh day of her illness, Fannie awakened, her once fat German body, now gaunt and lean. Her eyes stared out of dark holes in her head. She felt her husband's hand holding hers, but she had not the strength to press or stroke it. She closed her eyes. "Oh, Daniel."

She died that night at one-thirty. The moon shone down fully upon her window. Frost glazed the grass. Sounds of weeping and moaning swept up and out of the Yoder home. There was weeping and lamentation and great sorrow.

Because of the dreadfulness of the sickness, they could not even have a church funeral for this woman they'd loved so much, a warm, jolly-hearted woman, who seemed to know just how to put love and kindness to her husband and children first. She had not one enemy in the entire community. They all would miss their dear sister, Fannie Yoder.

Planning her funeral had been a grievous ordeal. The hearse that carried her body was drawn by four black horses. Six strong, straight-backed Mennonite men from the congregation carried her casket to the waiting grave in the Clearfork cemetery.

Frank stood on one side of his stricken father, Louella on the other. Daniel could not be consoled. It was good for him to express how he felt, this loss, this woman, rich in love and kindness, who'd managed his household so well. He could not even begin to think of what he would do without her. When he looked at five-year-old Aaron and six-year-old Ollie clinging to Dora on one side and Ida on the other, his grief almost overcame him. The little boys looked bewildered and lost at the uncertainty, the puzzlement of their mother's body being lowered into a hole in the ground.

Four of the six men who'd carried her coffin gathered close to the head of the grave, the bishop at their side. Opening a hymnal, they hummed their pitches, given to them by the striking of a tuning fork against the songbook.

*One sweetly solemn thought comes to me o'er and o'er-nearer
my home, today, am I than e'er I've been before. Nearer my
Father's house, where many mansions be; nearer today the great
white throne, nearer the crystal sea.*

Dora shivered as she glanced at the cloth-covered gray casket
hovering over the cold, dark hole in the earth. A flame from her
aching heart flickered, warmed by the sad harmony of the male
voices as they sang of our Father's house and a crystal sea.

No song on earth, thought Louella, weeping silently, could
ever move one and help one express the heavy sorrow within as
the funeral moaning rising out of the words and harmony of that
song, "One Sweetly Solemn Thought." She would never forget it.
Never.

Bishop Kauffman, serious and solemn, began to read in a
clear voice. The bonneted daughters, sturdy sons, two little boys
and grief-stricken father, hat in hand, looked on as they listened,
opening their hearts for the consolation of the Scriptures.

"For we know that if our earthly house of this tabernacle were
dissolved, we have a building of God, a house not made with
hands, eternal in the heavens."

The call of mourning doves drifted on the wind, even as
though nature itself joined them in their sorrow. The bishop
continued reading.

"Man that is born of woman is of few days and full of trouble;
he cometh forth like a flower and is cut down; he fleeth, also as a
shadow and continueth not. For all flesh is as grass, and all the
glory of man as the flower of the grass. The grass withereth and
the flower thereof falleth away; but the word of the Lord endureth
forever, in which word we have the promise of eternal life through
our Lord, Jesus Christ. Amen."

The body of Fannie Yoder was committed to the cold ground
as the black-clad bishop committed her spirit to God. His eyes
swept over the sorrowing family, clustered together against the
chilling spring wind, united in the attention they gave to his
words: "Look for the resurrection and the life to come through our
Lord Jesus Christ."

There was silence now, broken only by the thud of the horses'
feet against the soft earth. The bishop continued with a long
sonorous prayer.

"The grace of our Lord, Jesus Christ, and the love of our God, our Father, and the fellowship of the Holy Ghost, be with us all evermore. Amen."

To Louella no amen ever felt more final than that amen at her mother's grave side . She wanted to hold onto every word, every Scripture reading. She hoped the prayer would not end, but songs and prayers and Scriptures' all end, and even a life as lovely as the life of her mother, Fannie Yoder, whose body was left here on this lonely hilltop, had run its course. Mother Nature would heal the scar of the opened earth, bluebirds would sing in the cedar above, and the wind would whisper through the tall grasses, blessing the spot with its peace.

The perfection of a vine is shown by the clusters that load its branches. Apart from the vine, they can do nothing; the vine is glorified in them or disgraced in them, as they bring forth or do not bring forth fruit. And Christ is glorified or disgraced by his people as they bring forth fruit or fail to do so.

Daniel F. Yoder, 1896

5.

The Trial

Turning the team of horses at the end of the furrow, Daniel emerged from his reverie. Saturated by the agonizing experience of Fannie's death, Daniel's mind railed in anger at the power and ugliness of a disease like typhoid fever that wreaked such pain and sorrow. Confronted with the meanings of death and separation, he had searched his Bible. First Corinthians had the most meaning for him.

"But now is Christ risen from the dead, and become the firstfruits of them that slept .... a death where is thy sting? a grave, where is thy victory? But thanks be to God, which giveth us the victory through our Lord Jesus Christ."

The verse that coursed through his mind and seemed to soften the pain the most, however, was from the prophet Isaiah: "When thou passeth through the waters, I will be with thee; and through the rivers, they shall not overflow thee."

Bewildered by the loss of his mother, little five-year-old Aaron clung to Louella wherever she went. When he happened to lose sight of her, he grabbed Dora's hand. While Dora was helping with the outside chores, he buried his head in Ida's apron as she tried to peel the potatoes for their supper. No sorrow on earth can compare to the grief of the child who has lost its mother.

But merciful time is a healer, healer even of the ragged wounds of a premature death within this farm family.

Louella, whose talent for music had been nurtured by the congregation's singing of hymns and gospel songs in beautiful four-part harmony, gathered the children around her, Aaron on her lap, as she taught them to sing: *"Love one another, thus saith the Savior, children, obey the Father's blest command."*

She was stirred within her soul by the music. Without thinking, she often would burst out in song. She hummed when she ironed clothes with the heavy black sadirons, or when she picked string beans in the garden. Some of the people of the congregation were beginning to call her Singing Louella.

Sitting in the sewing rocker which had been her mother's, she rocked Aaron on her lap as they both watched the coals drop slowly onto the side hearth of the kitchen range and glow. She mused, her mind wandering to the notes of a new song she was learning to play on her piano upstairs. Oh, it was not a real piano. Heaven forbid! They were simple people. She had not even thought of seriously questioning their Mennonite teaching that pianos and organs were of the world and could not be used in the worship service. They were forbidden in the quiet, sacred sanctuary of those plain, wooden-floored, white-framed, clear-glass-windowed meetinghouses.

She'd gotten the piano idea one evening after school when she'd stopped by Elsie Burnwick's house to see Elsie's new piano. Her father had given it to her for her eighteenth birthday. It was a tall, magnificent mahogany piano. The white ivories gleamed in contrast to the black ebony keys and shiny carved wood.

When Elsie began to play the "Battle Hymn of the Republic," Louella wanted to move away from the piano and march around the room. But she did not. She was a plain, sober Mennonite girl, devoted to her family and to her church. It may be all right for this English girl to abandon herself at the piano keys, but not her. Louella's eyes, however, reflected how deeply she was moved by the sounds. The room was filled with rich, full harmony as Elsie's strong fingers flew across the keys, never making a single mistake. When Elsie began to play the chorus, Louella couldn't help herself, her face lifted, her eyes gleamed and her full contralto voice filled the room. They sang together: *"Glory, glory, hallelujah, glory, glory, hallelujah, glory, glory, hallelujah, his truth goes marching on!"*

By now Louella was so moved by the music that she'd forgotten her Mennonite composure. Her head and shoulders moved with the rhythm of the music. She began to tap her foot. Next she began beating to the four-four time of the march with her right arm and hand. When Elsie switched from the hymn to a frisky little number called "Rustic Dance," Louella's amazement was without bounds. How could anyone do what Elsie was doing? Her nimble fingers flew over the keys more rapidly than mice scurrying from old Tabby. Like the wind, Elsie's arms and fingers swept back and forth. The music crescendoed to the ceiling, up the stairwell, out the windows into the Missouri country calm. Louella forgot the time. When she finally got home, Dora had most of the supper cooked, had even looked at her a bit accusingly. Louella couldn't explain the feeling the music had stirred within her.

That night after the little ones were tucked into their beds, and Dora and Ida had gone to their rooms, Louella made her piano. She took a large pasteboard box they had placed under the shelves in the pantry. What were they saving it for? It didn't matter now. There was only one use, one purpose for this large, sturdy, flat-sided box. Getting the butcher knife, Louella sawed and cut it down to size. There! It fit perfectly on top of the small table in her bedroom. Next she got out the shoe-blacking and a wide-leaded pencil. When she'd finished her labor, chewing at her tongue in expectancy and excitement, she had made her piano.

It was after one o'clock before she finally went to bed, a disgrace for a hardworking country girl. But by that time she'd opened her hymnal, propped it above her piano keyboard and with halting, piteously slow fumblings of her fingers, moved them about to the sounds that she heard somewhere within, sounds somehow conveyed to her by the tiny black-flagged notes scattered on the staff lines of the hymnal page.

Her brothers, Ollie and Aaron sneaked up the stairs a few nights later. Only the cracking noises of a board or two announced their presence on the landing, waiting for a look in her door. What was it that kept their sister so occupied? Why did she go to her room every spare moment? What were those strange clucking and scratching sounds, intermingling with Louella's humming and occasional singing and foot pounding?

This night she had not locked her door securely. Gradually it swung open, slowly, silently as the breeze from a half-opened window caught it. With amazement, Ollie and Aaron stared at their sister, pawing and scraping at a box, her back straight, her head held high. She had a faraway look in her eyes as she strained with her hands and sang "Blessed Assurance, Jesus Is Mine." She was not looking at her hands, but straight ahead at the hymnbook propped between her box and the wall.

They did not let her forget her new musical instrument. Later, when they were in the backyard, headed for the barnyard, she heard them call. "Hey Louella! We're goin' out to saddle Old Dink. Think maybe he'd like to hear one of your songs. Play 'When the Roll Is Called Up Yonder.' " They then broke down in hysterics, pushing and slapping each other about the shoulders in their mirth. "Yeah, Louella," Ollie called. "I'm goin' out to get Old Roan and Bess. Play something that goes with the tinkle of a cowbell. Think maybe 'When I Ring Those Golden Bells' might do?" Louella laughed with them. She didn't mind her brothers' teasing. There had been enough sorrow and gloom in this house. For a moment, the sadness seemed lifted from the air. She was determined to learn to play.

In two weeks exactly, Louella stopped at Elsie's. With her heart pounding and rising in her throat, she asked Elsie if she could sit down on her piano stool. She opened her hymnal to "Blessed Assurance." Straightening her back she reached out before her, hands shaking. She looked at her notes, then down at her fingers. Her trembling stopped. While Elsie looked on, bewildered and amazed, her heavyset German friend haltingly, but surely, played through the entire song. Elsie brightened. "Oh, Louella!"

She bent down and hugged the beaming, sweating girl. "Oh, Louella, I hope that I can give you lessons."

Daniel was pleased that his children showed promise. He felt blessed, as he often sat by the fire in the evening listening to the trio, Louella, Dora, and Ida, sing from the hymnal.

Perhaps it was such deep caring about his sons and daughters that brought about the trial that changed the focus of his life. Daniel had often been told by Fannie that he'd have to be on guard. He was a dreamer, sometimes losing sight of the hard facts of human existence, the real day-to-day practical matters, needed, most certainly, if he was ever to be a success at running a farm.

Seeing the farm sale bill tacked to the side of the creamery in Garden City, Daniel Yoder decided to go to the sale. His attention was captured by two items listed among the numerous ones advertised. One was a walking harrow, which he'd like to bid on, as his old one had lost most of its teeth and had been repaired much too often. The other was the spring wagon, advertised as nearly new. The boys could use that, mused Daniel. A family as large as his could easily use another spring wagon.

So, on a late August afternoon, with Old Dink and Mort hitched to the wagon, off he went to the sale, in spite of the scorching heat.

By one-thirty, a sizable crowd had gathered in the yard of the Adam Powers' homestead. They were selling almost all of their household goods, farm stock, implements, and tools. They had sold their farm and were moving farther westward to Oklahoma.

Here and there, Daniel saw a sprinkling of his own people from the congregation. The women stood out with their severe dresses and black bonnets; the men less so, though with beards and hats without creases.

After hitching his team in the shade of the old, twisted mulberry tree, Daniel met his friends with his congenial eyes and spoken greeting. He moseyed around the yard looking at the goods for sale.

Then he saw it. A handsome parlor organ stood in the shade, protected from the hot rays of the afternoon sun. Hannah Stokley was pushing one of the pedals as her hand struck up a chord. The ivories gleamed white in the light. The melodious sound wafted across the lawn. Daniel stepped closer. Hannah moved aside, greeting the Mennonite minister.

"In the market for an organ?"

"Oh, no," smiled Daniel. "Just looking. Somebody did a fine job of wood carving on this." He moved his strong hand across the music rack and up the tall back. "Looks like beautiful walnut."

Daniel appreciated wood, its grain, the way it responded to the hand and soul. It could be smoothed, bent, carved, and chiseled.

Without giving it much thought, probably more out of curiosity, Daniel placed one foot on a pedal, pushed it a time or two, while with one hand he let his fingers dawdle up and down on the ivory keys. His spine tingled, almost as if he had a slight chill. "Ach, no." He smiled, remembering where he was, who he was. He turned away. But Eli Zook and his wife Lena both noticed that Daniel turned back to gaze at the parlor organ.

By three o'clock most of the household items had been sold. The crowd hovered around the round oak table with the huge pedestal. It sold quickly. The auctioneer moved over by the organ. Daniel Yoder moved back, behind the crowd, slightly under the shade of a tall cedar which was sighing and bending in a sudden wind. The bidding began. Quickly, like electric sparks, bids bounced around the crowd.

Later, Daniel remembered nodding his head, but he didn't recall actually making a decision to nod his head. Without a trace of a pause in his singsong, sweeping, cacophonous voice, the auctioneer picked up Daniel's nod, swung around to Nellie Swartz who'd raised her hand shyly. Next his gaze bounced off Henry Williams, who stood, red-faced, feet apart, intently concentrating on his bid for the purchase.

The bidding swung round toward the cedar tree. This time Daniel decided to bid. He nodded his head a hearty yes. Encouraged by the fast bidding on the clearly elegant organ, the auctioneer broke into a smile, his eyes gleaming. After the bidding swept half a dozen times around the widening circle of bidders, one could hear the "Going, going, gone!" accompanied by a clap of the mallet.

The crowd turned to look at Daniel who had just bought himself an organ. The English people seemed pleased, some even giving him a friendly pat on the back, a congratulation gesture for having stood by his bidding. He'd bid sixteen dollars and fifty cents.

Daniel felt a little uneasy, his mind bombarded by questions.

"What have I done?"

"Why did I make this reckless purchase when we so sorely need the money?"

"What about the church?"

But these questions merely skimmed the surface of his consciousness as thoughts, impressions, feelings, and sounds bubbled up into his awareness: his love for music, his daughters' trio, singing Louella and her cardboard box, the soft healing sounds that soothe old hurts and sorrows. It suddenly seemed clear to him why he'd been so impulsive and foolish this August afternoon.

When the sale was over, young farmer Moses Plank sidled up to the organ, rubbed his wide brown hand over the polished wood. Looking at Daniel, he seemed to understand.

"Brother Daniel, bring your team and wagon around by the cedar tree. I'll help you load it in the wagon." But young, music-loving Moses was the only one among the Mennonites at the sale who offered to help. Daniel hadn't even been aware of that until later; much, much later.

It was Louella, of course, who benefited the most from the purchase of the organ. But it was also Louella who worried more about her father, a Mennonite minister who'd bought a musical instrument. She was warmed, cheered by the way her father leaned against the doorway to the parlor, while she treaded away on the red-pedaled, walnut organ playing "Blessed Assurance" in perfect harmony without a mistake.

It was amazing how much she'd advanced with only two months training from her friend Elsie. She would keep up the lessons. A job of ironing and cleaning once a week in Garden City for the banker's wife gave her the extra money to pay for the lessons.

But there were stirrings among the people of the congregation about this impractical, evangelically inclined, smiling Daniel Yoder who'd been so impious as to drag a parlor organ to his home. Possibly, it would have been tolerated, had he not been a minister.

Already the ministers had met without Daniel. The visiting bishop, Brother Kauffman from Versailles, Brother Miller and Brother Helmuth from their own Bethel church as well as Deacon Zook and Deacon Heatwole.

It had not taken them long in their deliberations to review the traditions and positions relative to church worship for them to clarify where they stood. Clearly they were in the tradition of the Old Society of Friends and other groups, Amish and Mennonites, who had for hundreds of years kept to the simple life. This included the worship service. They all taught and believed that in the worship of God, their singing must be performed with genuine spirit and understanding, reflecting reverence and awe as they worshiped "in the beauty of holiness." Such worship did not permit the exhibition of instrumental or vocal talent on the part of a gifted few, excluding, therefore all instrumental music and choirs from their worship.

"The point is, though," said Brother Kauffman, as the five brethren pondered the problem, sitting around Deacon Zook's dining room table, "the organ is not in the church." Brother Kauffman was a lover of music himself, equally as much as Daniel Yoder. He could understand someone's longing for the melodious sounds of an organ.

"But, it's the example he's setting," said Deacon Heatwole, as Preacher Helmuth nodded in assent. "It's the example of worldliness being set for the young people. We cannot be too careful about the young people."

For more than two hours they exchanged their views, one of them even citing cranky old Cotton Mather, an early American Puritan pastor who'd held that the "instrumental music used in the worship of God is but a very late invention and corruption in the church of the New Testament" and "we must deny and decry it and consider it carnal." Brother Kauffman had a clear point of legality, however. "The organ isn't in the church."

"It's what it may lead to: the example! The example!" chorused Brothers Heatwole and Zook simultaneously, and with fervor. By eight o'clock that evening, they had reached a decision which would have to be brought before Brother Daniel Yoder. The decision was simple.

"The organ must go."

Change came slowly in Mennonite communities. It is true, perhaps had he not been a minister in the church, the little parlor organ would have been tolerated. Perhaps, it was not only the organ at issue, because, for some time Daniel Yoder had felt an air of distance from a few in the congregation. The two deacons had rigorously questioned him about his participation in the evangelical tent meeting held last summer over by Clearfork. Maybe he was dreaming, maybe he was being too touchy.

It was a golden September midday, two weeks later. At the Bethel church, mothers and daughters, white veiled or bonneted, Bibles under their arms, waited on the steps for the buggies to drive up where they could climb in, joining their husbands and sons. Louella, Ida, Dora, and Frank sat in their buggy waiting. What was keeping Dad? Louella was aware of a current wafted about among the people about their parlor organ. She was not aware that it had become an item of such concern and weighty importance.

Bishop Kauffman came down the steps, nodded, shook hands with the lingering few. Next came Brothers Heatwole and Helmuth. They joined their families in the waiting buggies. Deacon Zook came next, black hat set squarely on his head. He brushed its rim with his hand, smiled, and nodded to Louella. Then came her father. He walked slowly down the sidewalk. Without looking up, he climbed into the buggy opposite Frank, his son. "He's beginning to stoop at the shoulders," thought Louella, suddenly aware that her dear father, whom she loved, looked tired, old, and burdened.

Daniel had not agreed to sell the organ. He hardly spoke on the three-mile journey to their home.

In less than a month, the kindly old Bishop Kauffman came alone to the Yoder home. Daniel and the bishop met alone behind the closed parlor doors. Dora and Louella heard only muffled voices as they went about their evening chores in the kitchen. The Seth Thomas clock struck seven-thirty. There seemed to be sounds of praying behind the closed doors, mumbled phrasing that" as we all stand under the searching eye of God that we might follow the example of faith, that we might walk circumspectly and not as fools."

Soon the door opened and the two men emerged. The air was more relaxed. The bishop could tarry no longer. Daniel handed the black coat and hat to the noble churchman, who seemed composed. There even appeared a peaceful look upon his face, the wisp of a smile about his lips.

The bishop shook hands with Dora, then Louella, and lastly with Daniel, bid them the Lord's blessings, and was gone.

Daniel had been given the counsel of his fellow brethren in the Lord, the ministers, deacons, and bishop of his church. He knew what lay ahead. One week before communion, on Counsel Day, a day of soul-searching and making confession in preparation for the next week's communion service, he would have to declare before the congregation what his intentions were regarding the seeming violation of the standard of nonconformity to the world.

After supper, when the dishes were washed and put away,

Daniel asked his children to come into the parlor. There he handed Louella the hymnbook already opened to "Savior, Breathe an Evening Blessing," one of his favorites. Louella played. The beautiful melody filled the room, warm, soothing, comforting. Glancing at her father, Dora sensed he was regaining his spirits after her mother's dreadful illness and death. They began singing together. *Though destruction walk around us, though the arrow past us flies; sin and want we come confessing, we are safe if thou art nigh.* Then Daniel retired for the night.

A note of expectancy and concern hung in the air on Counsel Sunday. The church was packed. Wooden folding chairs had been placed down the aisles and in the back to accommodate the crowd of assembled worshipers.

They had sung their hymns. They had listened to the lengthy sermon exhorting them to search their hearts and souls lest on the coming Sunday they "eat and drink unworthily."

The time for testimonials came. First the bishop, then, Preacher Miller, followed by Preacher Helmuth. Now it was time to hear from the third minister, Daniel Yoder. Daniel stood behind the handmade pulpit. His blue eyes were at peace. Surveying the congregation, he began to speak.

"Dear brothers and sisters." He paused, turned toward the deacons and ministers behind him, and nodded to them. "It is with joy that I desire to come to the Lord's table with you next Sunday, to eat and drink at that holy feast. I have searched my heart and mind. I have listened to the good counsel of my brethren. I now stand before you to tell you that I am at peace with myself, have nothing but love in my heart for my brethren of this congregation as well as all mankind. I am at peace with my Lord and Savior, Jesus Christ, and do desire to partake of the emblems of his suffering and death, to take the bread, to take the cup as he taught us, 'in remembrance of me.' "

Then Brother Yoder sat down on the wooden bench with his fellow brothers behind the pulpit.

There was an electric air in the congregation. Too severe a hush prevailed. There were rustlings, clearing of throats, and manifestations of uneasiness. The ministers behind the pulpit, with the exception of Brother Daniel, rose, stood quietly conversing among themselves. They looked sad and stern as all but one sat down again.

Bishop Kauffman moved slowly behind the pulpit. He began to speak. Calm, but stern words fell upon the congregation. "Dearly beloved brothers and sisters of the Bethel congregation: inasmuch as our dear brother and minister, Daniel Yoder, has received both the counsel and prayers of the ministers and deacons of this church; inasmuch as he and his beloved family have been at the center of our hearts and prayers, we make the following statement. Brother Yoder has not kept counsel. It is our calling and Christian duty to remain pure, holy, and unspotted from the world. This we do in thought and deed and action. It is the belief of the ordained brethren of this congregation that an organ, a musical instrument, when used in the worship of the Lord is an instrument of carnality. Though the organ resides in Brother Yoder's home, and not in this house of worship, it is still a matter of grave concern, even so construed by the ordained brethren as constituting a direct violation of our holy doctrine of separation from the world."

Louella sat, her head down in sorrow, racked by sobs which she tried to silence with her handkerchief. Tears streamed down Dora's face. Ida twisted in her grief. The bishop continued. "Inasmuch as Brother Yoder has seen fit to deny counsel from the brethren, and assuming our full responsibility for the nurturing of the souls of this congregation, and for our concern that by word and example that the untainted gospel is preached from this pulpit, in sorrow and with great sadness we cast our vote to silence Brother Yoder as a minister of this congregation."

Absolute silence prevailed. Even the rustling of the catalpa leaves and the blowing of the wind were not heard. It was as if nature herself was shocked by this human decree. Restlessness swept over the people. Sorrowfully, but with authority, the bishop continued.

"We ask the prayers and support of this congregation that with us, the ordained brethren, we may so pray for our brother and his family, that his testimony in this community will again be that of one unspotted from the world. It is in our counsel that this period of silencing shall be for six months, after which time, and when Brother Yoder has met the conditions of contrition and obedience to the precious doctrines of the church, that is, our separation from the world, he again shall be instated in full fellowship, wherein he shall honor the Christ of his calling and again minister to his flock."

His sons and daughters had not expected this. Daniel, however, was not surprised. He loved these brethren, these sisters, children and young people, stern in their discipline. They were committed to their religion. He had suffered intensely the last seven months, John's onslaught of typhoid fever, the agony, sickness and death of his beloved companion, mother of his children. All this was coupled with his bent for dreaming, and now this, to be unfrocked. He arose, seeking to take his place on a front bench, to no longer remain with the ordained brethren behind the pulpit. Silently, he groped for a place to sit. He had overlooked how packed the church was. Humbly he walked down the crowded aisle. People of the congregation glanced at him with pain. Daniel couldn't bring himself to actually choose a place to sit. He was in the vestibule. Slowly his footsteps led him homeward along the country road where the sunflowers nodded among the bowers of purple asters and bursting goldenrod on that warm September Sunday.

Daniel prayed: "0 Lord Jesus, and God, our Heavenly Father, show me aright and keep me in the plain path."

6.

Giving Testimony

Life is composed of joy and pain, laughter and crying, exuberance and depression, love and hate, embracing and separation. Even as the preacher in Ecclesiastes long ago proclaimed: "To every thing there is a season, and a time to every purpose under the heaven: a time to be born, and a time to die; a time to plant, and a time to pluck up that which is planted; a time to weep, and a time to laugh; a time to mourn, and a time to dance."

Slowly, but surely, as the years passed, the Daniel Yoders became outsiders to the Mennonite community, unkosher, people of the world. Indeed, they had left the faith of their fathers and mothers. They were not completely forgotten, however, as their lives now and then touched the Mennonite folks of the Bethel and Sycamore Grove churches.

Even fifty years after Preacher Daniel Yoder was silenced from the ministry at the Bethel church, his grandchildren listened to some of the older Mennonite brothers and sisters talk about their carpenter friend, the old preacher at Bethel, his silencing, and looking away with lowered eyes and sad voices, murmur, "And it was the saddest thing that ever occurred at the Bethel church."

Daniel, though he did not compromise, bore no hate in his heart against the brethren who had religiously followed their unwritten regulations, their interpretations regarding the doctrine of separation

Jan Wouterss clearly spake:
This is the day of salvation.
Be silent, said the underbailiff.
Why should I, he said, forbear to speak?
My words are neither bad nor bold.
Adriaenken too looked forward,
To please her Bridegroom.
She rests now in the Lord
And has passed the fire's pain,
Through His bountiful grace alone.
Jan Wouterss placed himself at the stake,
Then laughed for joy, as a pious servant,
And thus commended his spirit
Into the hands of the Lord,
Who has his Refuge, Fortress and Castle.
Farewell, he sweetly called
To the brethren and sisters openly:
I will commend you to the Lord,
Who shed for us His blood.
These two lambs have now passed through,
Away tempest!
What were now all their sufferings?
They obtained the martyr's crown,
Which now they hold as their reward.

-Anabaptist Hymn, Dordrecht, 1570,
concerning the martyrdom of two loyal Anabaptists

from the world. He sat down at the old cherry desk that he and Fannie had brought to Iowa from Ohio, then on to Missouri, dipped a scratchy stick-pen into a bottle of black ink and wrote to the Reverend Blaise Grindlinger, bishop of the Methodist Episcopal Church, Columbia, Missouri. Daniel greeted him as a "Brother in Christ" then narrated the history of his Christian pilgrimage and his call to the Christian ministry.

"Due to a matter of controversy regarding my own purchase of a parlor organ for my home, and, also I believe, partially due to some of my evangelical fervor and more liberal interpretations of Mennonite doctrines, I have been silenced by this church.

"I have heard that you are in need of a pastor in the new Methodist Episcopal Church of Gunn City, Missouri. May I inquire if it would be possible for you to correspond with me about this matter, that is, my possible acceptance into the Methodist church as an ordained minister? Yours in Christ, Daniel Yoder."

In exactly three months, Daniel received the appointment to the small church. This was how the Daniel Yoder family learned to call the forlorn little prairie town of Gunn City, in northeast Cass County, Missouri, their home.

"I can see a white church!" called Ollie, a seven-year-old smiling, towheaded boy, sitting high on the mattress, as the wagon load of furniture wound its way around the dusty bend in the road. "Whoa! Whoa!" Daniel pulled the lines, holding his stomping team. There it lay, the tiny village. Indeed, it was scarcely one-half mile square, laid out in faith and optimism so current at the turn of the century in the American Midwest.

Louella, driving the buggy, called to Ida who had been standing to get a better view. "Sit down, I'm gonna' pass." She slapped Old Dink with her reins, and away they circled around the halted wagon. "See you in the city." She laughed merrily, knowingly making fun of the tiny village that lay ahead.

"Yes, we'll meet you on Grand Avenue," laughed Ida, pushing back her sunbonnet at Ollie, disappearing in the trail of dust as they left the wagon behind.

Indeed, Gunn City did have a Grand Avenue, and in 1899 it boasted a population of 250 souls. They had all roared in laughter as they looked at the county plot-map showing the townships and villages. The audacity of a crossroad village sporting such names for the dusty paths called streets!

Two of the influential Mennonite families who first built their homes on that northern Cass County prairie land were represented. There was Blank Street, the one that stretched past the Methodist church, leading directly to the school. Behind this was Zook Street, even more hopeful for it connected the Christian church with Richardson's General Merchandise down the street.

In addition, there were North and South streets, Main Street, Kansas and Davall streets, and most prestigious of all, Grand Avenue, fringed with weeds, stretched out in front of the school.

Scattered about the village just off the broad, plank sidewalks were white frame houses in various styles of Midwestern, rural architecture. The citizens occupying them would welcome the Daniel Yoders to their church and to their community. They were proud of their city. They could point with restrained pride at the hotel, the stock yards, Edmonson's Flour Mill, the post office, Richardson's General Merchandise, the livery stable, and, of course, the Methodist Episcopal Church South, and the Christian church on Zook Street. The Daniel Yoders settled into a story-and-a-half, unprestigious, white frame house at the end of Blank Street, just a couple of blocks north of the Methodist church. Large, whispering, dark green cedars in the front yard and gigantic drooping Bartlett pear trees at the back and side, as well as the picket fence around the yard, gave the house the aura of home.

The summer passed; the Yoders eased into the village life. Louella and Dora made new friends quickly.

"I do miss some of my old friends at Bethel," said Louella, as she and Amy Richards paused under the shade of the cedar by the picket fence.

"I would miss the singing most of all," replied Amy, who'd visited Bethel church once and never got over the way the magnificent singing moved her spirit.

"I guess I do miss the congregational singing a great deal," said Louella. The fact that she had focused her attention upon playing the piano at the new village church had been an inviting challenge for her.

"I hope we can do something about the attendance, though," she said. She was used to worshiping in a congregation with over two hundred, where whole families attended, fathers, as well as children and women.

In this tiny, new Methodist church, the crowd had never even reached seventy on a Sunday, even in the best of weather. Also, there was only a sprinkling of men seated here and there.

"I'm glad I stood by Dad, though," Louella continued. "He needed me, he and Aaron and Ollie. The others can take care of themselves." And of course that was true.

Frank bent his back working for farmers near Garden City. John went back to Kansas City to seek his fortune, much to the family's consternation and disappointment.

Ida and Dora slaved away washing, cleaning, and ironing for struggling farm families, east of Gunn City, needing help because of the new children added each year.

But Louella never really seriously entertained the thought of leaving her place as homemaker for her father and her two small brothers. Oh, Jake Still had walked her home from services a few times, but she knew nothing would ever come of that, slow and unpredictable as Jake was.

Later that year in November, Daniel's church called in a Methodist clergyman, Reverend Stephen Stallman, a noted evangelist who spoke with power and fervor. They would make a concentrated attempt to win souls, take constructive action about the attendance at their church.

The folks of Gunn City, Louella, her father and Reverend Stallman never forgot one particular night at the revival meeting.

It was Dora who had embarrassed herself with her silly giggling spell that lasted far too long. In fact, she became hysterical at the meeting.

The little six-year-old Aaron, out of his innocence almost brought down the house in the midst of the testimony meeting. It happened like this.

Dora had stopped by the Hunt home early one evening after work to visit her new friend Madge. Madge Hunt simply could not decide which dress to wear to the revival meeting. Before the mirror in her bedroom, Madge modeled, twisting and turning in a green satin dress. "Far too dressy for the meeting," thought Dora, not used to wearing hats and being accustomed to plain hairstyles and dresses. Dora, though, became fascinated by the decorative and fashionable prospects of ladies' hats. Madge socked a saucy pink velvet one on the crown of her head. Green ribbons bound its crown and fell down the back. Dora roared at Madge's impish face, the hat, the twisting and turnings.

"Here, try it on," said Madge, laughing and pushing it down to a side angle on Dora's head. Looking into the mirror, Dora saw a broad-faced German girl, hair severely parted in the middle and braided in the back, the straw-colored braids circling her head.

"Oh, Madge!" she screamed, holding her sides. "I, I, I simply couldn't wear this."

Hearing a clock chime six, Dora knew she'd have to hurry on home to eat supper and change for the meeting. She knew one thing. Let Madge wear the hat and the green dress, she'd settle for her simple blue frock, her second best, with its puffed sleeves and high neckband. And for her head? She guessed she'd settle for a simple dark-blue crushed velvet bonnet she'd made herself. She'd have to grow considerably bolder before she could wear a saucy hat like Madge's.

There is something in the air at a revival that makes people anxious. The air becomes electric with the fervent preaching. People pray for the unsaved, and in small villages and towns, even know them by name. If they could be nudged to come to the meetings, various methods would be used to encourage their salvation.

Dora and Madge sat near the third window on the right side of the church. They waited for the service to begin. Louella sat at the piano, prepared for the calling of a hymn. Her father and Brother Stallman sat behind the small pulpit. Dora looked at Madge who was wearing the pink hat with the green ribbons. She smiled to herself, remembering how ridiculous she herself had looked in it.

Madge glanced at Dora, chuckled softly, thinking of their fun earlier in the evening. She straightened her face though, as she thought, "I must settle down and not be impious; after all, I'm in church."

Brother Yoder called for hymn number twelve, "Work for the Night Is Coming." They stood. Louella, at the piano up front, played a short introduction. They began singing. Dora simply deplored such pitiful singing. Men, women, and children, all were singing the melody, not at all like the music she was used to where the roof fairly raised by the rich basses and tenors of the men, giving full foundation for the harmony of the sopranos and altos of the women. They, according to Dora's appraisal of the situation, "squeaked through the song." She began to giggle. She didn't want to laugh and couldn't understand why she had to giggle. "I must stop," she told herself. Straightening her face, she looked toward the pulpit, waiting for the reading of the Scripture.

Even when her father read the passage from the Bible, her body shook with two small spasms and tremors. She shoved her handkerchief into her mouth to stifle any sounds. "Mercy," she thought, "I must get hold of myself."

Following the Scripture reading and while they stood again to sing "Precious Promises," in walked matronly Bessie Reynolds, the village's leading socialite. Everyone knew Bessie Reynolds had to have the latest fashions that she could possibly manage to find in this isolated Midwestern country. Stately and poised, Bessie marched in, turned, and stood in front of the bench directly before Madge and Dora. On her head was a hat, a marvelous hat, more than two feet wide, made of dark brown straw. The brim shot up on one side where it was clasped by a gleaming ornamental pin to the round crown. Spreading outward over the front and flattened side of the brim was the major decoration for this masterpiece. It was a bird, an emerald cuckoo, prepared by some overly enthusiastic milliner to give its earthly years to the enhancement of a grand lady's hat. That lady now stood before Dora and Madge, nodding her head as she picked up the chorus with her loud contralto.

"0, Lord, no!" Dora prayed, earnestly, as she and Madge giggled audibly. They both knew they were teetering on the very edge of disaster. When they both attempted to sit down after the hymn, Madge clumsily dropped her songbook. Dora tried a cough to cover for her snickers. Looking toward the front of the church again, and groaning to prepare herself for the good brother's message, she waited, but the tail feathers on Bessie's hat wiggled with every slight movement of her powdered neck and shoulders.

Stricken, Dora looked at Madge. The folks in the congregation could hear a funny, stifled "pfffft." Some looked back to where the sounds seemed to be emerging and saw the two nervous, red-faced girls.

Madge managed to get control of herself, but somehow Dora couldn't stop. To make matters worse, the minister now said, "And now we shall open the service for personal testimonies to the Lord."

He stepped down off the rostrum, facing the congregation

eagerly. "Let us exalt the Lord with our testimonies of praise and thanksgiving, dear brothers and sisters in the Lord. Let us not be ashamed of our confession, but with strength and boldness speak of his unmatchable glories and goodness."

He proceeded to the first row and nodded to poor stricken Hiram Hodge. Hiram sat there for a moment as if he'd been caught stealing. Fear and pain were etched upon his face. Only the sharp nudging elbow of his thin, long-necked wife, Lena, got him off dead center. With fear in his voice, Hiram testified, saying the only verse he could remember: "God is love." This was the first time Hiram had opened his mouth in a public meeting in his entire life.

"Amen, brother, Amen!" intoned the evangelist, as his red-streaked, piercing eyes burned holes through Lena Hodge, next in line to testify. The agonized congregation cleared their throats and prepared as if their very lives depended upon it to get them out of this purgatory.

It became very clear to poor stricken Dora and Madge, that no one would escape" giving testimony."

"0 dear Lord in heaven, what now?" prayed Dora, as the preacher made his way down the aisle. She couldn't hold back the laughter. It welled up from way down somewhere within her, some deep cavern where all kinds of feelings-joy, humor, ecstasy, confusion, and bewilderment dwelt. It was as if a blasting wind was sweeping a bubbling current of laughter that she was powerless to control.

"What was that shaking?" The vibrations against her arm were Madge's trembling body as she tried to control the same disease that had overcome Dora. People stared at them. "Dear Lord," Dora continued in her prayer. Before she could get her head out of her hankie for even a breath of air, the minister's gaze had fallen upon her six-year-old brother, Aaron. But Aaron, an open and honest little lad, was not buffaloed. No, he knew his verse, and the congregation had shown him what to do. Leaping off his seat, he stood with eager eyes and loudly proclaimed, "God cried."

The minister stopped, rooted to the floor for a moment, stifling his own gasp with his hand. Little Aaron never understood that he hadn't said his verse, "Jesus wept," correctly. Didn't his version amount to the same thing? There was a loud ripple, chuckling and gasping as the adults, nervous anyway about testifying, responded to Aaron's verse.

Dora and Madge now were fit for being carried out on a stretcher.

Both had their heads buried in their laps. Some observers thought they were overcome with conviction at this meeting. Others wondered if they were sick, having gotten hold of some salmon salad a mite too old or chicken salad from a picnic in the searing heat. Again, choking herself with her hankie until she almost gagged, Dora decided that maybe she could stop laughing if she thought of dreadful events and things.

"0 Dear Lord, isn't this awful!" she prayed. She began to think of her mother's death, the coffin, the hearse, the funeral, and the mournful songs. It didn't help. Her body shook like an aspen leaf tossed in a mountain gale. She made her brains concentrate upon the grave and the ugly clods that rained down upon her mother's coffin. But, to no avail. Then catastrophe struck. The dear reverend had approached their bench. Madge was third and Dora was fourth down the row. Sister McClelland was intoning: "0 that men would praise the Lord for his goodness and for his wonderful works."

There was no escape. Like sitting ducks, they would be smitten now. This was the punishment she deserved for her sins. Yes, God was punishing her and Madge for their sins of pride and worldliness, the green dress, the hat.

Dora tried to straighten up, even managed to do so, only this time the beaded, blue-green eye of the flattened cuckoo splayed out upon Bessie's hat, beamed straight upon her, as if to say, "You've had it now, Dora, you're getting your just due." Dora cried. She laughed. She shook and held her sides abandoning herself to the uncontrollable, like a child abandoning herself, rolling down the haystack on a hot summer day. Tears streamed as Madge began to testify. Dora heard Madge's wobbling, high-pitched voice obviously out of control, gasp, "I love the Lord Jesus." It was said recklessly and desperately, then down bobbed Madge's head into her lap. Up bobbed Dora's. She felt the searching minister's eyes upon her. Looking straight ahead and without a break in the rhythm, Dora gasped, "Me, too!"

All the poor minister knew was that he now beheld two mightily stricken girls, overcome, no doubt, by conviction of their sins. His sermon, forthcoming and well prepared would edge them on to their soul's salvation.

The Yoder family never forgot the night that "God cried." Years afterward, at family get-togethers, they told the story. And if Dora was reluctant or slow in responding, someone would fill in for her:

"Me, too."

The God of Abraham, the God of Isaac, and the God of Jacob be with you, and bless this union abundantly, through Jesus Christ our Lord, and what God hath joined together let not man put asunder. Go forth as husband and wife, live in peace, fear God and keep his commandments. Amen.

Blessing at the end of a Mennonite marriage ceremony

7.

Down in Arkansas

Louella had always been her father's girl, and now that her mother lay buried in the coal-black dirt on the windy hill of Clearfork cemetery, she was not fully conscious of her dire need to support him. But her love and devotion were shown as she took more than usual care to fry his mush and eggs for breakfast, to dust his German leather-bound *Josephus* and the heavy Martin Luther translated family Bible.

We do not know what they said to each other, or whether Louella really could even put into words the loyalty she felt for him when he was unfrocked as a minister in the Bethel Mennonite church.

Where did they put their old German *Ausbund?* What about the four-part congregational singing reverberating in their hearts? Just when did Louella take off her prayer covering for the last time and place it in a drawer of a marble-top dresser, a drawer that smelled of spicy, ancient wood and tokens of things past?

Life is a process of taking off and putting on. Was what they were now putting on roomy enough? Did it have woof and warp sturdy enough to sustain the continued weaving of the fabric of their lives? In their grief and hurt, decisions were made that altered the character of their family forever. If Daniel and Louella Yoder ever felt the pangs of guilt, sadness, or remorse at their turning away from a religious and family heritage that linked backwards from generation to generation to the sixteenth century, they did not show it openly. Perhaps their silence about things Mennonite was the true indicator of their levels of discomfort.

On April 6, 1917, the United States declared war on Germany in the bloodiest war the world had ever known. Though the United States was in the conflict only nineteen months, it brought devastation and havoc to American families. By May 18, 1917 the Selective Service Act was passed, making all young men between the ages of twenty-one and thirty-one liable for service. Many young doughboys from American cities, rural villages, and farms were swept up in the fanatical frenzy surrounding the war. Thousands of young men lost their lives. Others were crippled and maimed for the rest of their days.

There was no provision by the U. S. government for conscientious objectors such as the Friends, Brethren, and Mennonites. Secretary Baker of the War Department had simply decreed that all conscientious objectors, when drafted, should report to the military camps where they would be segregated, not required to wear the military uniform, nor engage in drill. They were offered a list of services considered noncombatant by the Department of War, but they need not, it was said, accept any in violation of their conscience.

Those who could not accept any service under the military arm of the government would be held in detention camps to await such disposition as the government should decide upon.

As a result of this decree which gave conscientious objectors no alternative but to enter the military or go directly to prison, hundreds of Mennonites, Friends, and Brethren suffered death, torture, and imprisonment, including confinement in the infamous Alcatraz and Fort Leavenworth.

In the summer of 1917, Aaron and Oliver Yoder, sons of Daniel Yoder of Gunn City, Missouri, went off to war. They had entered the military as noncombatant conscientious objectors; however, they served in France with the regular military corps assigned to the Corps of Construction Engineers. Though they wore the uniform of the American soldier, they did not fight. They were, however, by the nature of their response to the draft, tools of the U. S. military machine. They did not take the radical stand that some of their Mennonite acquaintances had taken. Perhaps, however, this service in the Construction Engineers was a direct result of one of the Mennonite themes that had been kept alive in the Yoder home, though neither Aaron nor Ollie had grown up as Mennonites.

They, as small children, heard only the stories of the Amish of Iowa, or a verse or two of a "Dutch" song their kindly old preacher father sometimes burst out singing. Sometimes he told an anecdote or two about some near-forgotten episode at the Bethel church. Aaron and Ollie had been Methodists, attending the village church most of their lives.

Their brother John, however, was unfailing in his patriotism. He had entered the infantry where he suffered severe heart damage as a result of the gas warfare in France. Returning home after the armistice in November 1918, he lived off of his disability check, glorying in the tales of war and the honors of the American Legion.

No one could stop the march of progress as the wheels of invention began to bring about radical changes throughout the country following the war. Material progress, "the sky is the limit," became the prevailing air. The world had been made safe for democracy, supposedly, by the American sacrifice.

Preacher Daniel was now sixty-six years old, heavyset, bald, and white bearded. He often was found musing, thinking of his next sermon and his scattered family.

Louella, now a forty-one-year-old matronly woman, was known in Gunn City as the piano teacher, having taught most of the village children at least a hymn or two on her parlor organ or church piano. She'd never altered from her role as homemaker for her father and for whatever family she still had, as they came and went, weekends, holidays, and special events. She was known as a staunch and faithful Methodist.

John developed a country gentleman air as he walked leisurely down the rotting plank sidewalks of Gunn City to pick up the mail. Bald, and now thirty-eight, he threw back his stocky body, tipped his white straw hat as he met an occasional passerby. Swinging his cane, he would stop in some shade by the depot to swap stories and war tales with the town drifters.

Dora had become Mrs. John Flora. At thirty-four she had been the mother of three sons. The youngest, little Allen, lay buried beneath the sod, a victim of diabetes. The roles of mother and farmer's wife suited her well.

Ida, black hair parted in the middle and tied in a bun in the back, slaved alongside of her farmer husband in southwestern Cass County as they tried to feed their family of three strapping sons and one daughter. She and her husband, Hank Dahman, qualified as real Missouri dirt farmers.

Heading for Idaho and Washington state to make his fortune, twenty-five-year-old Ollie seldom ever returned to his Missouri home.

Louella, sweaty and tired from the walk and from canning peaches that morning, sagged upon a wooden bench in front of the combined general store and post office. She sorted the mail. "What's this?" A card from Aaron?" Turning the postcard over, she scanned the brief message from her brother.

"April 26, 1919. Dear Dad and Sis: Am enjoying my stay at brother Frank's. They serve good food and the weather here is fine. Wish you were here. Tomorrow Frank and I will plant some cotton in the valley. I'm told that Arkansas girls around here are pretty. I plan to find out. Aaron."

Louella looked away as she tried to picture the Arkansas scene in her mind. She was glad that Aaron had decided to visit Frank and Mae and their children.

Thirty-nine-year-old Frank had married a tall, slender southern Missouri girl. Together they'd settled on a rocky, hilly farm ten miles east of Batesville, Arkansas, among the southern hill folks.

On that rocky hillside, sprinkled with many acorns and a few razorback hogs, they sought to eke out an existence for themselves and their three girls, Mabel, Norma, Louise, and their son Bernie. The Frank Yoder family was pleased that the ex-doughboy, Aaron, paid them a visit upon his return from the war.

Aaron and his nephew Bernie sat on the grassy bank of the stream that rippled over the sand-rocks below their feet. Springtime in Arkansas was steamy and hot. They tossed round stones into the water as they chatted. Aaron, now twenty-two years of age, a well-built, fair-skinned young man with thinning blond hair looked directly at his smiling nephew with his blue eyes as he continued his story.

"We were threshing wheat over at Zook's farm," said Aaron. He explained the process from cutting the wheat to tossing it into the threshing machine to his nephew, who had never witnessed such an event.

"It was at dinner, though, when they tricked me," said Aaron, meaning the noon meal in the big farm kitchen. He proceeded to tell his nephew this most embarrassing moment, back in Missouri.

Standing in line behind the wash bench, which had been placed under a spreading maple in the Zook's backyard, Aaron waited for his turn to wash. He stood with his sleeves rolled up. When his turn came, he bent over the enameled wash pan, soaped his hands and arms, lowered his head near the pan to rinse his face, then reached for a towel. The moment of embarrassment came, however, as the dozen or more men sat around the extended dining table, forking in the hearty thresher's meal. Someone, sitting by Aaron, shook the pepper shaker. The pepper drifted across in front of Aaron's nose. He knew he was going to sneeze. Hastily he reached into his hip pocket, grabbing his handkerchief to stifle the explosion. "Kerchoo! Kerchoo!" There, he'd done it. Excusing himself, he started to put the handkerchief back into his hip pocket when the room echoed with the riotous laughter of the merry threshers. For there sat red-faced Aaron, holding a dark pair of women's stockings in his hands. The James brothers had sneaked them from the clothesline and slipped them into Aaron's pocket as he'd bent over to wash his face at the bench in the yard.

Bernie rolled upon the new spring grass, laughing at the hilarious episode and his bashful uncle.

After the chores that night, supper being over, the Frank Yoder family prepared for Singing School.

"Wait 'till you see her," teased Frank as they trudged up the rocky slope toward the New Hope School, which also served as a Methodist church. "Yes, Opel Slayden's the prettiest girl in these parts." Everyone liked teasing the blue-eyed, shy Aaron.

"I'm ready to look," said Aaron. "Remember, though, I'm from Missouri." They stumbled up the path through the brush toward the weathered schoolhouse perched in a bare spot on top of the hill.

Aaron thought of his only real experience at dating. He'd been out in Minnesota, where he'd dated a big and jolly Norwegian girl. They'd gone to an indoor variety show of sorts. Among the acrobatics and tricks was the lion show. Out ambled a gaudily dressed performer, dragging a tired, mangy-looking, old lion. Straightforwardly the ancient lion marched over to the edge of the stage, yawned, and before the trainer could yank him back, lifted a leg, letting a full quart of yellow urine fly right into Aaron and Zelda's laps. That was that! His first date.

Someone had already lighted and hung the lanterns which gave a dim glow in the small schoolhouse. The folks were gathering for the evening singing lessons. Frank, hymnal under his arm, moved up the aisle to a front bench. Aaron, not being much of a singer, sat near the back. The benches were filling up.

Then she entered, a small dark-haired, brown-eyed, Arkansas girl, dressed in pink calico. Turning to enter the aisle, her eye fell upon Mabel Yoder, Frank's oldest daughter and her best friend. She smiled, then seated herself.

Aaron fixed his glance. He was staring. "Pretty little thing," he thought. "Maybe I could ask to walk her home after the lesson." His eyes focused in the gloom. He then remembered his shyness and how hard it was for him to approach a girl and the humiliation of his first date.

Folks called her Ope. She was the last child born to Jim and Martha Slayden of their brood of thirteen. Opel loved the singing teacher, Frank Yoder, just as much as she liked to sing. Her soprano voice could be heard strong and clear as they harmonized on the old Ozark hymn, "Going Afar Upon the Mountain."

She was a wistful, sad-eyed girl. Whatever had happened to her, in her father's home, had taken its toll. Unless she could change her course, in a few more years, her back would be bent from chopping cotton and dragging the heavy canvas picking bags down the scorching rows. Singing made her transcend her silent and unvoiced sadness.

So Aaron and Opel met upon that night after Singing School, the Scotch-Irish Arkansas girl and the bashful farmer with a subtle sense of humor whose surname was Yoder.

They stumbled back down the rocky hill together in the clear moonlight, one about as shy as the other as they came to the rippling creek at the bottom of the tree-covered slope.

Arise, walk through the land in the length of it and in the breadth of it; for I will give it unto thee. Then Abram removed his tent, and came and dwelt in the plain of Mamre, which is in Hebron, and built there an altar unto the Lord.

-Genesis 13:17-18

8.

Back to Cass County, Missouri

Ted and Alden Yoder sat in the back seat of the dusty Model-A touring car as it chugged down a steep graveled road, walled in by tall pines. Ted, towheaded, fair-skinned and blue-eyed, had his arm around the yellow-orange and white collie dog lolling between him and his brother. Alden was struggling to roll down a window of the car to catch a breeze on this hot August day in 1936. Alden favored his mother, Opel, that is, as far as his coloring went. He was dark-skinned, brown-eyed like her, with thick dark hair. He was also exactly eighteen months older than his seven-year-old brother Ted.

The two boys were not at all bothered by the fact that their father had sold the forty acres that Grandpa Slayden had given to his parents soon after their marriage.

"We're movin' back to where the barns are painted red and the mud is black and sticky," Aaron said. He had often described the rich, black land in Missouri, land so fine for farming that one would have to search all day long to find one stone big enough to crack a walnut. Arkansas was a horse of a different color. Hadn't their father just last season cracked three ribs when his walking plow struck a rock, causing the plow handle to jolt up and give him a ferocious jab in the side. In Missouri, where they were going, the crops would be different, too. No more cotton. Chopping and picking cotton were two chores that neither of the tanned, barefoot, overall-clad boys would miss.

With her elbow hanging out of the right front window of the rattling car, Opel's mind wandered as she jiggled along in the heat. She was glad to leave Arkansas. She could not really say that she was tied to her side of the family. She'd vowed to give her boys more opportunities than she'd had. There had to be better schools than New Hope and Blue Creek, better neighbors than the hog-stealing Hagglers and the hair-pulling, shrill Parthine Hodge. There surely was better food to eat than wilted turnip greens and wild poke-salad with salt pork. Pshaw! She and Aaron half killed themselves stirring the rocks around each year, calling it farming. Her dad and sister could stay there, she'd take her family on to higher ground, back to Aaron's country. She wiped the sweat from her forehead as the car bounced along the road in the one-hundred-degree blasting sunshine. Time was on her side. She did not look her age. Her brown hair was combed back, ratted a bit with a comb, then rolled tightly at the back of her head. She weighed not more than one hundred pounds and looked no older than thirty.

Aaron guided the wobbling car. He sure hoped it didn't overheat.

He was one who didn't worry much about things as long as they seemed to work, squeak or no squeak. If something broke, bailing wire usually wasn't far away. Tires were another thing, though. A blowout could mean the loss of a couple of hours. "Blast it!" he thought, frowning, "that'd be hard medicine to take in this scorching August heat." They'd surely need the help of the Lord and a long handled spoon if they had a blowout.

Aaron Yoder looked older than his forty-two years. Now, completely bald on top, his remaining hair was streaked with gray. His once fair skin had been scorched red by the blistering summer winds. His calloused, scarred hands were large, showing powerful muscles, developed from gripping plow handles and heaving rocks. "I'm glad to see 'er go," said Aaron, turning to Opel, who was shielding her eyes from the sun.

"We should of had more money, though," she answered back.

Her one notable talent besides cooking and singing was her ability to stretch money. They'd received exactly four hundred dollars for their tiny pile of rocks they'd called a farm. A family of desperate, windblown and half-starved Okies had bought it, hoping for a new start in the land of opportunity.

Aaron drove with as much speed as the Model-A would permit without overheating its tiny clanking engine.

Aaron hoped he'd be able to rent a farm, that is if he ever got to Missouri. All they knew now was that they could rent a vacant house in Gunn City for a few weeks until he could find a farm. Aunt Louella had written that the house for rent was directly opposite the Methodist church on Blank Street.

Old Collie nosed Ted gently, arousing him from his daydream.

Ted had been thinking about his Grandpa Slayden and the cotton patch. He smiled as he remembered the trick his tall, weathered, tobacco-chewing, old Southern Grandpa had played on him.

The whole family, including some neighbors who had been hired for fifty cents a day were in the cotton patch chopping cotton. This was a job six-year-old Ted detested. It took strength and skill to walk with unbroken strides down a long cotton row, swinging rhythmically a sharp hoe, thinning the four-inch tall cotton plants. The day had been sultry and hot. Ted leaned his hoe against a tree. He simply did not have the strength to keep up with the others; besides, didn't they all call him Shorty? He'd rest awhile with Old Collie.

Lying there on his back in the shade, he suddenly noticed his towering, slender Grandfather Slayden staring down at him. His eyes were devilish and merry. "Why Ted," said his grandpa, startling the boy, "Why ain't you choppin' cotton?"

Afraid and in awe of this towering, powerful old man, Ted had replied: "Oh, Grandpa, I got too tired. Me an' Old Collie are gonna' rest here in the shade."

"Why Ted!" exclaimed the teasing old Southerner. "Don't you know that if you can't chop cotton, the least you can do is to put your hoe on your shoulder and walk up and down the rows?"

God had spoken. This must be the exalted and universal truth for all six-year-old Arkansas boys. With a frightened and anguished face, little short-legged Ted jumped up, shouldered his hoe and began to march up and down the red earth cotton rows in the scorching heat.

Ted blushed as he remembered how everyone had laughed at him. That, though, was one of his problems. Ted could never tell when someone was teasing him.

Next he thought of the house they were leaving behind. As far as he knew, it'd been a good enough house for ordinary folks like them. Only rich folks lived in houses that were painted white, and he hardly ever remembered seeing the extravagance of a barn painted red.

The house had been built on a hillside that dropped steeply to a winding creek in the back. Poles set in the ground held it up in the rear, forming a dark, cool cave under the house for him and Old Collie.

The front two corners of the house were anchored upon piles of sand rock. Poor folks in Arkansas did not have houses with poured concrete foundations. The weather-beaten house, made of native lumber, had no lathing or plaster on the walls. His mother had simply taken billing paper, tacked it to the walls to cover the cracks. They had cut small inch-sized squares of pasteboard to run the tacks through so that the paper would not rip out over the heads of the tacks.

The house sported three rooms, all dim and shabby-the kitchen, living room, and one bedroom where they'd all slept. Ted would never forget the morning that Alden, in the double bed just across the room, got tangled in his bed sheets trying to get out of bed.

"Mother, a snake, a snake!" Alden'd shrieked, fairly lifting the roof of the tiny house.

"Oh, I don't believe you. You boys better get up," called his mother from the kitchen where she was frying mush for breakfast. Alden's eyes bulged in his fear-stricken face. He was frantically trying to roll out of bed, but the more he struggled, the more he got tangled in the sheets. He emitted a shriek of pure terror. Sure enough, in the corner of the room, close to the foot of his bed, a black snake was crawling up, coiling itself around the barrel of his father's rifle, which was propped in the corner behind the trunk.

Well, they certainly could get along without the snakes. Ted hated them too. Often he had been frightened out of his wits by suddenly coming across or stepping upon a snake. There had been many. Scarcely a day went by, from early spring to fall, that they did not see a blue racer slithering speedily along, a king snake lying lazily in the sun by a fat rock, a long, evil-looking coach whip, striped garter snakes, and, down by the creek, the loathed copperheads and water moccasins. Maybe Missouri, the promised land, would have no snakes.

The dust-covered Ford came to a chugging halt. Aaron Yoder looked to the left and right, then eased the car up a grade of red gravel and sand. He turned onto the two-lane, gray streak of pavement stretching northward. The road looked lonely, forsaken in the dried-up drought-ridden countryside. The searing heat was depressing.

Ted leaned back against the worn, thin striped material that covered the springs of the seat. Wonder what Grandpa Yoder'll be like, and Aunt Louella? Will she be fat and greasy as his father'd described her? He pondered. Ted especially concentrated upon the old man he would see called Grandpa Daniel Yoder. He remembered his father telling him how old Granddad could sing a funny Dutch song and could show him how to do the bear-roll and rabbit dance.

Old Collie stuck his head out into the hot air to look at a dilapidated truck upon whose flatbed hunched a desolate, thin-looking group of people, their eyes staring, mouths open in their gaunt faces. These were depression times and the times were etched upon their faces. President Roosevelt hadn't rescued everyone yet.

By seven-thirty on the evening of that hot, dry and desolate August day, a red stock-truck loaded with faded mattresses, a couple of scarred dressers, a round oak table, its pedestal sticking up like a stricken windmill, a few odd chairs, baskets and tubs, turned the corner.

Behind it rattled and chugged the Model-A. Two dusty, exhausted boys, a bald, determined-looking man and his Arkansas wife, knees hunched up, leaned forward. They focused their tired eyes upon what lay ahead. One grimy and soured dog, tongue hanging out, managed a tired bark. They saw a crossroad village coming up. The main feature appeared in the dusty haze. It was the steeple of a tiny white frame church. A broken, wooden sign, set off by drooping telephone lines, sagging poles and tall, dry weeds read GUNN CITY POPULATION 72. The dented, rusty-red truck slowed, thick dust from the dry road engulfed it as it made a left turn on a weed-lined path that had, in more prosperous times, been labeled "Blank Street," after a leading Mennonite settler.

The dog, the exhausted man, Arkansas wife, and two tousled, wide-eyed boys named Ted and Alden Yoder, rounded the corner recklessly in a clattering old Ford, steam spouting from the overheated radiator. Old Faithful itself would have been jealous.

Both vehicles groaned and clattered to a stop in front of a gray, weathered picket fence that stalked and swayed across a patch of dead grass like a drunken sailor. Two giant green cedar trees whispered and cast a merciful shade. From out the sagging-roofed, story-and-a-half house with weather-boarding that gave just a hint that once upon a time it'd sported paint, ambled two people. One, named Louella, threw up fat, ungainly arms, her double chins circled and lapped in smiles. She wore an apron with a dark greasy center. More slowly, but with a beatific smile, hobbled a fat, bent-over little man, his pink head fringed with snow-white hair that perfectly matched his beard. He ambled and leaned upon two crooked hickory canes. Stopping, he raised one knotty stick into the air, proclaiming in a soft voice as he smiled, "Well, my land."

So this was Grandpa Daniel Yoder and Aunt Louella.

Yet setteth he the poor on high from affliction, and maketh him families like a flock.

-Psalm 107:41

9.

Uncle John

The Aaron Yoders lived exactly eight weeks in Gunn City before moving to a rented farm ten miles southwest, situated exactly halfway between the Bethel and Sycamore Grove Mennonite churches.

But during those weeks in Gunn City, wondrous things occurred according to Ted and Alden.

Grandpa Yoder sat in a broken-armed chair under the cedar tree and there, smiling, lifted up his white-bearded face with dim, nearly blind eyes and sang a Dutch song for his awestricken grandsons.

Sixty-year-old Aunt Louella unlocked the creaky door of the Methodist church, ambled down the dusty aisle, circled the potbellied stove on her way to the piano. It was an old piano, cracked and yellowed with age. Ted had never seen a piano before, and now that he was turning seven, he was certain that he beheld one of the seven wonders of the world. She began to play. First her fat, wrinkled, brown hands played "Blessed Assurance." Next she played "The Battle Hymn of the Republic." The sounds melted together, rolled toward the ceiling, crescendoed outward.

"Marvelous!" thought Alden, who was especially intent upon the fabulous musical instrument and the sounds it made.

"Play 'No One Loves Nellie Like I Do, Said the Saucy Little Bird on Nellie's Hat,' " cried Ted, overcome with enthusiasm, eyes beaming.

"Don't know it," chortled the heavy, potato-sack-like figure, bulging above the rickety stool. The request for the "saucy bird" song reflected Ted's fun-loving nature, his bent towards making merry, letting go in worldly abandonment. But his serious, reflective and even religious side was represented by a song taught to him by his Arkansas mother when he was five years old. It was" At the Cross, At the Cross, Where I First Saw the Light." Two themes, two natures struggled within Ted. Sometimes one almost overpowered the other, like Jacob wrestling with the angel.

So, Aunt Louella played songs on the ancient oak piano for her bug-eyed nephews. She played short songs and long songs, slow and fast songs, loud songs and soft ones. Finally, just as a cloud began to shield the sun, casting welcome shadows, she played a zippy little song she'd learned long, long ago named "Rustic Dance." The boys were spellbound.

But it was short, stocky, fifty-five-year-old Uncle John who stole the cake. Sauntering along on the rotting boardwalks that were left, pointing his cane and laughing, the old bachelor showed the two nephews the glories of Gunn City in the late summer of 1936. The scarred village clung to the parched earth as if to defy the hot winds to blow it off the face of the prairie. Uncle John set about to show his nephews the sounds and sights.

Less than a dozen houses were occupied. Most of these were cracked, peeling, and screaming for paint. These were desperate depression years. Only the white frame Methodist church seemed to emit a bright ray of hope amidst the grim, weathered buildings, weeds, and dirt roads called streets.

A dried-up pond, long forsaken by the bullfrogs marked the spot where Edmonson's Flour Mill once stood. The livery station, hotel and stockyards were marked by the remains, stone piles and a few scrambled bricks and rotted lumber. These mementos only gave hint of former glories before the flames engulfed them one stormy night long ago.

Richardson's General Merchandise rose gaunt and gray. The walls leaned in a bit as if straining to hold together a semblance of decency and order. Orange and green streaks from a board here and there on the Katy Depot reflected remembrances of former glory.

Following the tour of the town, Uncle John led his two

trailing, wide-eyed nephews back to their rented house where he began the painting lessons.

"Painting lessons!" exclaimed Ted in glee, as Alden and Uncle John spread some paper on a small, leaning table under the shade of a spreading maple tree.

"Why, yas," replied Uncle John. (He always said "yas" for "yes.") He handed Ted a quart fruit jar, "Pump some water there," he said, pointing his cane at the rusty pump.

Uncle John might just as well have opened a coffer and displayed costly jewels, spices, and gold, like the riches brought back by Marco Polo on his return from the fabulous East. The boys could not have been more amazed at jewels than they were over the brilliant yellow, red, and blue of the water colors.

"Here's how ya' do it," Uncle John said. He smiled, dipped a small brush into a tiny pan of red pigment. He rubbed the wet brush around a bit. "Now watch," he said, squeezing the dripping color into a small paint pan. Rinsing the brush, he repeated the maneuver, only this time, dripped yellow pigment onto the red. Mixing it, it turned bright orange.

"Well how about let's paint a sunflower," chortled the dark-skinned, sweating, bald uncle. He proceeded to splash streaks of orange on a sheet of rough paper, broad strokes, swirling and circling. Adding a stroke of green for a stem and a couple of dabs of paint for the leaves, he presented them with a glorious orange sunflower.

So, Ted, who loved flowers, every kind of flower, wild or tame, learned how to mix water colors and paint them, happily splashing away, overcome with excitement.-

Alden painted a picture of the train, the puffing, sleepy looking, tired little Katy train that wailed a couple of wavering lamentations, then rocked through the village once a day.

That evening the boys walked the two blocks north on Blank Street to Aunt Louella's and Grandpa Daniel Yoder's place. Aunt Louella was going to play some more songs for them, this time on the wheezy, dusty, little old parlor organ. It hummed, moaned, and moved their spirits. Grandpa Yoder sat in an old padded rocking chair by the window, head back, his dim eyes closed. He folded his hands over his round overall-clad stomach and smiled as he listened to the music, "Savior Breathe an Evening Blessing."

The night had cooled the earth hardly at all. Already by nine

0' clock the next day the blazing white sun blasted down on the dry and parched prairie. "There will be no relief from the heat today," thought Uncle John. What could he do to occupy himself, to pass the time?

He threw aside his *American Legion* magazine, grabbed his cane, tossed his cream-colored straw hat onto his bald head and sauntered out the screen door and across the sagging plank porch. There he came, Uncle John, strutting along, taking the shortcut across the lot. The two boys had known him for only a week or two and already they were intrigued by his fun-loving manner and overbearing charm and mystery. They laughed with him as he threw back his head while holding out his cane to split the air with a hearty, loud laugh, "Ah-ha-ha-ha-ha!"

"Hey boys," Uncle John called. "Wanna go for a train ride?"

Merciful heavens! What more unexpected wonders were waiting to be experienced by these two small, backward boys?

"Can we go, mother, can we go?" they cried, overcome by such a tantalizing invitation.

"See that yer faces are scrubbed. Mind the neck, though. Yer coveralls are clean, they'll do."

They could go on this great adventure, a trip of twenty-five miles to Holden on the awesome, rocking, puffing Katy train.

The three figures ambled across the dried grass in the vacant lots, catty-corner to the weathered depot. The hot sun glared down without mercy. Uncle John bought the tickets. They waited, glowing with excitement, as they stood in front of the tiny depot among the ragweeds and wilted sunflowers.

Soon they could hear the mournful wailings of the Katy as it emitted piteous warnings at the crossings, swaying determinedly into the Gunn City Depot.

Ted was spellbound. Settling himself into a seat by the window, he ran his hand over the faded, worn velour. They were the only passengers in the car.

Beaming smiles, the boys and Uncle John settled for the ride. The train snaked its way slowly out of the village, lurching along the track.

"How about some new clothes?" said Uncle John, pointing to Alden's patched overall knee with his cane.

"New clothes-a train ride and new clothes?" whispered the boys breathlessly. Would the wonders ever cease? It was almost too much to take in.

The train pulled into Holden, a town like all country Midwestern towns in 1936, beaten down, frayed at the edges and distressed by the drought and economic depression.

Sauntering along with his two acolytes in tow, Uncle John nodded and bowed to a few tired-looking country shoppers caught between little money in their skimpy purses and the oppressive heat.

The sinking, dust-covered sidewalk led to the Bales Department Store, a once prestigious building. The streaked glass display window was sparsely populated with three stilted mannequins, a few bolts of calico, shoes and boys' clothes scattered here and there. No particular theme drew them together.

"We'll shop here!" said Uncle John, holding open the peeling metal and glass door. The bell on the inside tinkled apprehensively.

"Oh, goodie!" exclaimed the perspiring boys, simultaneously, their bare feet padding through the door into the dim interior of the store. A thin clerk scraped and bowed as he came from behind a counter to meet the customers. He hoped, perchance, this odd trio would buy some merchandise instead of just looking and fingering the goods in his scantily stocked store.

"Good afternoon. May I show you something?" said the nervous clerk.

"Why, yas," replied Uncle John. The boys snickered. Their toes fidgeted on the oiled floor.

Pointing his cane at Ted and Alden, looking frightened and serious, he added, "Why, yas, see what 'ya got in the way of shirts fer them boys there," cane still pointing.

"Certainly, right over here," croaked the clerk beginning to brighten at the prospects.

"Nope, not that, that's a girl's color," said Uncle John as he dug through the motley assortment of men's and boy's shirts. Finding a blue striped boy's shirt, he asked the clerk to unpin it, shake it out, then hold it across Alden's waiting back. Uncle John was a careful buyer.

"Gotta make sure there's growin' room," he added.

Zealous by now, in the endeavors to be outfitted in new school clothes, they headed for the stacks of trousers. Uncle John and the clerk rifled through the pile looking for sizes that would fit the boys who stood in rapt attention.

"These ought to do, size eight." The clerk held up a brown pair of trousers in front of Alden. They seemed just fine, as far as Alden was concerned. "Try these out fer Shorty," said Uncle John, meaning Ted, as he handed the clerk a pair he'd selected. Sure enough, by holding them at Ted's waist they seemed to be the right size.

"Well now boys, we'd better try 'em on," said Uncle John. Ted and Alden stood anchored to the musty oiled floor.

"Try them on? Merciful heavens!" The stricken boys looked at each other, blanching.

Smiling and bowing, the clerk stepped across the back to the corner of the store. Never mind that there was no separate closet for trying on clothes. This corner would do, behind the counter. The clerk encouraged the bewildered boys, enticed by the prospects of a sale. There was almost total silence in the nook. The boys had never tried on clothes outside of their bedrooms in their entire lives. There were rustlings as they unhooked overall straps, the buckles clunking on the floor.

"Yep, try 'em on fer size, boys," urged Uncle John, leaning on his cane in the August heat.

The happy and expectant clerk and smiling Uncle John stared in at the two bare-bottomed boys, as they danced and kicked, trying to free their feet from the overall-legs bunched at their ankles. Their little male organs flopped and jiggled as they kicked. They stopped, ashamed, bewildered, naked as jaybirds from the waist down.

Uncle John cleared his throat while the clerk looked wan and worried. This was something Uncle John hadn't accounted for, the scorching August weather and no underdrawers on his nephews. A slight oversight, to be sure.

Red with embarrassment by the exposure, yet too near the goal to be completely disheartened, the boys shook out the trousers, hastily drew them on, then stepped outside the nook.

It probably was against the law to try on clothes for size without underdrawers on, but these were difficult and hard times. The clerk, Uncle John, and especially the excited boys were able to overlook such a slight matter as that.

The trousers fit perfectly and there was enough money left over to buy both boys a pair of striped suspenders. The clerk was beaming with pleasure. Money felt good in his hand as he transferred it to the cash register drawer. The boys could tell by Uncle John's look that he understood and had already forgiven no underdrawers.

A few years later, when times were more prosperous, Uncle John married a pleasant widow named Hattie. Hattie shared life deeply with him. Together they bought an ancient gunpowder-colored car, a Whippet. In this amazing, creaky car, they took the boys on picnics and fishing trips.

Now, each Memorial Day, someone from the American Legion places a flag on Uncle John's grave in the Clearfork cemetery where once stood an old Amish Mennonite church. He had his faults, but they were small compared with the way he rose above the despair of his times, hard, drought-stricken lean times, laughing heartily as he thrust his cane forward, Why, yas!"

Every kid needs an Uncle John.

How deeply was I moved by the voices of your sweet singing church! Those voices flowed into my ears and the truth was distilled into my heart, which overflowed with my passionate devotion. Tears ran from my eyes and happy I was in those tears.

-Augustine, Bishop of Hippo, A.D. 350

10.

Garden City

The riding plow squeaked and groaned as the straining team pulled it across the field. Aaron's furrows were straight and the rich black earth pulled loose and turned into overlapping folds like waves in a black sea. Nothing could match the intoxicating smells of spring, the aroma of the plum blossoms in the thicket by the fence, the savory warm air and even the sweet smells of the fresh-turned soil itself.

Aaron and Opel were pleased with the eighty-acre farm they had rented in the center of the Mennonite community. In fact, the farm was located about halfway between the Bethel Mennonite church to the south and the Sycamore Grove Mennonite church to the north. Long, long ago, Aaron's oldest sister had been baptized in the waters of Clearfork Creek flowing under the bridge by Sycamore Grove Church.

The dirt, hedge-lined road, running by their house connected the two churches. They were poor renters who'd planted themselves in the middle of prosperous farmers, whose farms reflected their thrift, skill, and industriousness. Though the Aaron Yoder family shared the same surname as several of the surrounding Mennonite families, there was a difference. They knew and felt that they were outsiders. They were ignorant of Mennonite tradition and belief, feeling slightly guilty and unworthy among these strict and orderly people. As far as the meaning, tradition, and heritage long associated with the Amish Mennonite name, Yoder, their name might just as well have been Stick-in-the-Mud.

Life was hard for this family of four, recent arrivals from Arkansas. Feeling the economic depression that had almost ground the country to a halt, being renters and facing the oppressive, humid Missouri heat, they still chose their present lot over raking through the rocks of Arkansas, calling it farming.

Aaron and the boys loaded the crate of eggs into the back seat of the dusty Ford. Next, Aaron lifted up the cream can, placing it between Ted's legs. Opel came out the back door, wearing her town dress, carrying her purse.

The car started. Aaron backed it up, then eased down the steep driveway to the graded, dirt road leading towards Garden City, where they would market their produce and buy their staples. Neither of the boys had yet seen the bleak town ahead, as it existed in 1936.

The car gathered speed as they chugged over the dark, freshly graded dirt road. Osage orange hedges leaned over the ditches, providing cool shade on the right side where Opel sat.

Beyond a break in the hedge came a wide green pasture, where a herd of Herefords grazed. Ahead on the right was a tall white building, shaded by some old catalpa and elm trees. Drawing closer, the boys pointed to the sign hanging above the double front doors:

BETHEL MENNONITE CHURCH. They chugged on. If Aaron was aware that this was where his father once stood behind the pulpit to preach, as a Mennonite, he did not mention it. The car coughed. Dust began to gather behind them ..

"Go careful, Aaron." Opel turned to him with a frown. The bump in the road had jolted the Ford. "Don't want no eggs broken." She had a serious look on her tanned face.

Aaron brought the car to a halt at the stop sign. After looking both ways, he let out the clutch and eased up onto the pavement that would lead them into town. The pavement ran parallel to an old railroad bed that once had connected Garden City and Clinton with Springfield, Missouri. Now it was crowded with sumac and elderberry bushes. Cows grazed here and there. A peeling sign ahead read, GARDEN CITY, POPULATION 840.

"Where's the garden?" asked Ted, looking ahead expectantly. He always became alert at any sign of flowers.

"Ah, there's not no garden, silly," replied his more practically bent brother, unaware of the double negative.

The forlorn town rose up starkly in the clear summer air. Heat radiated upward from the tired-looking buildings and graveled street. Tall weeds in the vacant lots were reminders of business places that had long disappeared through fire or lack of prosperity. The few shabby stores along the south side of Main Street were in stark contrast to a newly remodeled, glass-tiled Wilhite's Department Store. This store seemed to be Garden's City's major redeeming quality. Merchants and citizens alike had lost hope when the railroad that was to have brought prosperity and fulfillment was discontinued.

The boys sat on the worn back seat of the car, watching the few shoppers mosey along in the heat. Bent-backed men in faded overalls and straw hats dragged along the sidewalk. Their steps lacked a certain eagerness. Marks of the depression showed upon the town and the citizens. Now and then, a black bonneted Mennonite woman, purse over her arm, strode up the broken walk, appearing certain of her purpose in God's ordered world.

Aaron had ambled off to a tiny store at the opposite end of Main Street so Opel wouldn't know he'd purchased a plug of chewing tobacco. He dreaded the consequences, should she find out.

The boys, tired of waiting, joined their mother in Wilhite's store.

She bought only the most necessary items, a sack of flour, a twenty pound bag of sugar, a large package of navy beans, and a sack of cornmeal. Hastily she turned back to a shelf to pick up one-dozen jar lids for her Ball canning jars.

When Opel and the boys, who were carrying the bags of groceries, returned to the Model-A, parked by the dusty curb, they found old Mennonite farmer Troyer leaning in the window, smiling and trying to be neighborly to the wayfaring Aaron, whose father had once preached in Farmer Troyer's church, long ago.

"We've gotta go-gotta git home," said Opel, climbing in the Ford and slamming the thin door. Always in a hurry, she was already thinking about the green beans in her garden that might need canning.

There was little joy associated with those seemingly necessary weekly excursions. The routine was always the same. Get up, milk the cows, feed the chickens, eat breakfast, put the cream and eggs in the car, change into clothes just one stripe better than working clothes, then ride off to the dingy, little town, in the Model-A, with the mud dauber nests in the ceiling. There were no luxuries.

That fall of 1936, the two farm boys enrolled in the Clearfork country school, located one mile directly on the opposite side of the section of land from their house. They took the shortest way to school, down the cow path through the lot, across the pasture to the wooded area and creek. The creek was usually difficult to cross because of its high banks on both sides, mud and water below. Fortunately, nature had helped them out by uprooting a giant oak tree which had fallen right across the small chasm one stormy night. The trunk was wide and textured with bark, providing footing as they balanced themselves going across. Through a bit more pasture, across several fences, they meandered up a long hedgerow and across a wheat field to the school. In the wintertime or wet seasons it was a tiresome walk for Ted. Since his legs were short, contending with the mud almost got him down.

Alden could walk with skill in the sticky gumbo that sucked at his feet, almost pulling off the buckled overshoes, scarcely ever getting his overall legs splattered or mud encrusted. With Ted, it was different. His short legs splayed outwards, the heavy boots, embedded in giant globs of mud, making it agonizingly tiresome for him. By the time he was only halfway there, he could scarcely put one foot in front of the next. But, leaning into the wind, he swung his arms back and slopped on. But his pants. No matter how Ted placed his feet, or tried to walk in the mud, it would gradually rise up his pant legs like a slow incoming tide. Slowly, up over his overshoes, slime crawled and worked its way closer and closer to his crotch. He hated the mud and hated even more trying to scrape it off his clothes as it dried hard and brownish-white like cement.

The boys remembered their year at Clearfork School with fondness. Most of their classmates were Mennonite children who were both serious and fun-loving, studious at their lessons inside the school on a dim, dark day and happy and energetic on the playground at recess, where they played Tag and Dodge Ball and King of the Mountain.

It was their teacher, Miss Hartzler, though, who made all the difference in the world. This young, twenty-year-old Mennonite woman moved with grace and dignity through her classroom. Her naturally wavy, long hair was combed back, pinned high on the back of her head. With bright and cheerful eyes, she smiled at her charges. They all loved her. No angel could have been more beautiful to Ted. Lying his head on his arm, stretched over his geography book, his eyes focused upon her. Her kindness and beauty drew her to him. She dressed simply, according to the precepts of her church, but she would have been beautiful in any culture. She needed no ornamentation.

Later in the year, nearing Christmas time, Miss Hartzler selected Alden and Ted, along with five or six other small children, to be in a group choral recitation of the Christmas program. The boys diligently studied their lines, committing them carefully to memory. They all, however, needed one prop for the choral exercise, a large Christmas stocking which was to be folded in their hip pockets to be pulled out and displayed by all eager youngsters simultaneously on the closing line.

The Mennonite children, though, had mothers who had long been in the tradition of sewing, stitching, and quilting. Patching and threading were activities of little consequence to them. They were as natural as baking bread or cooking mush. But Ted and Alden's mother, Opel, though equally energetic and industrious, had no sewing machine and was too poor to buy one. She did her sewing by hand with needle and thread. There was no extra money, either, to waste on colorful prints, gingham or calico material for the Christmas stockings. Opel simply solved that problem by washing a couple of gunny sacks, ripping them open and cutting out the large stockings and sewing them together by hand and just in time, too, for the performance on the night of the program.

Standing with big smiles, the children, including Ted and Alden, wiggled and grinned, chanted their merry Christmas poem in unison.

"Better get ready," thought little overall-clad Ted, his arm creeping behind him to his pocket, tightly bulging out with his burlap stocking. Alden had his hand on his stocking too. Then the line came, "And for our Christmas stocking!" The Mennonite children, smiling, and in perfect unison, displayed long, brightly colored, carefully sewn Christmas stockings in front of them. They swayed and dangled to the floor.

Poor Ted and Alden. They tugged and grunted, they yanked and pulled. Finally, out of line and awkwardly out of rhythm with the meter of the chorus, their brown, thick, gunnysack stockings came loose. Sheepishly they dangled them forward. The audience roared, laughing at the two small boys. The children, not strong enough yet in their sense of self, felt humiliated and shamed by the laughing. They could not understand that the people were really responding to a funny situation rather than that they'd committed a terrible blunder.

One evening, while they were on the rented farm, Aaron came in with news. "There's a revival meeting down at the Bethel church," he said.

"I haven't been to a revival since we left New Hope in Arkansas," replied Opel, placing a skillet on the back of the kitchen range.

"We could take the boys and go. Accordin' to Dave Troyer, the preaching oughta be good."

Opel thought a moment, feeling apprehension at the fleeting thought of being a stranger entering a Mennonite congregation. She felt so different. Besides, Aaron had told her that not only did every woman have her head covered with a little white cap, but the women all sat on the left side of the church.

"I'd like to hear the singing," said Opel. She was beginning to worry about facing such a new situation.

The boys were glad to hear that they planned to go to a Mennonite meeting. Often, they stood in the yard or on the front porch waving at the pleasant Mennonite families that drove by. The women with their black bonnets looked happy and loving as they smiled and waved from the back seats of the cars. And, of course, the cars were something else. Their old mud-dauber-of-a-rattle-trap-Model-A couldn't compare with the Mennonite cars that seemed to maneuver the mud with such skill, humming and shifting gears as they swayed through the ruts on their journey to the church.

"Oh, what splendid cars!" thought the boys. There were

Plymouths, Chevrolets, Buicks, Pontiacs: cars they never hoped to have, but could only dream about.

That night of the revival, Opel wore her yellow Sunday dress, not realizing how much it would stand out among the plain and unadorned women of the Bethel church. She wore a small gray felt hat, close-fitting to her head, in keeping with the styles of the late 1930s. She'd ordered it from Sears and Roebuck for a dollar-ninety-eight.

Aaron wore the suit he'd been married in, back in 1919. It was shiny at the seams and fit too tightly over his arms and back but he wasn't one to complain. The boys buckled cleanly washed overalls over their blue, cotton shirts, freshly ironed and sweet smelling.

Ted and Alden eyed the marvelous cars as they parked on the church grounds. Already they were excited, but apprehensive as they noticed their parents' apparent nervousness about this venture.

An elderly Mennonite couple climbed the steps of the church, their severe clothing puritan and sterile. There seemed to be order and meaning here at the Bethel church.

They had decided to stick together. Opel didn't want to brave it all alone on the women's side. Seated on the men's side, they soon were surrounded. No one spoke. Only the creaking of the bench or floor at the weight of a body or foot broke the silence. The gathering people nodded and smiled to each other as they sat. They did not visit.

Ted turned to look at the rows and rows of white-covered heads on the women's side. There sat Miss Hartzler! She looked exactly like an angel to Ted, her white covering on her head, a gentle smile on her lips, waiting for the beginning song. His eyes fixed upon her. He was lost in silence and wonder.

Near the front of the congregation, a tall, heavyset woman, composed and orderly, walked to the very center of the women's side of the church, a hymnbook in her hand. "Number 296," she said, looking out at the assembled worshipers. Throwing back her white-covered head, she brought a small round pitch pipe to her lips. The boys could hear the clear tone. "HMMM, hum-."

She hummed two notes, the first a bit higher than the second.

Then the singing began-amazing, full-bodied, magnificent. The bench the boys sat upon vibrated with the deep bass and resounding tenor of all the men that sat around them. Never had they, in all their born days, heard such singing. The harmony of the alto and soprano reverberated from the women's side. Together the four-part singing rose in cadence and perfect volume like a cathedral organ. Opel was stricken with amazement at such sounds, haltingly, then with courage, she joined in with her beautiful clear voice.

Ted never forgot that first time he attended a Mennonite service, the awesome thrill, the way it had moved his spirit. Somehow, he'd been touched with a certain holiness of the atmosphere and the special sacredness of the service. Years later, even the lines from that opening gospel song still occasionally came to his mind, led by that tall, stocky, and plainly dressed sister of the church: *Father, I stretch my hands to Thee, no other help I know; if thou withdraw thyself from me, ah, whither shall I go?*

Beautiful Miss Hartzler came up to greet them following the service. She gave the boys an encouraging pat on the head, then shook hands with Aaron and Opel. Ted and Alden had sat through the service not knowing that many years before, their very own grandfather, Daniel Yoder, now old and blind, had once been a minister in this church.

The catalpa and elm trees outside had been less spreading then, but even so, they'd given comforting shade long ago when Daniel Yoder received the Order of Silence from the brethren of the Bethel church.

O heavenly King, feed and refresh us according to the spirit with thy heavenly meats, which never perish but abide in life eternal; for if thou shouldst withdraw thy food from us, all that we do would with ourselves be in vain and perish. But, through thy grace, we trust in thee, that we shall not fail .... I commend myself to God and His church; may He be my protector today.

-Anna of Freiburg,
drowned and burned in Freiburg, 1529. *Martyrs Mirror*

11.
Eating Your Sweetbread Now

The Aaron Yoders stayed on the rented farm between the Bethel and Sycamore Grove Mennonite churches only one year. Following this, Aaron rented the badly eroded one hundred-and-sixty acres of the old Barb Yoder place, about four miles northeast of Sycamore Grove Church. They were still in the Mennonite community, but more isolated than before. Even the Smith School, where the boys would now attend, had a dearth of social activities. In the year 1937, the enrollment consisted of six boys and one girl. These were the years of a gradual spiritual awakening in the preadolescent boys.

The hot, humid air pressed down suffocatingly upon the earth. It was a languid, dull Sunday afternoon. Aaron and Opel sat in their chairs- patched, old rockers bought in a bygone time at some rundown second hand furniture store. Ted lay on a piece of rag carpet, protecting himself from the rough edges of the board floor. Alden was wandering outside somewhere near the barn.

The strains of "Just As I Am Without One Plea," softly, plaintively swept over the drab room. This would be their worship service on this Sunday. The boys must hear the gospel broadcast over the Old Fashioned Revival Hour, sweeping through thousands of American homes, rich and poor alike.

"And while heads are bowed and Christians are praying," intoned the evangelist.

Ted felt uneasy. He wanted to swallow. He swallowed, surprised at the heaviness in his throat and chest.

Even more disturbingly, the voice went on, "Come sailor boy, you who are on leave, your mother's prayers are being answered for you. Get out of your seat and come. Come down the aisles to the front as you say yes to the Lord."

Though he liked the music, in fact, was deeply stirred by it, he wasn't sure of his feelings about the radio preaching, especially the call to Christ. Of course he loved Jesus. Of course, he had tried to live honestly and kindly and to do his best. Why, then did he have this gnawing, guilty feeling deep inside? The ages of eleven through sixteen are the years of physical upheaval and spiritual awakening in the adolescent. Ted was troubled by both.

Ted remembered walking with his parents and brother Alden to the Mount Hermon Methodist church when they lived in Arkansas. But now, there was no grounding for this family in a congregation of believers.

Sometimes Aaron drove the two boys over to the tiny wooden church in Gunn City, but Aaron never attended the service himself. Perhaps to him, religion was something for women, children, and weaklings. Maybe he would have attended, had at least a few men graced the benches;

Old Aunt Louella faithfully fulfilled several roles in the church which was often without a preacher, even a circuit one. Often, she played the ancient piano, then taught her nephew's Sunday school class. Sometimes, she was Sunday school superintendent. Ted and Alden though, were not deeply moved. Already they'd had enough teaching at Sycamore Grove Bible School to know that there was an intensity and devotion to church and belief deep enough to tie all members of a family together. In addition, Mennonite worship services were not only well attended by entire families, but the singing absolutely lifted you heavenward.

Ted's identification, slowly but surely, began to be in the direction of Sycamore Grove. Since grade three, he and his brother had attended the summer Bible schools held alternately between the Bethel and Sycamore Grove churches. There they'd memorized beautiful passages of Scripture from the Sermon on the Mount and from the psalms, passages that Ted sometimes pondered deep into the night as he made up the sermons that he hoped someday to preach.

Once, while Ted and Alden were sitting in the village church in Gunn City, listening to Aunt Louella tell the story of Joseph and his brothers, the weather started to change rapidly. Dark clouds covered the sun, a strong wind howled. Rain would soon be pouring down in a summer storm. Aaron had parked the rusty Ford down at the end of the street. He'd gone into the gray, weathered old home place to sit awhile with his feeble and almost sightless old father, Daniel.

Suddenly the church door opened. There stood Aaron. "Hey, boys! Come on! We've gotta' get goin'!" Aaron called loudly, his voice ringing throughout the church. Of course, they knew that he was right. If it began to pour, they'd have to abandon the car and walk. Ted and Alden felt degraded and humiliated by the incident. It seemed that poverty, the church, the weather, and the roads conspired against them. It was hard learning to be a Christian.

Two phrases that were sometimes spoken by his hardworking, anxious, Arkansas mother bothered Ted too. They were, "You're eating your sweetbread now," and "When you reach the age of accountability."

When tenderhearted, sensitive adolescents feel the dissonances between their family and the culture of the people around them, their agony is only increased. It was impossible for Ted to discover just which part of his sweetbread he was feeding upon that was so everlastingly good. Only his fantasy life and the woods, the healing woods, provided saving ballast.

What was sweet about driving the oldest rattletrap, mud-covered, tin lizzie of a car in the whole neighborhood? Or living three-quarters of a mile back in the center of the acres of ravaged ditches, erosion, wind and wilderness? Or the stinking, rotting smell of the falling plaster, caused by the faded paper-thin shingles on the house, dissolving in the wind? Both boys knew how to grope up the long staircase and down the hall to their bedrooms. Having a lamp or a piece of furniture other than an iron bed was out of the question. In Ted's room, he'd pushed the bed against the brick chimney so that on the bitter, winter nights, when the water froze in the bucket below and the fire in the wood stove burned to only a few glowing coals, some warmth still radiated from the bricks. He was comforted by a light shining from the hillside a mile back to the south. The friendly glow came from the house of Manasseh, the Mennonite bishop. Across the wheat field and woods it shone brightly, emanating a special warmth and hope represented by the Mennonites that Ted so deeply admired. Pondering at night, he sometimes thought in the anguish of his soul, "Oh, I'll put on my clothes and ride Old Major over to Brother Manasseh and tell him that I want to be a Christian."

A call to become a follower of Christ had not been given in the tiny church in Gunn City. How did one respond to a voice coming out of a box, with your father and mother sitting there, staring off into space? Ted felt the anguish of conviction and bewilderment over the spirit's birth and growth.

One day while Aaron was listening to the war news coming over the radio, the news broadcaster reported that a girl in France, in her spiritual quest and desire for peace to come to her land, had seen an omen in the sky.

Up in the clouds, she had seen a cross with Jesus upon it. "Oh blessed visitation!" thought Ted, who'd walked in just in time for the vision announcement.

Later that day he took a long walk into the woods, down over the bank where the papaw trees provided their refuge and shelter. Why was it some people were so blessed? Why did God seem to reveal himself so openly to a Catholic girl in France, but not to him. He wished, prayed, desired, and dreamed for some omen, some visitation from God that would give comfort in a frenzied world.

Strangely enough, dreams are sometimes the fruits of desire.

That night, huddled in the lonely, dark room, head by the chimney, Ted had a dream. Glorious white clouds began billowing and pouring into a gold and blue sky. In his dream, reverently and with awe, Ted turned his face upwards. There, where the clouds had split asunder, a cross was raised. Upon it was the outstretched form of Jesus. His omen came that night in his dream. He told no one. Like Mary, who was mysteriously visited by the Holy Spirit and carried within her heart the burden of her visitation, he too, kept silent.

Ted guessed that while he was finishing eating his sweetbread, he was simultaneously entering the age of accountability. He ached to say yes to God, but did not understand that God already knew the desires of his heart. He did not realize that his family's pattern of living, the social isolation, and the lack of a religious tradition and commitment were responsible for much of the frustration, guilt, and anguish over how to publicly announce his beliefs and what he wanted to do.

To my son: Oh regard not the great multitude, or the ancient custom, but look at the little flock, which is persecuted for the word of the Lord, for the good persecute none, but we are persecuted. When you have joined them, beware of all false doctrine, for John says: "Whosoever transgresseth, and abideth not in the doctrine of Christ, hath not God. He that abideth in the doctrine of Christ, he hath both the Father and the Son. *II* The doctrine of Christ is mercy, peace, purity, faith, meekness, humbleness, and full obedience to God.

-Maeyken Wins, burned at the stake for her faith
in Antwerp, Holland, 1573, to her son Adriaen

12.

High School

In September of 1943, Ted and Alden trudged across the wheat field, climbed barbed-wire fences, and routed themselves through a cow pasture. Picking their way across a stream, they hiked up a steep bank, trailed along the osage orange hedge, finally arriving at the graveled highway where they met the bus that took them to Harrisonville High School.

Usually they left home at six-thirty in the morning to avoid missing the bus as it wound its way through the country. The route took them eastward, then north to the crossroads village of Gunn City. There, on the old unmarked Blank Street, the bus stopped for a group of three or four teenagers, waiting in front of the Methodist church.

Down the dusty street to the left, hiding behind ancient cedar and pear trees, stood the old Daniel Yoder home, weather-beaten, looking as if it were slowly melting into the earth. Grandpa Daniel

Yoder had died in his bed at home in the late winter of 1940. Ted recalled the funeral which had been held in the small Methodist church. He remembered almost nothing except the trip to the Clearfork cemetery. He and Alden had ridden to the funeral through the deep ruts in their Kansas City cousin John Yoder's new Ford \'-8. They were awestricken at Uncle Harvey's oldest son's car. The day had turned bleak and gray by the time Grandpa's casket was lowered into the dark hole beside a weathering tombstone that bore someone's name whom Ted had never known, Fannie Troyer Yoder.

Occasionally, while glancing at the old Yoder house, Ted spied an aging, fat woman standing on the rickety porch in a loose, bagging dress. She smiled and waved as the bus turned the corner. It was Aunt Louella.

Ted was socially ill prepared for high school, since he moved directly from a tiny country school into the county's largest high school. It stood imposing and awesome on its shady, immaculate lawn.

His inquiring mind and willingness to learn, however, kept him afloat. He was not used to mixing with teenaged boys who seemed callous and . rough as they bragged about their sexual conquests, making sure to drop the names of one or two spirited girls of the town.

It was during these early high school years that a young Mennonite named Eli Eby befriended Ted and Alden. His red hair was swept back from his forehead, revealing fair skin, blue eyes, and clean sharp lines on his face. With a strong, athletic build, he exuded strength and health as he turned to smile. At his unbuttoned shirt collar, sandy-red hair curled outward. He was impressively mature for a sixteen-year-old.

Eli and Alden Yoder, both sophomores, had classes together, were keenly interested in music, and began to sing in glee-club and special programs, as well as enrolling in band. Alden, who had inherited his mother Opel's talent for music, learned to play with agility and skill an old, dented trombone he'd bought from a Harrisonville merchant's son for ten dollars. Eli rented the school sousaphone, and oompa-paad away as they harmonized with their instruments in the high school band.

Gradually Ted and Alden grew closer to Eli Eby. He appeared wise and all-knowing. Living on a farm that bordered the highway, he came from a prosperous Mennonite family that had survived the depression and was now secure and firmly planted. Eli and his brother Ray impressed their friends and acquaintances at school by driving into town in their father's new, gleaming Pontiac. To Ted and Alden, the car appeared opulent, and so outmatched theirs, there was no comparison. Their dad had finally traded the ancient Model-A for a 1939 two-door Ford V-B. Though an improvement over the Model-A, it was badly used before Aaron purchased it. The front grill, lacking two vertical bars, bore a toothless grin as it meandered down the road. The fact that it was a second-hand car and a cheaper make was clearly evident whenever it was parked in the vicinity of Eli's Pontiac.

One fall evening, a few weeks later, the orange school bus rattled over the rough limestone road, carrying its load of tired farmers' sons and daughters.

"Let's go to the football game," said Eli, as he leaned back facing Ted and Alden in the bus seat.

The two boys pondered, never having been to a football game in their lives. It really didn't interest Ted, but he could go along for the ride and the experience.

"We'll have to see when we get home," replied Alden. "Depends on whether we can get the chores done and get up to your place in time." He knew that he and his brother were not free to come and go as many other youth seemed to be.

"What time will you leave?" asked Alden, hoping that indeed the arrangements could be made. He and Eli had developed an interest in a couple of town girls whom they thought were strikingly beautiful in their short skirts, bobby sox, sweaters, and short hairstyles. There was a distinct contrast between the town girls and the Mennonite girls who dressed in homemade print dresses, wore long hair either braided and wrapped around the head or done up in a tight roll. They wore no makeup. Several of them wore long cotton stockings, as they had to walk a mile or two down muddy roads in the cold weather, then stand, waiting in the chilly wind for the bus. This set them apart even further.

Finishing the evening chores early enough, Aaron agreed that the two teenagers could drive the V-8 over to Eli's and go with him to the football game. Each boy with thirty-five cents in his pocket, was fortified for the evening spree.

The gleaming Pontiac floated into a parking spot by the

gymnasium. Out back, the bleachers were filled with cheering crowds. Ted hadn't expected so much noise. He thought the twenty-five-cent fee to get through the gate was dreadfully wasteful. Nevertheless, smiling and appearing happy, he seated himself on one side of Eli, his brother Alden, on the other. Down below on the field some strange game was in progress. Ted could see why it was called football because occasionally someone in an ugly, even grotesque, suit would kick an oblong ball, sending it soaring into the air. It appeared then that the other players scrambled and fought, trying to see who could knock the other down the fastest. There was no rhyme or reason to such a boring game, thought Ted. Then, suddenly, after a spell of stomping upon and strangling each other, the boys below gathered into two small groups, heads bent over, buttocks sticking up. Ted was even more puzzled. "Looks like they were rooting for worms with their noses," he thought, bored and feeling out of place.

The boys did not stay for the game to finish, as Eli announced that there was another football game at Butler, about twenty-five miles south on highway 71. The opulent car purred along on the concrete strip. Ted and Alden couldn't say no to this wonderful Mennonite friend of theirs who seemed so charming, powerful, and controlled. In the back seat of the Pontiac, Ted felt the guilt creep around him like a cloud. It seemed wrong and extravagant, going to another football game in such a faraway place without telling their folks. Already it was growing late.

When they reached Butler, they found that the game was past the halftime. No one seemed particular about collecting a fee. Eli eased them through the line at the east side of the field. This was one of the most boring nights Ted ever spent; he knew that he never would go voluntarily to another football game as long as he lived.

Bored and guilty, he began to feel depressed as he thought of the miles they'd traveled without bothering to inform their folks of this added excursion. He felt cheap and sneaky.

It was twelve o'clock by the time Ted and Alden sneaked the V-8 into the lean-to garage. The kitchen door squeaked as they pulled it open. Tiptoeing across the linoleum floor, they headed for the stairway door. Directed by the moonlight, they groped for the opening to the stairs, felt their way up the steps, then parted, each going to a separate room.

Quickly, they unbuttoned their shirts and trousers, pulled them off and hung them on hooks in their closets. Slipping into bed, they began to doze off, knowing that chore time would come far too soon. They were not aware that their suave, controlled, and dearly beloved friend, Eli, had turned back the odometer on the Pontiac so that his father, who had probably checked the mileage before the evening spree, would not know about the added sixty miles. But, such was life.

In matters of faith and life, Ted felt more and more at home with the Mennonites. He saw in their simplicity and ordered living the order and peace that he needed. His experiences at summer Bible schools had provided opportunities to not only learn about the Bible and the Christian message, but more importantly, he felt loved and touched by the warm and caring teachers.

Ted was overjoyed the day Eli invited them to come to the Mennonite young folk's Literary. The Literary Society, or Literary, as they called it, was the monthly fellowship held at one of the homes. The Literary featured talks and lectures assigned by the program committee. Games and party time followed this formal period. These were uproariously joyful and happy times of good, wholesome fun, with paper games inside if the weather was cold and action games outside in the spring and summer months. Ted and Alden, however, felt some apprehension about attending the Literary. Though they knew much about the Mennonite culture, they also knew that they were outsiders and would remain so unless they should happen to choose to become members of the Mennonite church.

Old Uncle John over in Gunn City, who sat and read his *American Legion* magazines would surely die of a heart attack if he knew his nephews were contemplating becoming Mennonites. Once he tried to set them straight. "Those Mennonite young men who don't go into the service to fight the Germans and the Japs are yellow-bellied-coward-no-goods!"

How did one handle the Mennonite concept of nonresistance in a time of war and struggle? Once they had heard Hitler's insane voice, ranting and raving as they listened to a broadcast, on their battery-powered radio. They also had cousins, Aunt Ida's two boys, Clarence and Alvin who were involved in the war in the Pacific. Ted and Alden were torn with the war agony and the sad sounds of strange places like Corregidor, Okinawa, Guam, and

Iwo Jima.

The historic peace position of the Mennonites sounded logical and consistent to Ted and Alden. It was not strange though that they experienced some inner dissonance since their cousins were involved in the hated war.

Literary that night was held at the Amos Schrock home. Eighteen-year-old Emma and her twenty-one-year-old brother John were host and hostess. Emma patted her neatly rolled black hair, checking to see if all the pins securely held. She smoothed her lilac dress, then walked over to the library table, struck a match to light the Aladdin lamp. John, ruddy-looking, hair neatly parted, closed the stairs door and entered the room. He was wearing his white shirt and Sunday trousers. He would wear no coat tonight, as the Literary was to be held inside. He needed to bring in some of the wooden folding chairs from the church. He'd placed them outside on the porch. The crowd of young people would probably fill the three rooms, kitchen, dining and living rooms.

By seven-thirty, dust began to gather at the far end of the lane as the first car, a blue Chevrolet, turned off the main road. That would be Mary and Elizabeth Hershberger. John hoped poor Mary wouldn't get flustered and crumple a fender getting her father's Chevy parked. "Good thing there are not many cars out there yet," he thought.

Next came an old 1930 Ford, chugging along in the dust. Floyd was at the wheel, his sister Eunice smiling from the other side.

Emma Schrock became nervous. "Oh my! Have I enough games planned?" she thought. "And how about the homemade ice cream? Is there enough to go around?" She concluded that they would just have to make do now. Already a small crowd was coming up the sidewalk.

By a quarter to eight, Eli and his brother Ray drove in and parked under the mulberry tree, completely forgetting how they were endangering the top of father's Pontiac, exposing it to the purple stains that would result from the birds perched above.

In the plush back seat of the Pontiac sat Ted and Alden Yoder, flamboyant ties cascading down the front of their starched white shirts. They had dressed for the occasion. Apprehensively, yet with excitement, they emerged from the security of the Pontiac.

Ted was feeling eager about one more link that just might help him in connecting with the Mennonites.

Both boys were glad that their jolly-hearted friend, Eli, had driven down the three-quarter-mile, narrow, eroded lane to their rented farm to pick them up. Eli was like that, he showed his concern for them, as well as kindness and generosity in providing transportation. They could enter the strange house among the Mennonite young folks, girded by the warmth of their friend and his brother.

If Emma and John Schrock considered the two new Yoder boys outsiders, they never allowed it to show. Smilingly, and with firm handshakes, they greeted the adolescent boys. The four young men entered the kitchen door John Schrock held open. They moved through the dining room into the parlor which would fill up first. Latecomers would be placed in the kitchen.

Ted and Alden sat by Eli and Ray, next to Samuel, the bishop's son. On the other side of the room, the Mennonite girls seated themselves. They were scrubbed and neatly groomed, sitting with their ankles crossed, Sunday hankies clasped in their hands which were folded in their laps. Ted hadn't considered this, men and women sitting on opposite sides of the room. The atmosphere seemed a bit strained as the two groups sat facing each other. Occasionally, someone turned to whisper a word, or clear a throat. The gathering was taken seriously. By eight o'clock, the president, Elaine Miller, stood up. Being a country school teacher, she leaned into her task with faith and confidence. Besides, Elmer Yoder over in the corner by the secretary had a small book of Robert's Rules of Order in case she strayed too far. Sadie Nuenschwander, the secretary, pushed back her metal-framed glasses, licked the end of her lead pencil and began to record the proceedings.

The Literary seemed to meet and reflect the two sides of Ted; his serious side, love for words and learning, as well as the holy hush of the sacred, religious atmosphere brought about by the singing of "Jesus Thou Mighty Lord" by a mixed quartet.

Ted's fun-loving side was typified by the title of a little song his father had taught him when he was a small child, "The Saucy Little Bird on Nellie's Hat," a side of him activated when the games began. The reserve of the group was broken. Dividing into teams for relays and numbering for partners, their laughter filled the house. It did not even begin to resemble the solemn group that crept in to begin the Literary. Everyone gave themselves fully to the warmth and cheerfulness of the evening so filled with fun and laughter.

Ted felt a security among these kindly young people who represented to him the very peak of Christian love and virtue. How could any group of young people be so good, so true, so orderly? They seemed both fun-loving and of single purpose in their love for the Lord. He envied them. He hoped this indeed would not be the last time for them to come to a Literary gathering.

Back in his dark bedroom that night, Ted relived every moment of the wonderful evening. He smiled, then chuckled out loud, remembering the games, the caring, and the merriment. The ice cream had been luscious. He did not know then that one Mennonite minister's daughter whispered behind her hand to Nellie Kropf, "What are those Yoder boys doing here? They're not Mennonites."

They would hear it later.

For our light affliction, which is but for a moment, worketh for
us a far more exceeding and eternal weight of glory; while we
look not at the things which are seen, but the things which are
not seen ... which are eternal.

-2 Corinthians 4:17-18

13.

The Fire

Louella Yoder, now carrying the poundage and etchings of
her sixty-seven years, lived alone in the tired old house eroded by
the ravages of time. It had not had a coat of paint since before the
great depression of the 1930s. The kitchen and front porches were
broken and sagging as the boards rotted and dissolved into the
ground. If she noticed how the planks bowed and bent, tilting to
the earth as she placed her obese body upon them, she gave no
hint. She was one who never complained. People noticed that her
fat, wrinkled face was usually smiling. Her graying hair was
parted, swept back and tied into the same old pile on the back of
her head. She'd worn it that way since the day of her baptism in
Clearfork Creek, way back near the turn of the century.

She stooped a little, looking ahead, one elbow bent, hand on
her side as she trudged along toward the tiny combined post office
and grocery to get her mail. Already sweat was dripping down her
dark, oily skin. She was hoping that today she'd get a letter from
her niece, Margaret, out in Nebraska. Margaret, like her, was a
devoted worker in the Methodist church. If her old age pension
check came, she'd buy a few groceries. A can of salmon, yes,
that'd be fine. She loved salmon patties. If they were out of
salmon, she'd buy sardines. The worn path led through the weedy

lot. If once there had been buildings there, perhaps she alone, among the scattered villagers, would have remembered it.

A sedan pulled up to the store. It was Martha Bradey and her two daughters coming in for the mail. She'd worked out at Bradey's every Wednesday for the past twenty years, doing the washing and ironing, chores for which life seemingly prepared her. She'd performed her duties without complaining or grumbling.

She found no letter from her niece, but was pleased that she'd received a postcard from her sister Ida out in Idaho. She ambled back along the street that led past the Methodist church. She shifted a small brown bag which held her can of salmon, a loaf of bread, and a half-pound of lunch meat. In the other hand, she held a torn slice of the spicy meat she'd slid out of the wrapping to nibble on as she ambled home. What need was there to wait until she got home? Her fat lips pooched forward, moving in and out as she nibbled the morsel with her remaining front teeth. Passing the church, she thought of her nephews Ted and Alden, wondering why they had been missing Sunday school lately, even when it wasn't raining and the roads were quite passable.

Her mind began to focus upon an incident a couple of years back.

Opel'd had surgery at a hospital in Kansas City. She'd had Chuck Bradey drive her out to Aaron's place to stay a week to do the cooking and help as best as she could. It had been the last of July. She had seen that the ripe tomatoes in the garden would have to be picked and canned, otherwise it would be a dreadful waste. So she and the two boys picked, peeled, and canned the tomatoes.

They'd sat in the sweltering July heat out on the screened porch of the rambling old farmhouse on the land Aaron had rented the last six or seven years. Even Aaron's rented farm seemed characteristic of the things that she experienced in her life-worn, eroded, old things; cracked dishes, a rusty, tin pie safe, the tiny black bowlegged kitchen range that went so far back in her family that she'd forgotten when they'd purchased it. Someday she might give the old parlor organ to Alden, her nephew, that is if he became a faithful Methodist. She still had two pieces of furniture that she knew'd been made by Amish hands back in West Liberty, Ohio. Musingly, she thought of her childhood back in Iowa. Whatever happened to her Aunt Mary Warey? or the celebrated

Sleeping Preacher, her Uncle Noah Troyer?

There was a surprise related to the tomato canning that she didn't know about for several months. After the canning, when she'd gone back to Gunn City, Aaron and the two boys were troubled by strange, disturbing sounds in the night. The silence of the darkness in the forlorn old farmhouse was shattered by eerie reverberations which came at frequent intervals. Dreadful booming sounds were followed by clattering and tinkling, like metal particles, or glass falling back to the concrete.

In the morning, when they'd gone down to the basement to investigate, the fermented stink of spoiled tomatoes rose up to greet them like the sour miasma of a swamp. Great splotches made by the soured tomatoes stained the ceiling. Glass particles and jar lids were randomly strewn. The cans remaining on the shelf stood there, foaming and hissing at the seams where the rubber bands and the jar lids met. It would only be moments before they blasted off. Before it was over, every single can of tomatoes took off for Mars.

The boys roared and howled with laughter, feeling that the hilarious situation was in keeping with what they considered to be the slovenly and careless ways of their old Aunt Louella.

A year later when she'd asked Aaron about the tomatoes, he told her bluntly about the night of the cannonading in the basement. She grinned, put her fat hand on her hip, smiled and said, "My land! Musta' done somethin' wrong."

Louella's musings were interrupted by the barking of the yellow mongrel biting the iron wheels of the farm wagon rolling and lurching by. Amos Sand rocked on the wagon seat, relaxed and almost asleep as the mules pulled the wagon towards the hay fields at the outskirts of the village.

"Howdy, Amos!" Louella called.

"How do," Amos replied, lifting his hat and nodding sleepily.

"Fine day, ain't it, Miss Eller?" Village folks often called her "Miss Eller."

Celia Carpenter stepped off her porch, swinging a badly worn broom across the broken sidewalk in front of her house.

"Well howdy, Miss Eller, any mail today?" she called. Louella cleared her throat. "Why yes, a letter from Ida," she called back.

Good news from out West, I hope?" queried the nosy neighbor. "Might say 'tis good." Louella stopped, poked around in her grocery sack for the postcard. "Here. I'll read it to you," she said, keeping in character with the way most of the news, good and bad, scandalous and innocent, was shared among the villagers.

But before Louella had her hand out of the grocery bag, she was startled by Celia's sharp cry. "Miss Eller, what's that?" Celia had dropped her broom as she pointed to a wisp of gray-black smoke wafting ever so gently from the kitchen roof of Louella's decrepit old house.

Stricken, Louella dropped her groceries, throwing up her fat arms as she fixed her eyes on the wisp of smoke, rising and falling, sweeping down, then up. Suddenly she froze in terror as she saw an orange tongue lick up at the sky, fall down again, then flame up and mingle with the smoke.

"0 merciful Jesus! Fire! fire!" she screamed. But her voice hardly rose above the wind, so constricted was her poor old throat.

Forgetting about her rheumatism, Celia staggered inside, turned the crank on her wall phone, giving it four long rings. "Fire! fire!" she screamed into the mouthpiece to whoever happened to hear her general ring for help. "Fire, fire! Miss Eller's house is afire!"

Sam Hodge, seeing the stricken Miss Eller in the middle of the dusty road, stopped his Ford to see what was the matter. Then he saw the flames roaring up through a hole in the kitchen roof of the ancient house nestled between the towering cedars and the Bartlett pear trees.

"A-ooo-ga, a-ooo-ga," sounded his horn as he leaned out the window, shouting for help.

Amos Sand, awakened from his drowsiness on his wagon seat, halted his mules, leaped over the side of the wagon frame and ran toward the house. His baggy overalls ballooned in the wind.

Five or six other villagers emerged from back porches, weed lots and privies, all gesticulating, straining and screaming as they ran in their various awkward and contorted styles toward the burning house.

By now Louella was halfway across the lot, her fat sides heaving and shaking. Her legs bent and buckled as she tottered along the path. "The organ! the organ! Get the organ first!" she screamed.

Pitiful and poor as were the ways of backwoods villagers, there was fear and fumbling, bravery and cowardice all mixed together as they tried to cope with the fire. Realizing that by now they'd better concentrate on getting a few of Miss Eller's things out, four men courageously entered the burning, smoke-filled building. Coughing and spitting, they emerged, dragging a tall piece of furniture out by the cedar trees. It was the old secretary brought by Daniel and Fannie Yoder from Ohio.

Before entering again, the men tied their red or blue farm handkerchiefs over their noses and mouths. They would save as much of Miss Eller's things as they could. The situation called for courage and they would try.

The air was filled with the shrieks, shouts, and calls of the humble villagers, bent on doing their best in a time of calamity. Their voices were accompanied by the barking of the village curs, the thud of falling timbers, crackling of the leaping flames plus shouting and cursing as the men struggled with another piece of furniture. They dragged it off the sagging porch. It was the ancient old desk, handmade, with the secret compartments.

"Dear Jesus," Louella prayed, tears streaming down her cheeks.

"The organ, the organ!"

The entire roof was in flames, black smoke, acrid and thick, poured out of the windows that had shattered in the heat.

Once more the men emerged. She knew this would be the last time. "Dear, merciful Jesus, give them strength," she prayed. Her eyes, burning with tears and smoke, tried to focus upon the struggling group in the doorway. She strained. "Yes, yes! Oh, dear God, they do have the organ in the doorway." Old man Beamer had fallen. She lurched forward. Celia and Thoni Mattson held her back. Coughing and cursing, old man Beamer found his footing, gave a mighty heave. The organ was on the porch. Fifteen-year-old Matt Snow ran to the porch and helped drag it to the forlorn pieces of furniture and a few stacks and piles of pitiful belongings that had been thrown from the burning rooms.

In less than an hour, all that remained of the old Daniel Yoder home, the source of refuge and security for Louella through the years, was a smoldering pile of ashes. Out of the ashes rose a sagging, melted iron heap. It was the old kitchen range with the side-hearth. It'd belonged to Fannie Yoder. Louella had kept it and used it all these years.

As the winds swept the ashes and smoke upwards through the

scorched trees, Louella stood, bowed and weeping. The stark, pain-ridden faces of the village women looked upon her. Their arms sought to comfort her in her hour of sorrow.

Though weather-beaten and old, the house had been her sanctuary through the years of joy and pain. She had risen above the agony of the times, years that jerked young men from families, sending them off to fight a war, grasshoppers eating up the crops, scorching droughts, bank closings, sickness, and death. Her heart had healed of its sorrow over the death of her mother who lay buried beneath the cedar tree in Clearfork cemetery. She understood that there was a time and a season for everything as she saw her father Daniel being lowered into the open grave beside her mother's mossy-gray tombstone.

She had not complained at her station in life, lonely and single through those years. By her faith she'd risen above clinging depression of the spirit, though she'd spent much of her life in poverty and hardship. She would rise above this almost devastating blow, the burning of her house, its atmosphere, its smells, its sounds, its cloak of comfort in the night. Like an old blanket, it had wrapped her in its security. She felt barren and naked without its aura of oldtime hominess and familiarity-the tick of her clock, the wind in the cedars at night, the crackling of the fire in her kitchen stove, and all of the sights and sounds of the crumbling, faded and now vanished house.

Late that afternoon, kindly villagers drove the sorrowing but not broken old woman out to her brother Aaron's farm. Maybe by being there a few days she could be assuaged from some of the pain, adjust to the reality of no home.

She stayed exactly one night. Somehow or other, no one seemed to know what to say. Ted hurt deep inside and agonized for his old aunt. If Alden felt anything, he hid it well. Aaron kept himself busy with his plowing and his evening chores. Opel cooked the evening meal, making lots of noises in her kitchen stoking up her kitchen range, opening and closing cupboard doors, rattling pots and pans.

When they ate by lamplight that night, it was largely in silence.

The only healing things about the evening seemed to be given by nature herself, the promise of hope reflected from the open hollyhocks nodding by the kitchen window in the yellow beam of the full moon that crept over the window pane. Out in the pond where the water turned cool by the evening winds, lusty frogs croaked, breaking the silence with their rhythmic croaks. They seemed to say, "More hope, more hope, more hope!"

If Louella anguished and wept on her bed that night in Aaron and Opel's rented farmhouse, no one heard her. She kept her feelings to herself.

The next day, Aaron had to get to the field and on with his plowing. Opel had to pick the green beans, then can the sweet corn, splitting the shucks right off the stalks in the garden.

"You boys take her back," said Aaron, looking off over the field as he stepped from the kitchen porch. He headed toward the barn to harness the horses. Opel allowed that since the villagers would be there to take care of their own, she'd get an early start on her green beans.

So they rode almost in silence, knowing that there had been a violation upon this earth. Their wrinkled Aunt Ella had been grievously smitten, but beneath her face of courage and pained eyes, one could see that indeed she would travel on, whether she felt like it or not.

She tried to put the boys at ease as they rattled along over the hard ruts and bumps of the road.

"Used to pick plums there." She pointed to a small thicket by the creek, meandering through a pasture.

"Yea, we did too, once," replied Ted, trying to fill in with conversation. "But, wild plums are bitter."

When the car maneuvered the bend in the road, old Aunt Louella lifted her face upwards to see if she could glimpse the village ahead. Yes, there was the white form of the Methodist church, and ... and ... down from the church a block or two ....

Her body seemed to heave a bit, then she shivered. She strained with her anguished, teary eyes, searching for the familiar outline that she knew was no longer there. She focused her tear-stained face upon the tall, dark green cedars that loomed ahead and the withered and scorched pear trees, sighing in the wind, the branches scraping, reaching out into the empty space for the familiar touch of the faded walls and boards of her old home.

They let her out where she told them to. She had the village men put her things in the empty house two weed-filled lots down from the church. She'd rent it for a small amount per month. She'd have to make it home, comforted that at least she was back in the village sustained by its sights and sounds and the poor, but kindly country folk.

That night Celia Carpenter turned and tossed. Coyotes howled in the fields to the south. What was that other sound? A moaning and wailing, bits of harmony. Could someone be in the church across the road? Rolling out of her bed, she ambled across the room and leaned out the open window. A tiny orange light glowed from the window of the house rented by Louella. Celia then could clearly hear the sounds from the wheezy, old parlor organ, moaning in the night as Louella played to assuage her spirit.

Come, ye disconsolate, where' er ye languish, come to the mercy seat, fervently kneel; here bring your wounded hearts, here tell your anguish; earth has no sorrow that heav'n cannot heal.

She played far into the night, blessing the rented, broken old house with the familiar sounds from her organ. All was not lost. She could stand her pain while bathed in the harmony rising from the keys. Only when her legs had reached exhaustion from the labor of pumping did she brave lying down to sleep without the sounds and feel and familiar walls of the rooms now vanished in fire and smoke.

My flesh and my heart faileth: but God is the strength of my heart, and my portion for ever.

-Psalm 73: 26

14.

The Literary

The Mennonite young people's Literary Society continued to draw the two teenaged boys' attention and interest.

"Let's have the Literary at our house," said Ted, the fun and exhibitionistic side of him emerging.

"In this old dilapidated place? Besides, we're not even Mennonites. What'd they think?" Appearance and acceptance were important to Alden.

"We can clean and straighten up," said Ted. "Besides, the wallpaper in the living room is halfway presentable."

Indeed, the living room wallpaper had one thing in its favor. It still clung tightly to the plaster, which, underneath, was smooth, unlike the cracks beneath the paper in the dining room and kitchen.

It was the blasting, searing heat radiating off the stove pipes that caused the paper to buckle, crack, then hang and curl on the ceiling and walls. They'd covered the cracked plaster with torn sheets, then pasted the paper over the bulges. The results, though, looked rough and bumpy. But not in the living room. Closed off during the long winter months, the wallpaper, though faded and old-fashioned in its gaudy, flowered print, was still smooth and straight on the walls.

"I don't know," said Alden, "the whole place hasn't been painted for twenty years." He was right. The house would look quite presentable, provided it had a coat of paint. It seemed to them that all of the Mennonite homes in the neighborhood stood sparkling in their coats of white, set back on emerald lawns. In fact, to Ted, everything the Mennonites had seemed stronger, cleaner, whiter, purer, and better.

Many of the Mennonites lived on graveled roads which provided easier transportation to town and church than this backwoods place, stuck off in the center of a hundred-and-sixty acres with a long three-quarter-mile cow path for a lane. It was absolutely impassable after only a moderate rain.

Both boys were still chagrined at the way their father, Aaron, had scolded them the night they couldn't get home from Literary. They'd stayed all night at Celia Roth's. During the games and fun at her house, it began to thunder. Soon it was raining. Wild, sweeping rain spread across the land in the April night. The mood of the party changed. Those who lived on the back, dirt roads, often poorly maintained, became concerned over how they would get their fathers' cars home safely. Ted and Alden knew in a few minutes that they'd stayed too late. Near the end of their long lane was the object of their fear and apprehension. Long ago, the homesteader Yoders had built a concrete and stone bridge, trying to arch the twelve-foot banks of a creek that turned and wound its way toward Camp Creek. There were no banisters or curbs to the bridge. Erosion, wind, and time cracked the cement, causing edges and chunks to fall off. The gullies by the side of the bridge were deep enough to bury several cars. Over this narrow, eroded spot, one drove very cautiously. In the past, when it was absolutely necessary to brave the slick mud, everyone got out of the Ford except Aaron, who would put it into low gear and then prayerfully ease across, hoping not to slide to the right and topple down into the fifteen-foot chasm. Many times they'd unloaded wagons full of rocks in the gullies approaching the bridge on both sides, but erosion kept fighting against them.

When Celia encouraged Ted and Alden to sleep upstairs rather than walk the three miles home in the mud and rain, they had consented. Then next morning, though the roads were black and muddy, they could drive by the light of day. They made it home safely, but Aaron'd been unreasonably angry.

"I didn't know if you were down in the hole off the bridge," he scolded, angry at events, weather, and poverty beyond his control. Why hadn't they called to tell their parents they weren't coming home? They had no telephone, though Celia Roth's house did.

The house on the Barb Yoder farm had not always been neglected, ravaged by time and poverty. Years ago it had been a showplace of prosperity and achievement. Sometimes when Ted went to the west pasture to get the cows in the evening, he'd stop, turn, and study the house. The eight front windows reflected an orange glow from the late July evening sun. There it stood, eleven rooms in all, the front porch with its balustrade and trumpet vine facing him. The view, softened through the haze and dust, always warmed Ted's heart.

He pondered the significance of the many-roomed house. Below the long kitchen was the cool basement with shelves and bins, and the furnace room with the gigantic furnace someone, years before, had ordered all the way from St. Louis. Now the furnace sat there in the gloom, the plaster around its pipes soured and rotting, the rusty pressure gauges unmoving and long silent, the enormous, corroded boiler humping there in the dark, unused and empty. Long, long ago, the steam heat system had given up the ghost in the old house. Sometimes Ted would lovingly move his finger across the cold brass-toned radiators in the rooms upstairs and imagine himself in a glorious city house, heated not by smelly, belching coal, or soured, wet and rotting wood, but by some hallowed mysterious force of steam coming from below, winding its way through the narrow pipes under the floors, hissing little clouds of welcome steam to heat the wide rooms against the chill winter winds beating against the weathered boards outside.

"We don't have electricity either," said Alden, remembering another strike against them if they wanted to have the Literary. "Can't see anything with our lamps."

"Oh, that's all right, I could go over to Mrs. William Hartzler's and ask her if she'd loan me her old Aladdin lamp. They used to have one before they got electricity." Surely kindly old Mrs. Hartzler would loan Ted the lamp. He would ask her.

"What'd we do for refreshments?" asked Alden.

"Mother'll bake some apple pies, and we can mix some ice tea with lemon. That'd do." Ted was determined to host the Literary. Besides, he became enlivened, almost ecstatic at the thought of leading the party games. Oh, the fun, the laughter, the joy of being together.

The program committee of the Literary Society agreed to have their next meeting at Ted and Alden Yoder's. After all, hadn't these two boys been coming to the young people's meeting at Sycamore Grove on Sunday evenings? Who knew? Maybe if they kept coming they might someday become members. Even so, it was said among some of their grandparents that Ted and Alden's grandfather, Daniel Yoder, had once himself been a Mennonite down at the Bethel church, and a preacher at that.

They began to work on the house, doing the things that they could do to remedy the ramshackle edges. They mopped and waxed the wide boards, gave the linoleum a coat of the stinky Glo-coat. The smell of it almost made Ted gag. The living room began to take on a presentable air. The sofa, purchased during the war, was built without springs, intended to "fit the body." Actually, it sagged, even had a respectable look in its blue upholstery. The huge upright piano standing across one corner had been loaned to them by their country school teacher who'd moved to Colorado. Storing her piano at their house, she knew that Alden, talented as he was in music, would enjoy it. Indeed, he played a fast, cheery little number on it called "Rustic Dance." Two others were "Aloha" and a new sheet-music song called "White Christmas."

Opel worked hard over the wood-burning kitchen range baking her famous Dutch apple pies for the event. They had a fifty-pound chunk of ice in the second hand ice box in the pantry. They'd chip ice 'from it for the iced tea.

Last Saturday when they'd made the weekly trip to Harrisonville to market the cream and eggs, Ted had gone over to the small library, located in a room in the courthouse. He'd checked out two books on party games, as he planned for the exciting time ahead. He did not want a dull party.

Ted had carefully cut squares of heavy paper, numbering them, printing his games and their rules on them. He liked things to flow smoothly, no wide gaps, hesitations, or dull spots. They would play Donkey and the Fiddle, Wink-urn, Animal Chorus, and several paper and pencil games that required pairing off in couples. Packages of Doublemint gum had been purchased for the prizes.

Preparing for the party gave Ted a feeling of belonging, of being needed and respected by this group of thirty or so Mennonite young people. Already, though he had not" confessed Christ before men" as the New Testament exhorted them to do, he knew what he felt in his heart. He wanted to belong. Someday the time would be right when he could make his public confession. He was convinced that he wanted to be a Mennonite. He liked the Sunday evening meetings at Sycamore Grove. The beautiful four-part congregational singing held him in pure rapture. Once he and Alden, Eli, and the bishop's son, Harold, had been invited to sing for the Sunday evening program. It was the first male quartet experience for Ted. He had been frightened as they stood in front of the congregation and sang an' old country favorite, "Life's Evening Sun."

Ted remembered also, with embarrassment, another time when they had responded to an invitation to sing at Abner Schrock's going-away dinner for the three young men who had been drafted into Civilian Public Service. These young conscientious objectors to war would be sent off to jobs in forestry and conservation. The entire church gathered for banqueting and prayer on the lawn of the Schrock homestead. Ted later wished that they had never consented to sing. He'd forgotten how sacred and holy the mood seemed among these people at such gatherings. Though the song they sang was innocuous, and even based upon a Bible episode, Ted had felt as if they had somehow committed a sacrilege. The song had been too foolish, too flippant, as it seemed to him, to sing at such a serious event as a going-away banquet for the young conscientious objectors who were making their stand in difficult war days. Their example of nonresistance would not have wide appreciation or understanding except among the Mennonites. War times brought serious moods, even sad ones at partings and good-byes.

The four youths had stood before the solemn gathering after they had eaten from the spread on the lawn. No sooner had they opened their mouths to utter the words, than did Ted feel the flippancy of the style of the song. *Peter, Peter, Peter, Peter, Peter on the sea, sea, sea, sea, sea. Daniel, Daniel, Daniel, Daniel, Daniel in the Ii, Ii, Ii, Ii . . . . Gabriel, Gabriel, Gabriel, Gabriel, Gabriel blow his trump, trump, trump, trump . . . . Who did, who did, who did, who did, Who did swallow Jo, Jo, Jo, Jo . . . .*

The rhythm, beat, style, all seemed inappropriate for the occasion. Ted was mortified as they, having started, managed to continue through the song. He often wondered, guiltily, about how seriously they had polluted the holy air of that austere gathering under the summer moon, with those Mennonite women, heads white-covered, staring straight at them, solemn and pure as the driven snow. Oh, for shame! And they'd had to listen to such foolishness. If he lived long enough, and perhaps prayerfully enough, he could redeem himself someday. Surely God and all of his holy angels knew that they should have sung a solemn, holy song like, "Lord Thou Hast Searched and Seen Me Through."

And Eli? that blessed friend, the one who had reached down his hand in brotherhood to them in their lowly station, foreigners, aliens in the land, to bring them nearer to the fold. What of Eli? Ted and Alden began to admit to themselves that at least two sides of Eli's nature were showing through. Ever since that evening escapade to the Butler football game, and Eli's snicker at how he'd turned back the mileage on the shiny Pontiac, Ted and Alden had become apprehensive. How could one be so gentle, caring, and good-natured and at the same time plan escapades, strategies that seemed devious, if not even deceitful?

It was a tragedy, but their belief in their faithful friend crumbled and soured. At the same time, he was the one who encouraged them, stood by them when they felt like outsiders, and he was the major person in leading them into the fold of the Mennonite young people. Strange, but true, the messages from God came in earthen vessels. In spite of his grace, wittiness, smile, and charm, Eli did have feet of clay.

Months later, when the four young men stood before the solemn congregation to sing, Eli, with a flowery, wordy introduction began narrating about the song they'd sing. Finally, after his embarrassing exposition, he had announced, "And now we'll sing for you, 'Headaches.' " There was some soft tittering in the congregation, at least a covered cough or two at the blunder. Ted, nervous and tickled by the Freudian slip, covered his mouth as he stifled his laughing. "Pffffft!" Alden was touched off too. God alone knows how they made it through the song entitled "Heartaches, Take Them All to Jesus." They had almost made themselves sick trying to hold back their laughter as they sat on the back row on the men's side during the rest of the meeting. They did not know that long ago their Aunt Dora, whom they loved so much, had once herself been stricken with the agony of hysterics in church, and at a testimony meeting, at that.

The evening of the Literary finally arrived. Ted stood on the kitchen porch overlooking the yard. They'd mowed the grass as carefully as they could with the rusty, antique push lawn mower, a difficult, almost impossible job. Cool shadows were cast across the lawn by the cedars. In the pasture, the pond reflected the white clouds floating toward the sunset. A few mallards quacked and paddled solemnly across toward the shallow side where the cattails grew.

Literary usually began at seven-thirty. In a couple of hours they'd all be here. The place looked presentable after all. Both boys appreciated the manner in which their parents had supported them thus far in the adventure. Mother's pies, lined up in a row on the cupboard, were crispy and golden. They had even driven over to get the wooden folding chairs from the church basement, as everyone did, for the Literary. The rooms looked presentable and spacious, somewhat lean and monastic in their bare-bones decor.

They hurried with their evening meal. Aaron washed thoroughly and put on a clean shirt and freshly laundered overalls. Opel wore her best print dress. They began the countdown, waiting for the beginning of this momentous event, the Mennonite Literary Society at their home.

The sun slid, red and sober, down the western cloud bank. The frogs in the pond outside began to croak, "Late enough, late enough, let's begin, let's begin."

Ted read through his stack of game cards, checking to see that they were in order. Alden checked the oil in the Aladdin lamp Ted had borrowed from Mrs. Hartzler. He reached up to straighten a small framed wall motto which read "He Careth for You."

It was almost seven o'clock. Then they heard the rumble, a rumble that only those who had spent their earthly days by dusty paths and dirt roads would recognize, the sound of car wheels on the beaten earthen road.

Ted ran to the west window. "It's Floyd and Eunice," he called back, as the dusty Ford slowed for the bend in the lane, then eased along the stretch before the front of the house, turned right and stopped. They heard shifting of gears and grinding. Floyd was searching for a parking place. There was plenty of room between the house and the huge, faded barn. The car seemed dwarfed and lonely parked by itself. The Yoders waited. No one got out. There were no doors slamming.

Presently they heard another car winding its way along. Far down the western lane, clouds of dust rose up into the azure sunset. More were coming.

"Why don't they get out and come in?" Ted wondered. So did Alden and Opel and Aaron. Usually at Literary people parked their cars, got out and went in, gathering over the span of thirty minutes or so. What was wrong? Three cars were lined up by Floyd's Ford: the blue Dodge of the Hartzler sisters, the Miller's Hudson, and the bishop's Chevrolet with Henry at the wheel.

Ted's heart began to pound. What had they done? Philistines and outsiders, they had overstepped their bounds. Oh, why had they been so eager to have this Literary? Aaron and Opel looked nervous and drawn. Alden checked the furniture in the living room again.

What was the matter?

Looking out of the dining room windows they saw that the half-acre between the yard and barn was filling with cars. But, it was quiet out there, almost silent. One could hear no voices above the mooing of a cow, or the rustling branches in the evening breeze. At seven-thirty sharp, there were creaking sounds, and car doors slamming outside.

It seemed that Floyd and Eunice were taking the lead. The Yoders hadn't known that the Mennonite custom changed when they gathered at non-Mennonite households. These serious, holy people must have felt like the children of Israel moving into a strange land.

A trailing crowd of about thirty young people was coming up the walk toward the kitchen door. Like Coxey's army, in a straight line and two abreast, they were solemn in their anticipation of what lay ahead. Ted opened the kitchen screen door, holding it back against the wall. He smiled and stretched out his hand to Floyd and his sister Eunice.

"Good evening," he said nervously as he shook their hands with as much dignity and formality as he could. He wanted to be a gracious host. Inside the door, Aaron and Opel nodded and said, "Howdy-do." The long line of these pious children of God continued up the walk, through the kitchen door. Alden greeted them again at the dining room and pointed with his outstretched hand toward the folding chairs in the living room beyond. It seemed as if the line came on forever. The entire group came in at once. All of God's people assembling en mass, united in their venture into this alien place, but willing to sit awhile with these outsiders whom God seemed to be moving toward his throne of grace.

The Mennonite girls began seating themselves on the west side of the room. That meant that the young men would sit on the opposite side. There were a few whisperings, greetings, and rustlings as they settled in for this novel event, the two Yoder boys having Literary at their house.

The meeting began. Eva Shank read the minutes of the past meeting. They were seconded and approved as read. The only old business was to conclude the discussion on the potatoes they were planting for their missionary project. There was no new business. The program began. Ralph Miller gave a talk entitled, "God Moves in Nature, or the Beauties of the Ozarks," based on his recent trip to the Shepherd of the Hills country. Leonore Miller stood, her knees shaking as she read her talk, neatly penned on ruled tablet paper, "Our Oldest Friends in the Forest," based upon the few remaining giants in the virgin timbers by the creek, one having a circumference of twenty feet or more, called the Old Indian Tree.

Things were going well, thought Ted. He was seated between the dining and living rooms, as he surveyed the gathering, trying to feel its pulse and mood. The president called for the special quartet. Marion Alderfer, Twili Yoder, and the two Miller boys stood in the center of the room to sing. They opened their hymnal to "Lord Speak to Me." Marion blew the pitch pipe; they hummed their pitches. Then they hesitated, they couldn't see the words clearly in the center of the room away from the glowing lamp. To Ted's mortification, Harold Hartzler got up, came across to the library table, picked up the borrowed Aladdin lamp, carried it carefully over by the four singers and held it, illuminating the hymnal as they sang:

Lord, speak to me that I may speak, in living echoes of thy tone: as thou has sought, so let me seek, thy erring children lost and lone.

The beautiful four-part harmony filled the room. The lyrics moved Ted's heart, already heavily strained from the events thus far. Oh, but their home was joyfully lighted by the presence of these holy Mennonite children of God. The glory of God shone through them. But, alas, the mortification of not having enough earthly light from the borrowed lamp! To think that someone would have to grab the lamp and hold it up for the singers! The

Yoders felt their poverty and their isolation from the Rural Electric lines.

Ted regained his eagerness, became spirited again as the mood changed. Time for games. His games were a joyful success. They rolled and rollicked with laughter. Henry Hartzler, when playing "Animal Chorus," stood and brayed loudly and lustily as he was directed to do, not knowing that all of the others had been instructed to keep silent. The mirth was overwhelming.

Opel's pies were delicious. The Mennonite girls nodded politely and said, "Thank you," as they were being served, allowing as how they would like the recipe. Ted made only one mistake with the serving. Being attracted to pretty little Brenda Kauffman, he had glanced up to her smiling face as he poured her a second glass of iced tea. She sweetly returned his smile as her tea glass overflowed. Cold iced tea oozed down between her tender young Mennonite thighs. But if it chilled her flesh or spirit, she never gave notice. There were apologies, bowings and scrapings, the offering of a folded handkerchief. All was forgiven. All was well.

The evening was a success. It ended the same as it had begun.

When refreshments were finished and the time seemed right to go, as there is a time and season for everything, and when these are known, there is no hesitation. They stood up, keeping themselves in close company with their own kind. Didn't birds of a feather flock together? Anyway, they sidled out the kitchen in twos and threes, the whole crowd leaving, heading toward the cars.

They had sat among the strangers, they had frolicked and made merry with laughter and fun. They ate the savory pie and drank the lemon-flavored tea, but they must not tarry in the land of the Philistines. They were God's people, duly nonconformed to the world by both their dress and actions. They allowed that indeed they'd had a wonderful evening, and if, Lord willing, it might happen again.

When they went to bed that night, exhausted, but fulfilled in many ways, Ted couldn't help wondering how they'd ever had the courage and fortitude to do it.

The Lord is the portion of mine inheritance and of my cup: thou maintainest my lot. The lines are fallen unto me in pleasant places; yea, I have a goodly heritage.

-Psalm 16: 5, 6

15.

The Revival

Nine years after the Aaron Yoder family attended the evangelistic meeting at the Bethel Mennonite church, they tried it again. This time, the revival was held at the Sycamore Grove congregation near the bend in the creek where old Aunt Louella had received her baptism.

This congregation, with its Amish Mennonite background, was an impressive church, with a distinct air of solidarity and purpose about it. It was unfair to compare it with the tiny village church in Gunn City where Ted and Alden had attended Sunday school since their move from Arkansas to Missouri.

Sycamore Grove seemed overwhelmingly large to Ted and Alden with its over 250 members.

The people who gathered there to worship reflected a kindly Quaker air, however, stern and puritan as well. The plainness of the building itself, the seating arrangement of men on the right, women on the left and the patterns of dress, particularly the women, reflected puritan themes.

Nestled in the churchyard among the walnut and oak trees in the foreground, the gigantic whispering sycamores providing a backdrop, the country church stood announcing piety, cleanliness, and order. Persons driving onto the church grounds when it was time for worship could see the older Mennonite women, five or six in a line, moving up the walk towards the women's anteroom, a small vestibule-like room provided for the sisters of the church. These older sisters climbed the steps one after another, plain black and gray skirts blowing in the wind, their calm faces reflecting an inner peace. Their black bonneted heads nodded and tilted as they entered the doorway. Here in the anteroom they would untie and remove their bonnets, hanging them on the hooks along the wall. If they were not already wearing their prayer coverings, here they would carefully place them over their immaculately combed, severe hairstyles.

They would then enter the sanctuary from the east side of the church, go up the aisle and take their places. The double front doors on the left, were used by most of the younger women, the double ones on the right, provided entry for the men. It did not matter that when opening the front doors to go in to worship that one faced the gathered congregation, and had to walk uphill, as the floor slanted upward toward the back. But, God be merciful to the stranger, the English, who, out of confusion or not knowing, may have entered on the wrong side. They had little recourse other than to nervously and frantically select a spot on the bench as quickly as possible, while every eye turned upon them. It took fortitude and courage indeed for an outsider to enter Sycamore Grove alone in those days.

So the Yoders went to the meeting. Ted was relieved. Being fifteen and feeling the warmth and support of the Mennonite young people through the Literary, as well as the backlog of training in attitudes and thought from the summer Bible schools he'd attended there, he was looking for a time and place to make his commitment.

This inner spiritual upheaval was stirred by the radio revival programs and the general knowledge that to be a Christian one had to make a "public confession of Jesus Christ before men." Maybe this would be the setting. However, Ted thought, "Wouldn't that be a hard thing to do in front of your parents? What would they say about him wanting to be a Mennonite?" This was something they never discussed or mentioned.

One hot September afternoon, following a heavy rain, Aaron propped himself against the railing of the porch on the west side of the old house that by now had taken on a decidedly "Peter Tumbledown" look. Ted mused, tugging at a heavy rope of the trumpet vine that had pushed its way through the porch floor. He didn't know whether or not he could even begin to risk saying what h/2 wanted to say. He swallowed. Somehow, he began to utter the words. As far as he could remember he and his father had never discussed religion. There was always an uncomfortable silence surrounding conversation of this nature. He began, "Dad, I believe I will become a Mennonite." There, the words had leaped out of his scratchy, tight adolescent throat. What next?

Aaron's neck and the back of his bald head began to turn a slight pink as a blush of anger began to creep up his face. Blowing a mouthful of tobacco juice over to the left, windward, he stared at his son, a frown upon his face. He probably did not even know the source of the anger. Was it the spiritual neglect that he'd felt in his own home? The ineffectiveness of the church in his life to make an important statement? Some, almost buried, trace of resentment of Mennonites and the church because of what had happened to his father, Daniel?

"Mennonite!" he said, almost scowling. "Mennonite? You want to be one of them?" He rubbed his white, two-day stubble with the back of his hand, spreading a small streak of brown juice downwards, over his chin.

Looking fully into Ted's face, he said to his sensitive and spiritually tender son, "Don't you know that Mennonite ministers are ignorant?"

What was he referring to? Perhaps only God and old Aunt Louella would know. Ted trembled, disappointed in his father's reaction, though not surprised. Life did not have a way of being easy for him. He tried to adjust quickly to its bruises and jolts.

Ignorant?

Ted was jarred. How can kindly old Brother Manasseh and Bishop Hershberger be called ignorant? Ted had never thought about ignorant preachers, those with or without theological training. In fact, he was so ignorant himself of schools of theology and colleges that he could scarcely have named more than one or two at the most. But, layer by layer, the impressions built, as he internalized his experiences among the Mennonites, their simple ways and kindly faces, even though at times they were also stern. He had an adolescent need for a belongingness, for a faith and a commitment and psychological order that seemed seriously wanting in his life as it was. If it was a matter of a clergyman trained in theology and churchmanship, versus a simple unlettered follower of Christ, radiating a love and peace, Ted'd take the latter.

Their 1939 Ford with the two missing grill teeth rolled down the country road toward the church. Dust clouds ahead announced that other carloads of persons had traveled this way. Alden was disgusted and anxious. When he'd backed the Ford out of the dirt-floored garage, it lurched and bumped sideways. A flat tire! Why was it that when they were most intense and geared for a journey, the Ford seemed to give them opportunity for the improvement of patience and fortitude?

By the time they'd managed to change the tire, then clean up, they figured that they'd be late. Since they were all wearing their Sunday best, an attempt would be made to get to the meeting. By chance, perhaps, it might start a bit late, who knew?

They left the tree-lined road as Alden turned the dusty car into the church grounds. He slowed almost to a stop. Opel tightened her body, reached up to straighten her hat. She'd remembered to wear something on her head so as not to shame or be ashamed. She herself had taken a look at St. Paul's teachings in First Corinthians, chapter eleven.

"Where shall I park?" croaked the anxious sixteen-year-old driver, surveying the grounds, already overcrowded with a varied assortment of cars.

"Try over there by that hickory tree," Aaron said, pointing his work-worn hand toward the far edge of the church grounds. After all, outsiders need not try to edge in among the cars of those who really belonged here.

Alden put the Ford in gear, the car lurched ahead, grinding toward the spot. They parked. Opel, nervous and even looking a bit frightened, straightened her hat again with one hand while she tried to smooth out a wrinkle in the skirt of her dress with the other. They all began to wonder, "Why did we come?" Suddenly the summer evening air was permeated by sounds-magnificent, resounding sounds rising up within the high-ceilinged frame church, sounds that caught on the wind as they emerged from the open doors and windows, saturating the eventide with an atmosphere of reverence and holiness: *Savior, breathe an evening blessing, ere repose our spirits seal; sin and want we come confessing; thou canst save and thou canst heal. Though destruction walk around us, though the arrows past us fly, angel guards from thee surround us; we are safe, if thou art nigh.*

The words rose up as a spiritual offering to God, to the universe, to any wayfaring wanderer who might perchance hear and turn in to join with the swelling choral response to God.

The Yoders were stunned. The magnificent four-part singing moved them. They were late. It had taken them too long to change the tire and get here. Now what? The boys looked at each other worriedly.

Opel's fidgeting increased. Aaron became firm and resolute as he viewed the wide open double doors on the men's side of the building. He knew what lay ahead. Entering, walking uphill, and facing that church full of worshipers with his Arkansas wife and two awkward sons trailing behind him was too great a challenge for him.

"Let's get goin," he said, turning a tight, worried face to Alden, the chauffeur.

"Naw, we can't do that," said Ted from the back seat. His voice quivered with nervousness. He was shy at times, but life presented times and places for fortitude and commitment, and this, he felt, was one of them.

"Start up the car," said Opel. Her dark brown eyes stared out like two acorns in her sunburned face. She straightened her hat. "We'll try it again tomorrow night."

So the Aaron Yoders started up the dusty Ford and headed for home, feeling, of course, beggarly and forlorn, not really fully understanding the underlying feelings of unworthiness and displacement as outsiders, tardy ones at that. One thing was certain. If they ever found courage to come again, they would not be late.

Surprisingly enough, they attempted it again, the very next evening. Aaron was pleased with the seeming scholarliness of the evangelist (imported from Indiana, whose last name also happened to be Yoder). Opel and the two boys were amazed as ever at the a cappella singing in the crowded church, feeling as though they were surrounded by a heavenly choir. The boys had additionally been strangely moved at the end of the service when the invitation to come to Christ was given.

Accompanying this invitation, a quartet of solemn men stood to one side in the crowded building, blew a pitch pipe, hummed their pitches and began the invitation song: O *weary wanderer, come home, thy Savior bids thee come; thou long in sin didst love to roam, yet still he calls thee, come.*

The evangelist pleaded for any uncommitted to raise their hands and acknowledge Christ. Ted's heart thumped like a stricken animal as it bumped against his rib cage. He wanted to swallow. "Gulp." He did. What a loud noise it made. He became short of breath. Was Alden feeling these palpitations too?

The melodic voices of the men in the quartet surrounded them.

Ted wanted to thrust up his hand and said "Yes. Yes! Yes."

It's what he'd been wanting and waiting to do. "Do it, do it before your heart tears through your ribs, leaving a gaping hole and thumps up the aisle on its own," he thought. But somehow, he couldn't. Alden too was just as deeply moved. They both sat.

Why couldn't they make the necessary response? Why? Perhaps it was because their dad sat just a few seats back. Had there been more of a united religious focus in their home, some common dialogue between them, not just the abortive staring straight ahead with the blaring of the Old Fashioned Revival Hour at your back. And Dad and Mom-what about them? Which church would be theirs?

These questions remained to be answered.

The next Sunday, Ted and Alden informed their dad that they were going to Sycamore Grove for morning worship. Aaron said nothing. He scarcely looked up from his paper. Already they felt more and more as though they belonged to the Mennonites, yet, they knew what they had to do.

Brother Hershberger, the bishop, preached a long and moving sermon. At the close of the message, he paused, mentioning that he was sorry that some persons hadn't "come to the Lord during the past revival." He felt certain that there were those whom the Spirit was calling. He added, eagerly, that he would again give the invitation to Christ. "Would the congregation please join in as the chorister leads in 'Just As I Am.' "

During the third verse, the two Yoder boys raised their hands simultaneously.

Riding home, the brothers were silent. Each one reflected on the meaning of the experience. It had been a sincere and true conversion for Ted. At long last he was relieved of the pent-up feelings of unworthiness and guilt. Now a formal statement had been made publicly "before men."

Brother Hershberger and Brother Hartzler met with them privately in the church basement following the service to give them both blessings and instruction required for new converts in the Mennonite faith.

Brother Hershberger had clasped their hands, asking God to bless them for their stand. Then while they were seated around the children's Sunday school table in the damp basement, a stark naked bulb illuminating the darkness, he read to them: "For I am not ashamed of the gospel of Christ: for it is the power of God unto salvation to every one that believeth; to the Jew first, and also to the Greek."

Ted was so relieved, so overjoyed, he felt home at last deep within his soul. He began sobbing as tears of release and contrition streamed down his face. Having been caught short for want of a handkerchief, he had no recourse other than to pull from his suit coat pocket the small silk decorative handkerchief with which to stifle the flow. Looking through the tears at the silk handkerchief, worn for worldly display only, he was aware of its flimsy, worldly superfluity. He would now begin to put away worldly things.

This was a noble start in beginning to build the bridge of faith. For even now, at the moment of their confession, had not the chasm been bridged. Ted's mind reflected on the homecoming words of Saint Peter, words of intensity and belonging. They coursed like healing waters over his soul. To be a people, to belong.

"But ye are a chosen generation, a royal priesthood, a holy nation, a peculiar people; that ye should shew forth the praises of Him who hath called you out of darkness into his marvelous light. which in time past were not a people, but are now the people of God; which had not obtained mercy, but now have obtained mercy."

They drove home in the dusty Ford in silence. How would Aaron greet them? Though joy filled their hearts, would their parents understand? Would Aaron and Opel also cross this bridge? What does one do with religious brokenness within a family? God's work was not yet done. They did not know that the healing wind of God was not yet finished blowing over their family.

16.

The King Place

Though Ted and Alden had made their public confession of Christ in the early fall of the year, the weather and roads conspired against them. Cold, blowing fall rains kept the dreaded narrow lane slick and treacherous. They had not been able to go to a Sunday morning worship service at Sycamore Grove for three or four weeks. Finally, there was a touch of Indian summer, as hot winds dried the ground. Warm, hazy sunbeams filtered down through the autumn skies, highlighting the goldenrod and marigolds growing in wild abandonment along the roadsides and fallowed fields.

Then, one Saturday afternoon, the rumble of a car was heard, lurching and shifting gears, maneuvering over the hardened rough edges of the ruts in the road. Rounding the bend between the house and the barn, it came to a stop by the crumbling buggy-stile. Brother William Hershberger and Brother Manasseh Hartzler got out. They were dressed in the black plain coats required for the ministers of the Mennonite church. They walked up the broken walk, Bibles under their arms, Brother Manasseh's head tilted to the side.

Stepping up onto the porch, Brother Hershberger knocked on the door. Ted opened the door, feeling slightly tense and anxious, not knowing fully what to expect. He greeted these revered men from the holy order of the Mennonite community. Already his faith was working, knitting, binding him closer.

"The Lord bless," said Brother Manasseh, grasping Ted's hand and bowing deeply. He repeated the same greeting to Alden and Opel, then later to Aaron when he emerged through the back screen door, and with a shy, puzzled look, sauntered into the room.

136

Nothing remains but a memory
Of the home of my childhood days
Gone is the rippling laughter
And the hours I spent in play.
Gone is the rambling farmhouse
Staunch, and sturdy and strong,
A house inviting a child to explore
When the winters were cold and long.
Gone are the times I spent in the woods
Chasing the squirrel and the lark,
But the trees are there
That shall forever wear
The brand of my knife in their bark.
Never again shall I go in the spring
To the blossoming redbud tree
And break off a branch and carry it home
To hold proudly for mother to see.
Never again shall I take my pail
And around through the brush to wind,
To gather the first ripe berries
That only a child could find.
Never again shall I take my ax
And bring home the Christmas tree
And open presents on Christmas morn
With quite so much laughter and glee.
All is gone but a memory
Of the days I spent as a child.
Only a lasting memory remains
Of my home that stood by the wild.

Gathering in the dining room, Brother Manasseh and Brother William were asked to sit in the two old painted rockers. All four Yoders pulled straight-backed chairs from around the oak dining table and seated themselves. There was an uneasy pause. Then Brother William cleared his throat and began.

"We just thank the Lord Jesus for your stand." He addressed the two teenagers. They smiled uneasily, then shyly looked down at their scuffed, high-topped work shoes.

"We'd like to begin instruction classes as soon as we can," added Brother Manasseh.

This was new territory for Ted and Alden. However, like Philemon, who also had expressed a new faith in the Lord Jesus Christ and toward all the saints, they were willing and eager to learn. After all, they had been instructed in Mennonite summer Bible schools for six or seven years and they were familiar with much of the new faith.

" And how about you folks," said Brother Hershberger, encouragingly, addressing the middle-aged parents.

"Yes," encouraged Brother Manasseh, "our church doors are open for you too." It was clear that they had come, hoping that the entire family might be of one mind in this matter. The truth was, Aaron and Opel's last church membership had been at least ten years ago in the tiny Mount Hermon Methodist church, back in Arkansas. It'd stood a few miles up the road from the little forty-acre farm given to them by old Jim Slayden. In the ten years that had passed, the church had long since burned to the ground. If there were any records at all, they were now beyond retrieving. Aaron and Opel were typical of the rural poor of the depression days, no land, no social security card, no birth certificate, and no church record. What was to be done? "What is recorded on earth is recorded in heaven."

How would this Arkansas-born woman sitting on her hard bentwood chair, who didn't like crowds and was unused to the goings and comings of the people in this community, cope with this? She shifted her position and looked over at her overall-clad, baldheaded farmer husband. In her heart, she knew that she wanted her family to be united. Though she and Aaron had talked about it only in the most scanty terms, she knew what they must do.

"Why, can you take us in on a letter?" queried Aaron,

evidently on the same wave length as Opel. His eyes lowered with uncertainty.

"Yes. Yes, we do," answered Brother William. "We do take in members by church letter." Aaron and Opel were not aware of the collective respect that the community already had for them. Though the Mennonites knew in general that these particular Yoders went to the Gunn City church, they really had little knowledge of the levels of their commitment.

By the time the short, amicable meeting was over, vast mountains had been moved, much to the boys' astonishment. Wonders were taking place before their very eyes. What was that in the parable about the mustard seed?

It had been agreed that Aaron and Opel could be accepted into the Mennonite church upon verification by someone in Arkansas who had also been a member of the Mount Hermon church, long burnt to ashes.

Ted looked at his parents, his mother-could she make it? Would the hurdle be too great? She'd never worn jewelry other than a simple gold wedding band. She also had always worn her hair in a simple style, combed back, rolled up and pinned in a roll at the base of her head. Would she be able to surmount wearing the covering?

And Aaron? What about his tobacco chewing? Though Ted was acquainted with the fact that a few of the Mennonite men did use tobacco, he knew that it was officially forbidden and considered a mark of worldliness and uncleanness.

Now their family was being challenged by a call to a faith that would unite them in a new way, offering a grace and sustaining force such as they'd never before experienced. They would have to wait and study and pray. What lay ahead? Could they all survive the converts instruction class? God moves in a mysterious way, his wonders to perform.

In addition to the spiritual blessings and growth being accomplished in their household, there had been another event, powerful in its confirming force for the Yoders in this particular community. Working, as described in Genesis, by the sweat of his brow through the years as a laborer and farm renter, often, no doubt, feeling disenfranchised among the landholders around him, Aaron had slowly, but surely achieved a tour de force. Starting out with three or four white-faced Hereford calves, he built up a respectable herd of beef cattle. When he had marketed the thirty or more, he had finally realized enough for a down payment on an eighty-acre farm about two miles through the woods from the Sycamore Grove church. To make it even more wonderful, the farm sported a sturdy, clean, two-story, square frame house and even more blessed yet, the farm was located on a graveled road. Redeemed at last from the mud!

They moved to their new farm called the King place, in February of 1945. Emma King, owner of the farm on Clearfork Creek, was a first cousin to Aaron, though he'd never visited her and never, as far as Ted could remember, talked about her as being related to him.

It was almost as if Aaron had no family. Emma Yoder King, wife of Milo King, was the daughter of John R. Yoder of West Liberty, Ohio, brother to preacher Daniel Yoder, Aaron's father. There had been fourteen children in the family of "Red John" D. Yoder, Aaron's grandfather, who'd married Anna Zook, back in West Liberty. Red John Yoder was the son of "Big Dan" Yoder who'd married Anna King Smucker. Big Dan was the son of Christian, "Der Dick Christel" Yoder, who'd married Magdalena Hooley. Christian Yoder was the son of "Strong" Jacob Yoder who'd married Anna Beiler, and Strong Jacob Yoder was the fourth child of Jacob and Barbara Yoder who'd set sail from the canton of Bern, Switzerland to find a new home in Pennsylvania. Tragedy occurred, as Jacob Yoder died at sea, leaving his Amish widow, Barbara, and her nine children to begin their lives in America without their husband and father. Ted Yoder, new convert to the Mennonite faith, did not know that he was a direct lineal descendent of his great, great, great, great, great grandfather Jacob Yoder whose body'd been slipped over the rail of the *Francis and Elizabeth* sometime in 1742, buried in the great, gray and troubled ocean.

Legends arose regarding the strength of Strong Jacob Yoder, son of Jacob and Barbara. This Amishman's physical strength became a focal point for conversations and tales among the Pennsylvania colonists.

Many years ago, a group of Amishmen were at the mill carrying grain, along with Strong Jacob and his sons. They were carrying three bushel sacks of grain up a long flight of steps at one mill. A young man tweaked the sons' beards as they passed by with their loads. They reported this to their father, Strong Jacob, who decided to take the next load up. Grabbing the offender, he carried him with his three bushel sacks up the remaining two flights of stairs and dumped him. They carried the remainder of the wheat unmolested.

Ted recalled an event involving his own father, Aaron, and his physical strength. It'd been threshing time a year or so back. With his wagon fully loaded with wheat bundles and heading toward the threshing machine, misfortune struck. It was there on his own farm, too, where he could ill-afford to be the one to hold up the work while his neighbors sweated out in the fields helping to get the job done.

Aaron'd had no recourse than to unhitch his team, tie them to a tree, then begin the repairs himself. Ted, who was water boy, riding Old Major out to the field, saw his father, under the wagon. Suddenly he strained and heaved, his shoulders under the front quarter of the wagon floor. Holding it up, under great strain, he kicked out the broken part by splitting it some way, he'd strained, lifted the wagon bed again, and managed to ease the repaired crossbeam into place. Ted'd felt for his father on that day. The only help he'd given his father was to ride back to the shed for the hammer, a part of a two-by-four, and some nails. Though Ted did not know the legends of Strong Jacob Yoder, it seemed that, indeed, the genes programming muscles and physical strength had carried down the line.

How fragile and nondescript their household possessions looked, loaded onto farm wagons as they headed up the yellow clay hill toward the King place.

Ted and Opel had gone on ahead, trying to maneuver the slope before the ground had become completely unthawed. Never mind the unlicensed driver. They'd waited too long, though. The Ford began to slide in the slick, wet clay. Quickly, Ted counter-turned the wheel. The car shot abruptly towards the ditch. He turned the wheel again, his elbow striking the Aladdin lamp his mother was holding, shattering the mantel. "Watch it!" she exclaimed, fearful that they might yet end up in the ditch.

It was apparent by the end of the day, when all their furnishings were arranged in their newly purchased farm house on its eighty acres, that their hearts beat with wordless joy and pride. Never had they lived so nicely before. They were all filled with thankfulness and anticipation for the future.

They had not moved the gigantic wood and coal heating stove that blasted the paper off the ceilings. This house had a hot air furnace, squatting in the basement below, with its huge pipe funneling the heated air up through the three-foot-square register in the dining room floor. Though far from modern, the furnace seemed like a fabulous and welcome friend to the Yoders. One didn't even have to go down to the basement to regulate the fire. There were two small chains by the baseboard near the register. Pulling and adjusting the chains regulated the furnace dampers below.

Though the house had not yet been hooked up to the rural electric lines, it seemed luxurious, sturdy, and very respectable in its coat of white paint and green metal roof.

They had not moved from the old Barb Yoder place without some longing and regret. After all, for nine years it had been a place of refuge. It had added to their lives. To Ted, it was a familiar old friend. He would miss the magnificent woods. Though there was a small woods and creek where he could fish on the King place, it was not the same.

It had been the sanctuary of the woods, the giant oak and hickories, the papaw groves, the sheltered fishing spots on Camp Creek beneath spreading hackberry and sycamores that had nurtured him in times past when he felt lonely, afraid, and unsure. He had been touched and comforted with the healing brush of the growing things, the murmur of the water, the call of the doves, and the wind in the cedars on the hill above the creek. It seemed that nature itself nudged him, lest he give in to that part of his nature causing him to be poetic, too impractical, too metaphysical.

Out of his hesitation to leave the rambling old farmhouse in the wilderness and eroded land, he had written a poem that expressed his feelings for its sanctuary, rough and spartan though it had been. Why, they had even dared to have the Mennonite Literary there, even when they, like Peter pointed out, were "no people."

The old farmhouse was torn down within a few months after their move to the King place. The pipes and joints from the long unused heat system, so out of place in the backwoods environs, were purchased by a plumbing company in the local county seat.

A few months after they moved, Ted, looking over the horizon toward the north, beyond the hedges of osage orange, could see the tall red bank barn that folks said old preacher Daniel Yoder, his very own grandfather, had built. But there was an empty space in the scene just to the left of the cedar trees. The two-story, rambling, weather-beaten house was gone.

Ted's poetic nature was moved. He felt a sadness sweep over him for old home things now lost. This was life, a reaching out and a giving up. He was lost in a reverie of woods and wind and grasses, and the sweet sighing of a hazelnut bush by the winding creek. He must look to nature here, here in the King meadows to fill the emptiness-cedar trees on a hill, the evening sunset over the western woods, the call of the whippoorwills in the dusky evening. And just over yonder beyond the woods stood the white meetinghouse, amidst the giant sycamores, sweeping in the wind, inviting "come, come."

Question 19. To what are the members of the church of Christ obligated by baptism?

Answer: To the act of burying their past sins into Christ's death and of binding themselves to Christ in a new life and conversation- a life of obedience- in order that they may follow his will, and do what he has commanded them.

-Matthew 28:20

17.

Baptism and a Bridge of Faith

The Sunday school at Sycamore Grove was just over. Ted noticed how the elderly brothers and sisters slowly arose from their seats. Their classes had gathered on the short benches of the raised platform on each side of the pulpit. There, in front of the entire congregation, they greeted each other, some with the holy kiss of peace, as they prepared to move to the main part of the sanctuary for the worship service.

Ted and Alden, seated on the men's side of the church, though comforted by the growing experience of their new religion, still felt the misgivings of novices as they sat expectantly and nervous. Their former status as outsiders was slowly eroding at the edges. Brother Zook, with his clear blue eyes and balding head announced a hymn, "Number 563, '0 Could I Speak the Matchless Worth.' " The harmonious volume of the men's voices around the boys could be felt in vibrations through the church benches. Suddenly, on the chorus the clear, vibrant voices of the women ascended the choral scale, sure, certain voices of these country women who complimented their husbands' foundation bass and supporting tenor. It seemed as if they were surrounded by an angelic choir. Ted was moved as usual to the very core of his being.

When the song finished, without hesitation, short, amicable little Brother Manasseh jumped off one of the three chairs behind the pulpit, stood beaming at the gathered congregation and said, "While the next hymn is being sung, we'll ask the converts to come forward to the front bench for instruction."

Oh, the strange newness of the Lord's ways in the

145

congregation of the righteous. Ted's heart skipped a beat or two. Alden swallowed and turned, nervously. What next? What new turn of events in the road that leads to faith and holiness?

The chorister began the hymn: "Christ Receiveth Sinful Men."

Sounds rolled upwards, swelling out over the high ceiling. The two boys struggled as though the bench was reluctant to release them for this new pilgrimage. But, they did manage to get up and begin their journey, across knees and feet of faithful brothers sharing the same bench, then down the sloping aisle to the front bench, directly before Brother Manasseh and the pulpit. He stood waiting, certain in the beatitude and blessing related to the instruction of new converts.

Sweating and with trepidation, the two teenagers seated themselves, looked up with apprehension and self-consciousness as they waited the further revelation from God. This was God's house. They were among his holy people. Never fear. Little matter that no one forewarned them of this necessary journey to the front of the church and what the status of a convert really was. Weren't they two brothers who had been nobody-ignorant pagan outsiders? Now they were being instructed in the finer points of doctrine and tradition. Their spirits opened to receive the spiritual bread of life that would nurture their soul's salvation. Oh, blessed hour!

Never mind the thumping of the heart against the rib cage, or the loud gulp and swallow coming from Alden. They were" drinking at the fountain," soon they would be authorized and duly declared citizens of Beulah Land.

Brother Manasseh descended the steps below the pulpit and cleared his throat. He began the catechism lesson on nonconformity to the world. The boys strained with earnestness and trembling lest they miss a point and, like the foolish virgins, be caught short. After all, who knew? Maybe they would be questioned before the hallowed congregation, queried before the saints seated all around them, not a single one of whom would miss an answer. No, they must ardently receive the instruction from the Lord presented before them.

"For my people are a peculiar people," intoned Brother Manasseh, lost in his rapture at instructing the newborn.

Surely their adolescent lives would take on new meaning. Their feet would follow new steps. Had not Ted read and marked well in his Bible the evening before, "How beautiful are the feet that preach the gospel of peace."

There must be no more lusting after the things of the world. (Had there ever been? Their lives had been Spartan in appointments and sparing in exposure and experiences.) Their sins were the sins of adolescent longing.

There would be no more picture shows. They had only gone to four or five free shows at East Lynne in their entire lives. Here in this decrepit little village, the struggling merchants banded together to sponsor a free movie on summer evenings, once a week. There, sitting on a railroad tie, looking with upturned heads at the sheet stretched across a frame, willing to suffer the agonies of a stiff neck the next day, the two boys had been instructed in the ways of the Cisco Kid and other Western heroes.

"Be sure your sins will find you out," though and that is just what happened. While riding in the Mennonite minister's Chevrolet to Bible school the very next morning following the free show, Mary Edith Snow, one of the "gentile" children from a family on relief, turned, beamed at Ted in the car filled with pious children, she pointed her dirty little finger at Ted, grinned through her yellow teeth and said, "I seen you at the free show last night."

Oh, the mortification and shame of exposure! Ted wanted the door of the Chevrolet to open enough for him to slide out into the ditch where he then could crawl through the punishing thorns of the hedgerow. No, here in the holy order of the righteous there would be no shows or dances, no worldly frivolousness or unquestionable amusements. No wearing of jewelry or giving of the mind to vain philosophies and nebulous earthly pursuits. "Worldly pleasures vainly call me, I would be, would be like Jesus."

Brother Manasseh, smiling and bowing, pleased with the eager attention given by the two sweating converts, brought the session to a close, ascended the rostrum to stand behind the pulpit.

Their instruction continued each Sunday until the holy day of their baptism. In addition, there had been a dozen or more weekly sessions held at their home and the home of Sally Kauffman, another convert.

Since Opel and Aaron were also becoming Mennonites, the sessions included them. They all had been faithfully instructed in the ordinances and doctrines of the Mennonite church, doctrines that if applied, would enable them to live out the daily routines of life, the Christian way of life, as interpreted historically by those of the Anabaptist faith.

Ted's Bible was marked with a red pencil, especially the verses pointing out the call to separation from the world, and the holy ordinances that symbolized the walk and faith of a holy people. The ordinances were: baptism, communion, the washing of the saints' feet, the devotional covering, the Christian salutation, also known as the greeting of the holy kiss, anointing with oil, marriage, and ordination.

Both teenage boys memorized and committed themselves with the strength of young hearts to the sacred foundation doctrines of the church. The doctrine of nonconformity to the world, emphasized their call to put away worldly foolishness, tangible non-essentials and to become committed as faithful brothers, who walked by faith in the light of the Lord.

They had no ideological difficulty with the holy doctrine of nonresistance, wherein Christians were exhorted to "love your enemies, bless them that curse you, do good to them that hate you and pray for them which despitefully use you, and persecute you; that ye may be the children of your Father which is in heaven."

But, these were the middle years of World War II, and they had, a month or so back, received a letter from their Aunt Ida from way out west in Idaho, telling them of her three sons, their very own cousins, who were fighting bravely for the Allied cause in the Pacific theater.

When Deacon Miller arose to address the Sycamore Grove congregation regarding the giving of the tithes and offerings for C.P.S. (the Mennonite boys who entered Civilian Public Service rather than serve in the military) both boys felt a dissonance, a tug at their loyalties. The Bible was clear in its statement about the Christian turning the other cheek. They placed their nickels and dimes in the offering plate, and passed it on. God would understand the tumult of their hearts. It took time to become a Mennonite, time to internalize the full meanings of doctrines accepted and practiced by those around them in an unbroken chain back to the days of the sixteenth-century Anabaptists and the drowning of the first Anabaptist martyrs in the lake at Zurich, Switzerland.

Even their own relatives would not be fully gracious and understanding. Old Uncle John, still fervent in his loyalties to the

American Legion, sat in his gunpowder-colored Whippet car on the square in Harrisonville, confronted Alden, pointing his dark-skinned finger at him, and gave Alden his firm opinion of those who not only mingled with, but who joined the Mennonites. There was no doubt in Uncle John's mind, they were "cowards and yellow-bellies."

Alden, silently and painfully endured the humiliation, comforted by the words he had memorized; "Blessed are ye when men shall revile you and persecute you and shall say all manner of evil against you, falsely, for my sake."

No, both young men would gladly and fully agree that the process of deciding, fellowshipping with and receiving the instructions to become members of the Mennonite church were worth the sacrifices of enduring the slurs of Uncle John, and whatever other misunderstandings or puzzlements occurred on the part of their relatives.

If old Aunt Louella in Gunn City ever felt a pain at their discontinued attendance at the village church that she and the boys' grandfather had labored to build, she never mentioned it. Only years later was there a direction on her part that may have implied her position.

By late spring of that year, the bishop and the ministers of the congregation agreed that the converts were properly instructed in the doctrines and ordinances, that they had made a genuine response to the walk of faith in Christ and were indeed fit candidates for baptism.

On a Saturday, a week and a day before the scheduled baptismal service, Aaron drove home from Garden City on the dirt road past the Bethel church. He turned the car into the lane of the Kauffman farm, close to the bend in the Clearfork Creek, by Sycamore Grove.

Opel got out of the mud splattered Ford and ambled up the sidewalk. If she had had any serious misgivings about the doctrines of the Mennonites, she did not mention it. A saintly looking elderly woman greeted her at the screened porch, dressed in Quaker gray. Smiling broadly, she invited Opel, with a sweep of her arm, into her kitchen. In about ten minutes, Opel returned with a small envelope in her hand. She smiled, waved to the old Mennonite sister in her gray dress and white apron.

The Yoders drove home in silence. Opel's new purchase

folded in the envelope, would prepare her for her necessary steps in "becoming a Mennonite." According to her instruction in the faith, there were two required behaviors yet, on her part. One was a taking off, and the other was a putting on. She would be required to remove the plain gold band on her third finger so as to be in complete compliance with the doctrine of separation from the world, as instructed in First Timothy 2:9, "In like manner also, that women adorn themselves in modest apparel, with shamefacedness and sobriety; not with braided hair, or gold, or pearls, or costly array." And First Peter 3:3: "Whose adorning let it not be that outward adorning of plaiting the hair, and of wearing of gold, or of putting on of apparel; but let it be the hidden man of the heart, in that which is not corruptible, even the ornament of a meek and quiet spirit, which is in the sight of God of great price."

The other act that would be required of this little, hardworking Arkansas-born woman, mother of two adolescent sons, was the putting on of her new purchase in the plain white envelope. This item was her devotional covering. At home in her bedroom, standing in front of the old mirror on the dresser she and Aaron had purchased from some used furniture dealer years back, she opened the envelope, took out the white newly sewn cap, made of netting. Unfolding it, she placed it on her head, fitting it neatly on her auburn hair. She pinned it to her hair in the front, and inserted pins at the sides. It fit her head with the grace and dignity required for such verses as First Corinthians 11: 5: "But every woman that prayeth or prophesieth with her head uncovered dishonoureth her head: for that is even all one as if she were shaven. For if the woman be not covered, let her also be shorn: but if it be a shame for a woman to be shorn or shaven, let her be covered."

Opel glanced at herself in the mirror. "Yes," she agreed to herself, "I can do it." The small white cap, though somewhat quaint, added a neatness to her style and presentation of herself. Yes, she allowed as, next Sunday, when they'd all be taken into the fellowship of the Mennonite church, she'd not be caught short. Smiling, she removed her covering, placed it carefully on the dresser, tied on her apron and walked briskly out to her kitchen to begin the supper.

Two events detracted from the anticipated, holy event of baptism of the two Yoder boys and Sally Kauffman and the receiving of Aaron and Opel into the membership of the

Mennonite church.

Aaron, while attempting to round up the cows for the morning milking, slipped on a corncob in the barnyard one rainy morning. Down he went with a jarring thud, as his boot slipped out from under him. He heard a snapping sound, as a bone broke in his leg. Grabbing a fallen limb from the locust tree, he managed to pull himself up, painfully, and hobble to the house. This unfortunate accident meant that when the announcement for the converts to come forward, Aaron would have to hobble down the long aisle on crutches. But, never mind. He was used to broken things, an old Ford car fixed with baling wire, a wagon box held together by old pieces of boards nailed haphazardly. He'd never been one for pomp and show. Didn't the neighbors all know Aaron as a somewhat shy, though very direct person? What matter if his toes stuck out from a plaster cast? Pshaw, he hardly felt any pain at all. The congregation would just have to wait for him to drag to the front on his crutches.

There were complications for Opel as well, for the very next Sunday after Opel had purchased her covering, she decided she would wait until she arrived at church to put it on. Entering the anteroom on the east side of the meetinghouse, she found it crowded with large, severely dressed Mennonite women. Some of them were removing black bonnets, reaching up to hang them on wire hooks on the austere walls. Tiny, wiry Opel had trouble getting aligned with the small wall mirror, where one could check such a legitimate item as a prayer veiling or bonnet. (The mirror must not be large so as to invite copious standings and primpings and the wasting of time in such frivolity.) Just as she dug through her purse to find her folded white net covering, something bounced out of the gaping purse jaws. She heard a "ping, ping, ping," as a tiny object rolled on the floor in a circle, then came to rest by black-shoed feet of the black-stockinged sister with the severe gray crepe dress. On the floor, Opel's wedding ring, which she'd removed in the car, glittered in a beam of sunlight from the clear window. Mortified and embarrassed, Opel walked over, bent down to retrieve the forbidden object before the onlookers, who'd turned at the sound of the pinging, thinking, perhaps, that it was a coin lost momentarily from someone's grasp. With curious eyes and gentle faces they bent forward, willing to help the unfortunate in any disaster, and like the widow in the Bible who lost a piece of silver, lighted a candle, swept her house and looked diligently for it, they were willing to help Opel find her ring.

It would take time to learn all the ways of holy living. Opel knew she'd never be able to speak in the funny Dutch-accented, sometimes backward sounding sentences as did these sisters-to-be, surrounding her. Such phrases as "the butter is all," "come here once," and "h'us come?" were enigmatic to her. Nevertheless, these comfortable and seemingly contented women seemed to know their places and stations in life. It would remain to be seen whether or not Opel could align herself with them, or not.

Finally, the Sunday of the baptism service arrived. The hymn had been sung, the converts, faith and conviction reflected in their eyes, marched forward. Aaron crept slowly down the aisle with his crutches, holding his leg with the plaster cast off the floor. Pink swollen toes stuck out of the gray cast. Opel sidled up the women's aisle, finding her place by Aaron at the divider on the bench that marked the women's side from the men's. To her left sat Sally Kauffman, the other teenaged convert.

There was a pause in the proceedings. Something was wrong.

What next? First the baptism had been delayed due to rain and muddy roads. Aaron's broken leg kept him home a Sunday or two, holding up the works. Now what?

The bishop and two ministers stood behind the pulpit. No one came forward to take the lead in the service. What was the matter? Was there some new teaching, or some not yet understood doctrine to challenge them further?

Suddenly the bishop stepped to the pulpit. He cleared his throat, looking sad and a bit worried, as he turned his face to address the congregation.

"Dear brothers and sisters in Christ," he intoned. The mood was serious. Ted wondered in apprehension. Then he glanced at Sally Kauffman, sitting by his mother on the women's side. Her hair! She should have done up her hair. There sat Sally with her shoulderlength strands swept back in curls, hanging loose. Her devotional covering perched high on her head. She did not appear dressed in full modesty with her modern coiffure. What would they do now?

The bishop continued. "We regret to inform you that we will postpone the baptismal service today. We, the ministers of the congregation, apologize. We are sorry and we do take full responsibility in this circumstance."

A silence swept across the congregation. Religion was serious here. Commitments given were commitments kept. There was the sound of clearing of throats.

"We are sorry that we have been negligent in teaching and in instructing in the Word," continued the bishop. He did not specify Sally's specific indiscretion that delayed the baptismal service. It was obvious.

"We will continue instructing our dear converts, and will look forward to their baptism in the future."

Then the bishop called for the chorister to lead a hymn as he sat down, preparing himself for the sermon.

Indeed, becoming a Mennonite was no small undertaking. Ted had faith in his heart, though, that it was worth the efforts. Day by day, the feeling of being a part of a caring and loving community grew within him. He understood some of the meanings of his act of faith, bridging the gap left by one generation in his family. Now, he too, with the seal of the water of baptism, would stand in the tradition of the Anabaptists.

But, even more than becoming one of the Plain People, with their strange ethnic and cultural ways, was the truth of the doctrines they taught. Nonresistance seemed to Ted and Alden to be a basic foundation for any Christian. Surely, the world would be better if it carried out the implications of Brother Manasseh's recent sermon where he'd stated: "We need to simplify our lives in order to have more to give."

For the third time, the baptismal service was rescheduled. Sally Kauffman had received counsel, along with her father and mother. Together they had, with the bishop and ministers, looked carefully at the implications of the teachings of St. Paul in Corinthians, the verses specifying sisters in the church to adorn themselves with the "ornament of a meek and quiet spirit," giving themselves to the church's faithful interpretation of the word.

So, on the following Sunday, while the congregation sang, *Take my life and let it be consecrated Lord to thee; take my moments and my days, let them flow in ceaseless praise,* Aaron stumped forward the second time on his crutches. Opel joined him on the same bench where they'd sat a week before. Sally Kauffman sat by Opel, her hair tightly rolled up and fastened with pins, her covering secured tightly enough for an Atlantic gale. All seemed in order, maybe they would make it this time. Ted and Alden strode forward, serious and expectant.

Ted did not know on that day of his baptism that just over fifty years ago, a few rods down the shady road, his old Aunt Louella had too been a receiver of baptism in the Anabaptist tradition. However, she had knelt in the muddy waters of Clearfork Creek. Here Ted knelt with his brother Alden and Sally Kauffman as the bishop stepped before them.

"Upon the confession of thy faith, which thou hast made before God and these witnesses, I baptize thee with water, in the name of the Father and of the Son and of the Holy Ghost."

During the intonation of these words, Brother Hershberger had cupped his hands as Brother Manasseh poured water from a pitcher into them. He then placed the cupped hands upon Ted's head, opened them and the cool water spread across his head and dripped down.

So, the three were baptized: Ted, Alden, and Sally Kauffman.

They then were exhorted to arise, wherein they were greeted as brothers and a sister in the church. Brother Hershberger kissed Ted and Alden with the holy kiss of peace, in the Anabaptist tradition. The bishop's wife came forward and kissed Sally.

Next, the bishop turned to Aaron and Opel, read from his manual the words for the proper reception of members by transfer of church letter. They too acknowledged their faith in Christ and answered in the affirmative.

"Do you confess that you are of the same mind with us in the doctrines and rules of the church? And do you promise to remain faithful and obedient in the same until death?"

Aaron also was kissed by the bishop, while the bishop's wife, in similar manner, greeted Opel.

Ah, happy day! No longer were they a family without tradition.

No longer would Ted suffer the agonies of the spiritually uprooted. Though it had taken several months, at last they stood in front of the sacred congregation in the full declaration of membership. As in Romans eleven, they were "surrounded by witnesses." The family that had torn itself away from its past was now connected with the traditions of the historic Anabaptists by a bridge of faith. They, by their response, had recaptured the ancient blessings and heritage of their family.

The Yoders did not know that day wherein their efforts and struggles of faith and will to become Mennonites were honored, that in less than thirty years the Anabaptist message would have so been carried to the nations of the world that by then Third World peoples would comprise more than one-half of the church. No longer would Mennonitism be defined or interpreted from the quaint, ethnic, German tradition. Anabaptism is spiritual movement, transcending cultures and ethnic folkways.

Serve the Lord with gladness: come before his presence with singing. Know ye that the Lord he is God: it is he that hath made us, and not we ourselves; we are his people, and the sheep of his pasture.

-Psalm 100: 2, 3

18.

Night of the Angels

Before Ted and Alden's association with Sycamore Grove, they had not known the authority or the persuasiveness of the church. One thing became increasingly clear to them both, here the church was taken seriously.

Sixteen-year-old Ted began to serve by teaching a Sunday school class for junior age boys. The class gathered on the first and second rows on the men's side of the church.

More and more, Ted was aware of the forces within, directing him toward his future. This included his desire to become a minister and a teacher. He'd not forgotten that when he was six or seven, he'd draw up an old bentwood kitchen chair, climb on the seat, open a Bible, and announce, "And now I'm gonna' preach a sermon."

Ted seemed to experience a presentiment regarding future events.

A few times, while sitting concentrating in worship, listening carefully to the sermon being delivered by Bishop Hershberger, he would be overcome with a strange knowing, an intuitive feeling. He found himself thinking, "Someday, I know I will stand behind that pulpit and preach." He blocked the words from his mind, feeling ashamed and presumptuous to so project himself. Years later, Ted realized the folly of not understanding his needs and interests and of not assuming responsibility in developing these important aspects of his nature, not only his deeply religious side, but his need for the aesthetic, love for drama, art, literature. But, this community had not yet acknowledged the full worth of these enterprises, often quickly labeled worldly.

Ted's other venture at teaching was accepting a position to teach in the summer Bible school. Actually, this was an extension of the same activities he was doing with the junior age boys. However, to him it was even more challenging and interesting.

The internal workings of the Mennonite church kept revealing themselves to the Yoders. There were many surprises. One of them was the free and certain manner in which persons were elected to church or Sunday school appointments and offices. This seemed to happen with surety, abruptness, and finitude.

The first experience of being involved in such an appointment, was at the yearly business meeting for the reorganization of church and Sunday school. A portable blackboard had been brought to the front of the church with the positions listed. Among them were:

Sunday school superintendent, assistant superintendent, primary superintendent, chorister, ushers, Sunday school secretary-treasurer, librarian, and others. Among the church offices to be filled were, trustees, alms committee, church choristers, conference delegates, and ushers.

Nominations began from the floor. Ted sat up abruptly. Old Brother Schrock had called out his name as a nominee for Sunday school secretary-treasurer. Ted swallowed. His heart thumped. This seemed like a monstrous job, more than he cared to do. What should he do? No one was declining a single nomination. He guessed the only thing to do was simply to sit and let the Lord do the leading. The Lord did and Ted was elected.

The sixteen-year-old youth found it to be a difficult and time-consuming job, which involved keeping the register of all twenty-five or so classes, the weekly attendance, amounts of offerings from each class, a counting of the money, rolling the coins for the bank, depositing it, and sending letters and checks weekly to whatever charity had been designated by the deacons. In addition, Ted was required to sit conspicuously up front on the side bench each Sunday while he tallied the attendance, then stand by the register on the wall and post the correct attendance as well as the amount of the offering. This had to be done before the closing of Sunday school, when one of the superintendents came to the pulpit to summarize the lesson, and the chorister led the group in a final hymn.

Alden, talented and interested as he was in music, was elected chorister, a position for which he was well suited. He would do a superb job.

Neither of the boys questioned such direct appointments by the church. No person did. It was very rare indeed when someone, nominated from the floor for an office or committee, refused the honor or responsibility of the nomination. What was contracted there was contracted in heaven. So they were all taught. Who would dare to be contentious and deny the Lord one's talent and service?

It was as Brother Buckwalter, who'd preached at a special service, had told them, half humorously, but yet making the message clear, that a Christian needed to be "one who could preach a sermon, pray, or die at a minute's notice."

And that was the way the Aaron Yoders experienced their newly adopted church. They soon noticed that almost every man was expected to be able to pray in public. Only the unusually shy male, or one whose manner of living was in question was omitted from the call to lead in public prayer. So Ted and Alden both quickly learned to drop to their knees and pray in public.

There was one assignment which Ted never forgot. Committees had to be appointed by the congregation for the district conference, as their church, Sycamore Grove was to host the conference on their grounds. This was a task of considerable responsibility, requiring careful planning, commitment, and organization. Suddenly, Ted heard his name announced from the floor by Brother Kauffman. He had been nominated as one of four members to serve on the Grounds Committee.

As events would have it, he was elected. Never mind his qualifications. Having scarcely any notion at all regarding what the Grounds Committee would do, Ted soon found out. Why hadn't he been appointed to a committee more suited to his interests? Well, he guessed the Lord called people to exercise themselves in every manner, both mentally and physically.

When conference time arrived, Brother Eli Schrock,

committee chairman, drove by in his truck. He'd called ahead to Ted, telling him to be prepared with a shovel, that they'd be driving to the woods to get sawdust. Sure enough, they lurched through the brush and undergrowth, crossed a creek, following a trail that led to a large pile of sawdust. Here, Eli, Ted, and Howard Hartzler slung the soured granules of wood into the back of the pickup with their shovels. The day was hot and humid. Sweat rolled down their backs. When Brother Schrock agreed they now had enough, they hauled it to the church, shoveling it through an open basement window by the two giant furnaces.

Ted, bewildered by his lack of interest in the task at hand, and his feelings of inferiority when he worked around farm men, who seemed so skilled in every kind of physical maneuver, tried to be compliant, a good committee member.

Next they drove to East Lynne, where they loaded up four or five hundred pounds of ice from the ice house. Covering the ice with thick blankets and burlap sacks, they sped back to the church. The sessions of the conference had begun. Cars lined the roadsides, the parking lot overflowed. A huge tent, stretched out on the lower level of the ground in front of the church, loomed high among the sycamores. There was no doubt about the significance of the occasion.

Brother Schrock ground his pickup into reverse, backed it up to the basement window. The Lord had called some for the inside labor of the worship hour, the preaching, teaching, listening, and singing, but today, the Lord had called Ted to unload ice into the church basement. He grunted and strained. His ice tongs slipped. There was a resounding thud as a corner of his block of ice hit the metal side of the pickup truck. He strained and sweated as they placed the chunks inside the two giant furnaces, covering half of the remaining ice with the sawdust and burlap.

Fans had been attached to the furnace to pick up and circulate the cooled air into the crowded, hot sanctuary above.

While they were unloading the ice, they were suddenly surrounded with heavenly music. The swelling sounds of the four hundred or so worshipers rose up within the sanctuary, streamed and billowed out the open double doors in the front of the church, and cascaded out the open windows. Ted's skin tingled. No people on earth could sing like these. His heart swelled with joy and pride. He was happy to be one of them, a Mennonite himself.

Though he had been miscast to serve on the Grounds Committee, and had felt sorely unsuited, God had blessed him with this sacred event which he never forgot, the blessing of that magnificent hymn bathing Ted and his fellow committee members as they strained with the ice: *But I know whom I have believed, and am persuaded that He is able to keep that which I've committed unto Him against that day.*

The end of the conference week finally came. Ted had time to attend some of the sessions. He had been touched not only by the magnificent hymn singing, but also by the preaching and the concern and interest that seemed to be reflected from the gathered brothers and sisters.

The languid hot August crept past. Farmers began plowing the ground for their fall planting. The huge round August moon shone down on the golden wheat stubble surrounded by the hedgerows of osage orange. It was a night beautiful enough for the very shining angels of God to sweep down from heaven and fling themselves through the gilt-edged cloud bank in the western sky. Eons of light years away, stars twinkled against the indigo sky. The earth was pastoral and serene. An occasional cow lifted up her voice to bellow a comforting word to her calf.

Martin Stutzman and Wilbur Hershberger drove up the darkening lane toward Ted and Alden's house. Wilbur's Chevrolet shifted gears and scooted the gravel as he accelerated up the slope.

Turning off the headlights after he'd parked in the small grove of oaks in front of the square frame house, he waited for Ted and Alden to come out.

Soon the two brothers were in the back seat of the Chevy. Wilbur and Martin, free at last from most of the hard summer's work, felt the rush to travel some unknown road or path. "How about going for a ride?" chuckled Wilbur, glancing back at the two Yoder boys. "It's okay," Alden said, leaning back on the seat. Ted rolled down a window. He too, was game for a ride through the country, especially on an evening like this.

There was no particular plan. Martin Stutzman said it'd be nice to drive over to East Lynne and get a pop or ice cream. Ted felt in his pocket. Yep, he had a dime. The car, doing forty or fifty miles an hour rounded the two sharp corners on Highway Number Two. Ted felt a little queasy. Was Wilbur trying to show off?

They began discussing the girls of the congregation. All of

them, being church members, would not seriously consider dating a girl other than a Mennonite. The church took a firm stand on marriages or dating outside the faith. If the outsider in the marriage did not convert to the Anabaptist belief, then usually there was such a forceful psychological feeling within the closed communion that the couple took membership in a church of another denomination. Mixed marriage (of differing faiths) was viewed by the Mennonites as representative of "the unequal yoke."

The spirited farm boys shared stories about the country girls.

"Anna Rose is lots of fun, isn't she?" said Alden, speaking of the slender young Mennonite teacher who taught the neighborhood school. He himself had stopped in one evening after school, finding Anna Rose still grading papers. She'd agreed, yes, indeed, to accompany him to church the next Sunday night.

But Anna Rose, being from the Bethel church, teetered on the outermost edges of the standards regarding plainness in dress, as interpreted at Sycamore Grove.

Her need for individuality was so great that, in spite of the doctrines and traditions of attire, she had cut her hair. Worse than that, however, she even dared to wear lipstick. They all agreed, though, that Anna Rose was beautiful, as she sauntered down the church aisle, her covering bouncing on the springy auburn curls on her head.

Martin Stutzman, a bit jealous, couldn't stop talking about school teacher Deborah Kurtz, and how she'd been taken home from conference one night by that burly Mose Kreider in his shiny new plush-seated DeSoto. Wasn't that something?

Then there were the Heatwole sisters, kind, considerate, and hard-working. Edith Marie, the oldest and largest, seemed to have been born big. Ted could remember her, way back at Bible school in 1937. Even then, not more than a fourth grader, Edith Marie stood head and shoulders above her peers. Her single, thick braided pigtail hung down her back. She had a heart of gold, was fun-loving and as stable as a prairie buffalo. God had blessed her with a happy disposition. Then, there were Carla and Hester, her two sisters who slaved with true Mennonite commitment at farm tasks and the challenges of the Missouri mud slinging up their calves as they plodded out to wait for the school bus. All the young people enjoyed Sunday afternoon parlor visits with them.

Wilbur had stopped the car at the crossroad. He looked both ways, then turned toward the sleepy little village of East Lynne. "Let's stop and scare Earl!" cried Martin.

"Sure," said Wilbur, excitedly. He knew they'd be driving past preacher Manasseh Hartzler's farm. That'd be young Earl plowing by tractor light, late into the evening, as he tried to finish tilling the wheat field.

Ted wasn't too interested in the proposal, but, since he was a rather nonassertive person and the excursion called for little more risk than getting his pant legs full of cockleburs, he nodded his head in agreement.

They'd amble over the ditch and into the field to scare Earl as he concentrated on finishing his plowing.

The boys began to snicker as they crept down the dark hedgerow.

Ted, became more animated, sensing excitement in the air after all. "This is as much fun as a snipe hunt," he thought to himself.

Alden ripped his shirt on a branch from a hedge tree that Wilbur let fly back too fast, but what matter now? They were traipsing, slinking, one after another down the hedgerow. The idea of scaring Earl grew funnier and funnier. They stifled their snickers and coughs.

"Ouch!" cried Martin who'd punctured his thumb on a barb from the barbed-wire fence. Martin eased on across, took out over the dark shiny-edged furrows. The others followed.

They could now clearly hear the groaning of the John Deere tractor as it gouged the earth, pulling two shiny plow shares. Earth turned like water before the bow of a ship. "Hurry," whispered Wilbur, hoarsely, hastily looking back at the three darting figures behind him. "If we can reach that ditch, we'll be right at the end of the furrow where he will turn around."

Sure enough. Wonder of wonders. The events of the night were falling into place. A party mood and frivolous spirit coursed through the boys. Nothing could stop them now. The lights of the tractor glared closer. It's motor chugged and strained. A man's figure could now be seen bouncing and jostling in the air as he, tired and growing listless from the long day's plowing, edged the behemoth machine toward the end of the furrow. Closer and closer came the tractor. The driver bounced high as an arm reached for the hand brake, preparing for the strain of the turn at the furrow's end.

"Now," whispered Wilbur, hoarsely. Then pandemonium broke loose. Wilbur, Martin, Ted and Alden rose up like resurrected ghouls from the bowels of the earth. Their unearthly shrieks and yells were punctuated by their upturned faces and flailing arms. "Whooooooeeeee! Yeeee-eeee-eeee-eeee-ahhh-ahhh-ahhh! Yaaaaaaaa-aaaa!"

The figure on the tractor seat rose straight up with the speed of one who'd just sat upon an electric wire. Like Ichabod Crane in Sleepy Hollow, the hat fell from his head, his mouth fell open in seeming terror. Arms flailed and pawed the air, then grasped wildly for the brake. The tractor lurched to a stop, front wheels on the very edge of the chasm.

"Oooo-oooo-oooo-ooooh, Oooo-oooo-oooo-oooooh!" The sounds came from the dark hole between beaming owl eyes in the face staring down at them. It was then that the quartet of young night raiders saw the extremities of their folly. For it was not Earl at all standing on the tractor above them. It was their dearly beloved Mennonite preacher Brother Manasseh himself. "Dear Lord! Merciful heavens!" The shocked youth stood fixed in the night, their feet stuck to the earth, their spirits frozen within, feeling doomed to perdition.

When they'd gasped a time or two, they began to climb up the edge of the ravine to the tractor and the stricken preacher above them. They bowed and scraped ashamedly as they tried to apologize.

"Oohhh-oohhh-oohhh! Ah, ah!" Brother Manasseh was laughing nervously. "Oh, my! Oh, my, my!" he said, as he saw the faces of the four youths of his parish grinning through their embarrassment. "You know, the only thing I could think of," chortled Brother Manasseh, "was that I'd been surprised by the very angels of God."

Ted ever after remembered that night of the scare as the "night of the angels."

Perhaps no minister on earth would have taken the startling experience with such even humor and kindliness as did dearly beloved Bible-quoting, bandy-legged little Preacher Manasseh.

And the joy we feel in the solemn service of your house brings tears to our eyes, when in your house we read the story of your younger son, that he was dead and lived again; had been lost and is found. Indeed you rejoice in us and you rejoice in your angels who are holy in holy charity.

-St. Augustine

19.

Counsel Meeting

The October Missouri days, tangy and crisp in the morning, grew warm and balmy by evening. The blazing red of the oaks contrasted sharply with the vivid yellow leaves of the shagbark hickories. The whole earth was a sweep of color. Nature was turning the varied seasons as the wild Canadian geese winged their way southward in the gigantic V formation.

Ted loved the autumn, the morning haze, and the smell of wood smoke in the air.

Events of significance held in the church in the fall were counsel meeting and the communion service. The Aaron Yoders experienced these realities for the first time in the congregation of the Mennonites. They would search, travail, and transcend as they participated in the ordinances. For now, they comprised one sister and three brothers in the church.

Counsel meeting was always scheduled one week before the communion service. This solemn and protracted meeting provided an area where, as the poet Scollard said, each individual could search and experience "rapt converse with thyself from sordidness and self, a sanctuary, swept by the winnowing of unseen wings, and touched by the white light ineffable."

Only after the individual examining-where the members of the congregation searched their hearts and souls and confessed their sins in prayer and by public confession, should such stringent measures be necessary to cleanse the soul and restore one to the holy faith and fellowship of the beloved-only then would they participate in the fellowship of the communion.

Following the breaking of the bread and the drinking of the cup, brothers then would demonstrate the example of servanthood as taught by the Lord Jesus himself and wash their fellow brother's feet. The sisters would wash each other's feet on their side of the church.

With solemnity, counsel meeting was understood by all to be in keeping with the Scripture in Second Corinthians 13:5: "Examine yourselves, whether ye be in the faith; prove your own selves."

By keeping this austere observance twice a year, since the sixteenth century, these Anabaptist were keeping alive the doctrine of nonconformity to the world. God's people were to be "unspotted from the world."

The autumn light glared through the windows in the meetinghouse. That stark light was softened only by the tones of grays, browns, and blacks of the assembled worshipers. Since the two sets of double doors in the front of the church were closed against a chilling wind, they were cut off from any soothing overtures of nature, the rich smells of the earth, the blessings of the bowing trees, the aroma of dried corn and autumn flowers, or the touch of wind upon the cheek.

The church was crowded. Members had made stringent efforts to be present. Only the bedfast among the elderly remained at home.

They stood to sing. With skill in his hand and holy light in his eye, the chorister led them through the swelling hymn. Why did it move Ted so? *Lord, Thou hast searched and seen me through: Thine eye commands, with piercing view, my rising and my resting hours, my heart and flesh with all their powers.*

Who was this God who pierced our hearts and knew our every thought even before such thoughts were our own?

Suddenly Ted was aware that they were singing the Amen. The hymn was finished. So let it be: this prayer-song had focused upon the perennial warmth yet searching eye of God who saw and

knew their earthly passions, yet understood and forgave. This was
the hour for forgiveness.

The hymn softened the mood set by the austere building,
wooden floors and benches, high ceiling, and white painted walls.
The harsh light broke through the undecorated plain windows.
Ted needed no one to convince him. He truly felt surrounded still
with God. His heart began to beat more rapidly. He'd sensed the
need for his own soul's deference to the hour. He waited patiently.

Stern Bishop Hershberger rose to the pulpit, bronzed and bald
by both the sun and heredity. His serious passion for the church
was vivid, reflecting from his eyes. He surveyed the congregation.
Behind him on the bench sat three other ordained brethren, but
Bishop Hershberger needed no backing. He looked strong and
staunch enough in the Lord just by himself. One could tell by the
exacting look in his eye that he was prepared to deliver a powerful
sermon.

The sisters halted any moving of their heads or hands, looking
up with tender eyes, willing and eager to learn from the Lord.
Brethren cleared their throats and adjusted their gray and black
clothed backs to the unyielding benches.

Backed by his Bible verses and the force and strength welling
up within him, he delivered his sermon on their need for
nonconformity to the world, and for confession where they had
sinned against God and others.

Brother Hershberger stopped. He surveyed the solemn
assembly.

There was a pause. Pheobe Miller's baby whimpered. She held
it close to her brown clothed breast, soothing it with a brush of her
cheek.

The bishop continued. "And now, my dear brothers and sisters
in the Lord," his voice had softened, his face looked caring and
beseeching to this congregation that they might truly examine
themselves in order to be worthy of communing at the Lord's
table.

An angular shaft of sharp light, coming from the south
window, penetrated the austerity of the room. Suddenly a gust of
autumn wind gained momentum. There was a rushing sound as the
gigantic sycamores outside were swept and bowed by the sudden
gale. Nature was shaking the debris and useless leaves from the
limbs. Branches, left white, purified by the light and cold wind

reached into the air to await the resurrecting touch of spring.

Ted adjusted himself on the bench. He looked over at Alden who crossed his legs and swallowed.

The intensity of the hour settled upon him, and now the minister was exhorting each one of them to do individual searching, sweeping and winnowing the useless chaff out of their lives. The minister was saying: "Therefore if thou bring thy gift to the altar, and there remember that thy brother hath ought against thee; leave there thy gift before the altar and go thy way; first be reconciled to thy brother and then come and offer thy gift."

All the members of the congregation knew that there had been" serious rift among the members last summer when Silas Heatwole had sold forty acres of his land to Eli Bender. Both brothers had verbally agreed upon the price. Something happened when Brother Bender, who discovered that, indeed, he'd offered good land a bit below the current rate, raised the price. After all, it adjoined Brother Eli's farm. Changing the price to keep it in accord with the going rate would be understood by any reasonable man. They had not even yet made up a contract. There had almost been an excommunication over this quarrel.

There were negotiations and prayers. Through visits by the deacons and the prayers and leading of the bishop, the impasse had finally been overcome, Brother Silas Heatwole being convinced that their verbal agreement did take precedence before God and people. The episode had generated restive feelings among the members of the extended families on both sides who were now scattered throughout the congregation.

There was silence. Ted could hear the ticking of the oak-cased clock on the wall. Silence.

The bishop's voice continued, as he surveyed the congregation.

"We are all admonished to prove this time for our spiritual benefit. We have endeavored by prayer, meditation, and the reading of the Scriptures to come near to God, to purge out the old leaven of sin and impurity that yet might beset us."

He paused, his voice imploring. Then the most serious and difficult sentence of all. "Is there any among us who need public confession?" The sentence girded the congregation in the exercise of searching.

Though Ted could not think of any specific sin that urged him to public confession, he began to pray silently the words of the hymn that came to his mind in moments of contrition: "My sins, my sins, my Savior, they take such hold on me, I am not able to look up, save only, Christ, to Thee."

The penitential, searching mood was broken by a sound coming from far back on the women's side of the church. Did someone sneeze or cough? Indeed, what was that sound? Benches creaked and groaned as the gathered worshipers turned toward the sound. Again it came. An anguished cry? Apprehension and uneasiness clutched Ted.

Suddenly, Deborah Kurtz, school mistress and friend to many, rose from the hard bench on the women's side of the church. Her head was bowed and tears streamed down her cheeks as she thrust her head into the harsh beam of light. She groaned in her efforts to unite her mind, soul and body in readiness for the pilgrimage she must make to the front of the congregation. Deborah Kurtz, too, had been hearing that refrain for the last ninety-seven days: "My sins, my sins, my Savior, they take such hold of me."

Deborah would have to come forward before the sacred congregation. It had happened four months ago on a summer evening. A hardworking and faithful daughter to her widowed mother, she'd taught her pupils in the country school, hoed garden, and canned what she'd reaped therefrom. The only event breaking the chain of servanthood and work was going to church on Sunday.

Mose Kreider, who was known for his careless attendance at services, had approached her after one evening program at conference. "Would you care to go for a ride in my new DeSoto?" he'd asked. Then, of course he'd offered to take her home. Mose was reckless, earthy, and handsome. She knew he was not considered to be one of the young pillars of the church, but she liked him anyway.

Now, Deborah was pushing her feet through the space in front of the bench. Holding onto the back of the bench in front of her, she struggled over legs and feet toward the aisle. She glanced ahead. Her throat was on fire. The aisle lay seventeen miles ahead. "Oh, God," she prayed somewhere within.

Since her father's death when she was but a small child, she'd never really been close to a man. She'd missed her father's strength and warmth when he held her on his lap. And she'd had no kindly grandfather to brush her silky cheek with his whiskers. Mose Kreider seemed earthy, but generous in spirit. She'd taken the ride on the violet-colored, plush seats of his DeSoto. No, she hadn't protested when he drove down a long forgotten lane by Sugar Creek under a stand of sycamores, where the silvery moon peeped through. She'd had two years of college, but her only dating experience had been an occasional escort to church on Sunday night. She had limited her spinster dating only to young men of her faith. She even feared she'd become a spinster and grace the bench near the back of the church where the unmarried sisters sat.

The stricken undulations of her body and her dragging, scraping feet upon the planks beneath her finally pushed her to the aisle. The aisle. She looked at it, hazily aware of the open way it provided, leading somewhere. She must not forget. No, she would not forget the way, for the way ... "straight is the gate, and narrow is the way, which leadeth unto life, and few there be that find it."

With hands, red from dishwater and calloused from the hoe handle, she braced herself against the edge of the bench by the aisle. Could she let go? Her clutching fingers relaxed their hold. She stood, facing forward. From somewhere within she received strength for the journey ahead!

When Mose had parked the car under the July moon and white branches above, he'd removed his tie and opened his shirt collar. The heat had been sweltering. She'd noticed the curly mat of hair spilling out of his collar. She'd cleared her throat, her right hand toyed nervously with the buckle on her belt. Mose reached out a dark hand, brushed with hair. Gently it enveloped hers. It was then that she'd discovered something about the universe that she'd not had time to notice before. A force. A strange, warm force pulsed and throbbed through every living thing. Though apprehensive and even frightened, a part of her acknowledged the warm current pulsing through her.

Ted Yoder turned, looking over his left shoulder toward the strange . sighing, scraping sounds coming from the sisters' side of the congregation. What was Deborah Kurtz doing, wan and pale, standing there in the aisle? Dear, beautiful Mennonite Miss Kurtz had been his Bible school teacher years ago when he was a small child in the third grade. She'd taught him the poem, "All Things Bright and Beautiful." She seemed to epitomize the very poem itself. Maybe she was indisposed and would turn, three-quarters of the way down the aisle, towards the anteroom and walk on out to the women's privy, surrounded by the large spirea bushes. Yes, that must be it. Miss Kurtz was overcome by some indisposition of a physical nature. The eerie silence in the congregation, the waiting and the scraping of her feet told him otherwise.

Miss Kurtz's trouble was the agony of her spirit. True, it coursed through every fiber of her being, including her bowels. She was coming to the mercy seat.

Come, ye disconsolate, where'er ye wander, come to the mercy seat, fervently kneel.

Miss Kurtz's golden braided hair gleamed through her net covering as her head edged into the shaft of harsh light. Her mouth was slightly open, her eyes, strange and disconsolate stared far into the wilderness ahead. What did she see?

"What is my name? Oh, yes, Deborah is my name." She remembered it now. Named after Deborah the prophetess whom the Lord raised up to judge Israel. Only she was not here to judge Israel, but to proclaim her sin to Israel. Today Israel would judge her, lest she be cut off from the land of the living. Who was that, standing far, far down the way in the distance, light years beyond this beam of light dazzling her mind. And why weren't they singing some song like "Come ye that love the Lord and let our songs rejoice"?

That man standing in front of the pulpit was Bishop Hershberger in equal agony with this sister of his congregation. Silently, he prayed, with painful eyes and aching heart, that mercy and grace be administered to her.

Hail, Mary, Mother of God, full of grace and truth; the Lord is with thee.

Blessed art thou amongst women, and blessed is the fruit of thy womb, Jesus ....

Into Deborah's feverish mind flashed the memory of her Catholic friend, Erma. They had roomed together one summer at college. Erma often said her Hail Marys. Deborah was strange to the ways of Catholics. She was a Mennonite, a Mennonite who'd walked circumspectly and not as a fool month after month, year after yearexcept for that one summer evening.

Since it was coursing through her brain, the Catholic prayer would do. "Hail, Mary, Mother of God, full of grace and truth." Ah, yes, it seemed related to the Magnificat-only the cry of one sister to another as told by Saint Luke. Elizabeth, great with child, sang to Mary, who held the unborn Jesus, quickening in her womb.

Oh! What had she to offer for her folly? No child-no fruit of the womb, only a flat stomach and a penitential, contrite heart.

The planks in the aisle sloped forward. The hard wooden heels of her Sunday shoes clonked on the floor. Why should the sounds and scrapes of the penitent be softened by rich rugs and the sweet sounds of the organ and smells of incense and flowers? No! Better to stagger down the aisle in this plain, austere meetinghouse while the thuds and scrapings of her heels, reverberating beneath her, announced to God, the angels, and to this assembled congregation that a penitent had begun her pilgrimage. Where to? To Jerusalem? No. Just to the front of the church. She must not lose her way. Somewhere it was out there in the haze. Over yonder, above the heads of the bowed, white-covered women, and the waiting brethren. Over there somewhere loomed the pulpit before which she must stand. Ah, yes. It loomed ahead like Mount Pisgah, looking down upon the desert of her soul. Water. Cool water. Her mouth was as dry as the parched sand drifting in her mind and heart. "As the hart panteth after the water brooks, so panteth my soul after thee, a God," she prayed.

If she stopped this weary journey and just turned around, she could lead the kindly sisters and brothers in a hymn. Of course. *On Jordan's stormy banks I stand and cast a wistful eye.*

The loneliness of her living the way she did with her old mother left her vulnerable. No. She must not excuse herself. Her mother was God-fearing and virtuous and had instructed her well. She had simply answered the force, and part of that force came from her. The other part was the hard and warm comfort of the chest and body of that man. There was a joy and union in being held, but oh, the burning agony of her soul now. If only Mose would be standing up there ahead under the burning sun and below the peak of Mount Pisgah, waiting for her in all his earthy maleness, maybe this journey would seem less desolate. Why should she sojourn a desert path alone? *Must Jesus bear the cross alone, and all the world go free? No, there's a cross for everyone, and there's a cross for me.*

Deborah's pilgrimage had taken her now to where the aisles on the women's side crossed. The left aisle led to the anteroom and down the steps to the outside. To the right, in the unfocused distance, rose Mount Pisgah, the altar. "Come to the mercy seat, fervently kneel."

She had not flaunted herself naked on a rooftop like Bathsheba before David. She had simply taken a ride and discovered a force within her, and strangely enough within another living being. Their merger was unsanctified, abortive, unfruitful. Mose had soon skittered off to try ranching somewhere in Montana. She had to lurch up this weary aisle alone.

Deborah turned to the right, her eyes searching then focusing upon the altar. She had tried to dismiss it all, to keep it to herself. But, she was a Mennonite, a child of God who knew her Bible well. Like King David, it boiled and raged within her. The more she had tried to bury it in the depths of her subconscious, the more parched grew the desert within. *When I kept silent, my bones waxed old through my roaring all the day long. For day and night thy hand was heavy upon me; my moisture is turned into the drought of summer. Sela.*

Bring waters from the Jordan, penitential rain. *Here bring your wounded hearts, here tell your anguish; earth hath no sorrow that heaven cannot heal.*

Instead of Mount Pisgah, it was the faithful, sturdy, hand-hewn old pulpit from which she'd been taught the proclamations of God. She'd listened prayerfully beneath it, joined with her people. Her hands now clasped before her, the soggy handkerchief caught between. Could she even say the words? That word? The one that was so hard, sharp, and ugly sounding, grating like rusty, corrugated tin torn from the barn by the wind? Was the roaring within or without? "Through my roaring all day long." The autumn wind had broken loose again. It swept the eaves of the angular, stark country church where ordinary flesh and blood mortals were having rapt converse with immortal powers. Roaring down and in a mighty undulation, the wind anguished itself among the white branches of the sycamores outside. They writhed in the same agony of the cypress trees in a Van Gogh painting. Nature herself palled, anguished at her broken, contrite heart.

Will confess my transgressions unto the Lord.

Suddenly Deborah's face lifted. Facing the congregation of stricken, blanched, tense faces, her eyes fell for a moment upon the form of a heavy, old, black-robed woman, her organdy covered head bowed in her hands, weeping. Her mother. Her eyes brightened as they focused. They swept back and forth. Once, twice. Silence. Her mouth opened to the words her heart emptied out. It would not stop. She had not planned to say the verses, but the Holy Spirit surrounded her. *For the Spirit also helpeth our infirmities; for we know not what we should pray for as we ought; but the spirit itself maketh intercession for us with groanings which cannot be uttered.*

Her words became audible in the awful silence of the room.

"Have mercy upon me, a God, according to thy loving-kindness; blot out my transgressions. I stand before this fellowship, the members of this congregation because I have sinned."

One hand hung by the side of the dark dress of penance she had chosen to wear. The other wiped the flowing tears.

Ted and Alden sat fixed. They watched Miss Kurtz as the overpowering forces of counsel meeting and confession engulfed them.

Then came the ugly word. I have committed .... " But before it could be uttered, the body itself had to fortify the individual members thereof for their express duties so that the utterance might be proper and audible, expressed plainly before the brothers and sisters of the congregation. Her diaphragm drew in, her chin lifted. The mouth opened slightly, lower lip bent in just a trifle, enough to brush the upper front teeth, gleaming white in Miss Kurtz's mouth. The Cupid's bow of her upper lip turned out as the small explosion gave birth to the word "FORNICATION" Then began the verses: "For I acknowledge my transgression; and my sin is ever before me. Hide thy face from my sins, and blot out all mine iniquities. Create in me a clean heart, O God; and renew a right spirit within me."

Bishop Hershberger stepped down from the pulpit to stand by her side. His cheeks glistened with tears. Silence. Then with compassionate kindness he looked into the sea of faces before him and implored, "You have heard the confession, the prayers and the contrition of our dear sister. With full courage, she has taken it upon herself today to make public and full confession of her sin. She has not spared herself. If it is your desire to exercise the grace of forgiveness to our dear Sister Deborah, you will manifest it by standing."

The benches cracked and groaned as they gave up the weight of their loads. Even the old, the halting, and the arthritic unfolded themselves slowly from the benches, standing like stricken windmills.

The bishop nodded to his severely dressed wife and helpmeet, acknowledging her duty to come forward and welcome Sister Deborah with her gentle embrace and the graciousness of the kiss of peace. After all, there was no need for an excommunication. Sister Deborah's sorrow and contrition were evident and soul-shaking.

The bishop nodded to the chorister. "Let us now have a hymn." *Wash me, O Lamb of God, wash me from sin; by thy atoning blood, make me clean; purge me from every stain, let me thine image gain; in love and mercy reign, o'er all within.*

The service wore on. All of the ordained brethren stood giving lengthy testimony to their spiritual status as they understood. Then they knelt on the hard floor for more prayers. Three brethren had been asked to pray. Fifteen minutes had gone by and Ted and Alden were still kneeling. Twenty minutes, twenty-five. Their knees ached from the cracks and ridges beneath them. At last there came the bishop's final Amen.

An awesome silence prevailed before the searching question. "If you have examined your hearts and minds, and can truthfully say that you stand in peace before God and your fellow brothers and sisters, and before all people, and that you have truly searched your hearts and confessed your sins and desire to eat of that bread and drink of that cup with the fellowship of believers next Lord's Day, you may manifest it by standing."

Though having undergone a psychic rent, brought on by the pain and confession of one of their members, they'd banded together with forgiveness to stitch it up with healing and mercy. Each one had been reminded of his or her own fallibility and proneness to err. In unison, they responded to the bishop's question. They would meet again here next Sunday for the holy communion and the washing of the saints' feet.

20.

Communion and the Washing of the Saints' Feet

While they were still under instruction to become members of the Mennonite church, Ted and Alden learned that they would be observing closed communion. This would be a communion for the brethren and sisters of like faith, who had kept their commitments to the holy ordinances and practices of the Old Mennonite church. How could he forget that agonizingly long meeting of last week called Counsel Meeting, wherein they had searched their hearts and minds and declared their peace with God and man? It was a sincere, austere, and solemn time of the year. Ted had not yet been able to put to rest the searing pain and shock of Miss Kurtz's public confession.

The church was even more packed on communion day. Members, who for some reason had missed last week's meeting were now given an opportunity to make confession and to give a statement that they were at peace with God and desired to commune with the congregation. These dozen or so, plainly robed members scattered through the congregation, stood to their feet, confirming their readiness for communion. There was now a commitment and unity from every member present to partake in the holy celebrations of the hour. Ted felt a slight relaxing in his back and legs. The hard work of searching and confessing was past. Surely the sacred rituals and emblems would bolster and support their expectant spirits.

The smell of feet, clean washed and prepared, farmer feet of the brothers and sisters of the meetinghouse, rose up like the earthy smell of newly dug potatoes. How perfectly they were reminded that they too belonged to the earth, received their sustenance from the fields, and depended upon the service of one another within the community, then, one day they would all return to the earth.

It seemed to Ted that the women were dressed even more severely on this day. There was no outward sign of frivolity or worldly display. Saint Paul himself could have sat among them and indeed confirmed that, judging by the externals, all were in accordance with his standard: "In like manner also, that women adorn themselves in modest apparel, with shamefacedness and sobriety; not with braided hair, or gold, or pearls, or costly array."

The mood of holiness and the memory of the Christ who had given freely of himself upon the cross was set by their voices. *Forbid it, Lord, that I should boast, save in the death of Christ my Lord; all the vain things that charm me most, I sacrifice them to his blood.*

"Yes Lord, forbid boasting or worldliness of any kind," Ted prayed silently, as his thoughts merged with the song of sorrow and of Christ's passion, calling for "my soul, my life, my all."

There was a soft thudding as hymnals were slipped back into their racks, the clearing of throats, and sounds of settling wooden benches as the communicants awaited with open and forward faces the reading of the Scripture from Matthew, chapter twenty-six.

Deacon Kauffman read the agonizing story of Jesus who told his disciples, "Verily I say unto you, that one of you shall betray me."

Ted felt the force of his love and the fervor of his commitment here in the congregation of the Mennonites. He felt his gratitude for the new order and blessings that had been brought to his family through the church. He prayed that he would be sincere in giving himself, for the hymn had expressed his feelings. "Love so amazing, so divine, demands my soul, my life, my all."

The sonorous tones of the deacon's voice were clearly heard in every corner of the meetinghouse.

"And as they were eating, Jesus took bread, and blessed it, and broke it, and gave it to the disciples, and he said, Take eat; this is my body. And he took the cup, and gave thanks, and gave it to them saying, drink ye all of it; for this is my blood of the new testament which is shed for many for the remission of sins."

Following the deacon's lengthy prayer, the bishop rose to give the communion message. The sincerity in his voice was evident as he exhorted his flock, reminding them that the eating and drinking together at the Lord's table is expressive of the communion and unity of the church as the body of Christ.

Then, holding his large black, leather-bound Bible in his calloused, farmer's hands, the bishop read First Corinthians 11:23-29. The seriousness and the intentionality of this meeting was expressed in those words: "For he that eateth and drinketh unworthily, eateth and drinketh damnation to himself, not discerning the Lord's body."

Nodding to the other ordained brethren, the bishop stepped down to the communion table in front of the hand-hewn pulpit.

When the small white cloth was removed from the emblems, Ted could see an ordinary loaf of homemade bread, cut in slices. It was not even unleavened bread, especially prepared for holy communion. Beside it was a pitcher of grape juice and four or five large, but ordinary drinking glasses or tumblers. The severity of the people's dress, the plainness of the meetinghouse and the solemnity of the moment would be matched by the almost drab ordinariness of the communion emblems and vessels of service. The bishop holding a slice of bread that the deacon's wife had baked raised it up and offered a prayer of thanks, concluding with the words, "This is my body which is given for you; this do in remembrance of me."

The sun, breaking through a cloud, sent shafts of light through the windows in the front of the church, as if God himself was providing a special illumination for celebration of the crucifixion of Jesus.

Five ordained brethren were distributing the bread to the standing members. With their calloused and bronzed hands they broke the crusted bread into bits and handed them to the stern and silent communicants. These were people of the soil and they received the emblems of the soil from hands that tilled and subdued the earth. The air was not graced by the lovely sounds of words like "silver tray and chalice." Only the murmuring of the eternal words of the Scriptures, due appointments for communion, punctuated the giving of the particles of bread.

With anticipation, Ted awaited his turn. One could hear the low murmuring of the voices of the ordained men as they quoted their verses from the Bible while distributing the broken bread. Dear and beloved Brother Manasseh was coming down the aisle. He looked directly at each communicant. Ted, remembering both the warmth and humorousness of this man, felt suddenly eased, somehow, that he would receive his first communion from his hand. Brother Manasseh had evidently forgiven and transcended his rude shock of the "night of the angels." In his priestly role, Brother Manasseh handed him a broken morsel of the coarse bread. He spoke as he handed it to Ted, "Take eat, this is my body." Placing the morsel in his mouth, Ted chewed it slightly, then swallowed. The slightly sour taste of yeast and wheat-flower lingered in his mouth, ordinary emblems of the life and existence of God's people.

The same procedure was followed with the plain kitchen tumblers filled with grape juice. Holding one in his hand, the bishop again offered a prayer: "The cup of blessing which we bless, is it not the communion of the blood of Christ?"

Then distribution to the standing congregation of people began.

There was silence. Again, the faint mumblings of verses from the lips of the ordained men as they passed the glasses of grape juice to their members.

If Ted was surprised at all during his first communion, it was over the everyday drinking glasses being passed down the bench aisles from minister to member, from member back to the minister, then again to another member until they all had drunk from the glasses. Only a fleeting thought about the sanitary condition of drinking from the glass upon which so many had pressed their lips swept through Ted's mind. Quickly he dismissed it, buried it. This was a holy day, a holy ordinance and celebration. If there were germs they surely would not survive the glory and light of God during this holy service. He felt better as he handed the glass back to Deacon Kauffman. The words were still coursing through his mind. "This cup is the new testament in my blood which is shed for you."

So this was the Lord's Supper. Ted looked at Alden. They sat as the deacons covered the emblems on the communion table and the bishop took his place again at the pulpit. Ted was still caught up in his own pondering of the meanings of what he had experienced as the bishop exhorted them "to remain faithful in the service of God, walk humbly, and exercise meekness and love toward all men."

Ted knew that as long as he lived he would not forget this first communion, the one where his family stood united in the church.

He smiled with thankfulness as he awaited the next service, the washing of the saints' feet.

The Aaron Yoders had learned their Mennonite catechism well.

There was not a one of them who did not know the interpretations, intentions, and meanings that were associated with the ceremony of foot washing. Did not the Lord Jesus himself institute this ordinance of humility? Did he not in addition command his disciples to do to one another as he had done to them? In spite of learning the lesson from the catechism well, there was a nervousness and slight misgiving among each of the Yoders. Not a single one of them had ever witnessed a foot-washing service in a Mennonite church before. It had taken Opel a long time to admit to herself that indeed she could do it. In their new church, which already seriously challenged these novices, they would try, in spite of uneasiness and lack of experience, to emulate the Lord Jesus when he took upon himself the role of a servant and washed his disciples' feet.

Both Ted and Alden had scrubbed their feet carefully the night before. Ted's young, adolescent toes gleamed white, nails trimmed, as he pulled fresh socks over them that Sunday morning. Not a callous or corn marred them. Neither were they old, wrinkled or disgraced by joints covered with unsightly hair.

Ted wondered what precautions his mother had taken. Knowing her, she would be ready, though. He stifled a smile as he remembered her tiny size-five foot and how it must appear among feet of these big German women, twice the size of Opel. And Aaron, his father? Well he guessed that Aaron would have the attitude that they would have to take his feet as they were. Everyone acquainted with Aaron knew that he was a simple man of the earth who preferred work overalls and work shoes to any other garments. He did buy an inexpensive blue suit for the day of their admittance to the congregation, though. His shoes, freshly blackened with polish, showed scuff marks and worn places from their years of humble service. Ted had no idea at all about the condition of his father's feet. He'd surmised that by the way he had stomped out to the porch in the moonlight, hobbling on one foot when the other leg had gone to sleep, all for the purpose of secretly throwing away a tobacco cud, that Aaron's feet were slightly bruised, blistered and calloused, crude feet like those of

Peter the fisherman.

Bishop Hershberger was reading the passage of Scripture that related to the ordinance they would soon keep. "He riseth from supper, and laid aside his garments; and took a towel, and girded himself. After that he poureth water into a basin, and began to wash the disciples' feet, and to wipe them with the towel wherewith he was girded .... So after he had washed their feet, and had taken his garments, and was set down again, he said unto them, 'Know ye what I have done to you? If I then, your Lord and Master have washed your feet, ye also ought to wash one another's feet. For I have given you an example that ye should do as I have done to you.' "

Ted's uneasiness grew as he waited in anticipation of the coming event. What if he made a mistake? Was he supposed to take off both shoes and socks or only one? This ordinance called for utmost concentration. Well, he'd just have to observe and "do as the Romans do." His heart increased its beat.

The tall farmer chorister stood to lead them in a hymn. *Christ in the night He was betrayed, for us a plain example laid; he to a private room retired with those he afterward inspired. He rose and laid his garments by, when towel and water were brought nigh. To prove his love divinely sweet, he stooped to wash his servants' feet.*

That morning the deacons and other appointed brethren of the congregation had brought large milk cans of heated water and had placed them in the basement before the service. These same brethren, as the hymn began, rose and quietly moved to the rear of the church and into the basement. By the time the assembled worshipers were singing the last verse of the hymn, two of these brethren had already started down the aisles with foot basins, large, wide, shallow pails over their arms. Ted watched, intrigued, as they placed them before the benches in the very front of the church.

Another hymn was announced. They kept on singing as the foot-washing basins were brought into the meetinghouse and distributed at other points throughout the building. Silently, a deacon laid a number of white folded towels by each tub. If Ted was impressed at all, it was with the fact of the total organization and smoothness by which this service was flowing so far. His uneasiness quickened, though. Foot washing. Even the words sounded plebeian and earthy.

More than a dozen basins had been placed throughout the meetinghouse on both sides of the building. Ted glanced over on the women's side, wondering how discreetly the sisters of the congregation could keep such a bold ordinance as washing feet? But, were they not called by the same call as Paul and Barnabas to "wax bold"?

Would the sisters keep their stockings on? Somehow, it seemed immodest to even think of these kindly, pious, plainly dressed women bending down to unhook their stockings, let alone strip them off, here in the meetinghouse at that! Surely God would provide. Ted trusted. What was Opel going through? And, these sisters had been so careful about the clear teachings of Saint Paul, too.

The bishop's voice trailed off. "Now let us keep the ordinance as instructed by our Lord and Savior, Jesus Christ: For I have given you an example that ye should do as I have done to you."

Slowly and silently, the men on Ted's side of the congregation began to rise. Apprehension gripped Ted. What was he to do? Better wait. Watch. There must be no mistake. Men were turning to one another. They mumbled something to each other. What was it they were saying? The bishop, ministers, and deacons near the front were turning and nodding too. They were asking one of another, "Will you wash with me?" Brother Miller and Brother Heatwole already, near the front of the church, sat on the oak bench near a waiting basin and towels. They began untying their shoes. To the right of Ted, near the aisle, another two brethren were doing the same. How was he to get involved in this? Would he be left sitting here chosen last? What should he do? Men were pairing off in every direction. Now lines were forming as they waited in front of brethren who were already keeping the ordinance.

Old Brother Schantz sat by the basin while Brother Helmuth, kneeling in front of him, reached out, took the gnarled foot, barely touched the calloused sole in the basin of water. With another hand, warm water was lifted up, once, twice, again, over and around the foot, then, removing the dripping appendage from the tub, the farmer's calloused foot was patted and dried, then set to the side. The same work began on the other. As soon as this was finished, the men changed places and repeated the ritual with solemnity and skill.

Ted had forgotten about the ordinance of the holy kiss. The bishop, deacon, and ministers kept it every Sunday, but now having finished washing each other's feet, the two farmer brethren grasped one another by the right hand, and kissed each other soundly upon the lips, commenting to each other, "The Lord bless you."

Thirty-year-old Thomas Hartzler tapped the restless Ted on the shoulder. Smiling, the tanned young farmer said, "Will you wash with me?" The die was cast. Ted must move on to keep this ordinance of this newly adopted church. The "spirit was willing but the flesh was weak." They waited in line for five minutes. Ted cast a glance over to the women's side of the meetinghouse. Poor Opel, like a babe thrown into the pond, would she be able to swim all the way across? He began to pray silently, "Oh, God, show me aright ...."

He must not look at his brother, Alden, nervous as they both were. A hysterical chuckle might rip loose. That would never do. Ted knew that it would be absolutely disastrous if that happened.

Yes, Opel on the women's side was apprehensive too. Turning to the big German woman twice her size on the same bench, she asked, "Do we take off our stockings?"

"Oh, yes," replied the stocky woman, already reaching under her dress to undo her garter for the other leg and foot. Poor Opel. These Mennonites had been reared from their mother's bosoms with their customs. What was sacred and ordinary in their religious ritual was strange and awkward to the novice. She had tried so hard to be a good Mennonite.

"Well, here goes," she said to herself. She straightened her face, bolstered her faith. She would not let her sons down on this matter either. After all, didn't Ruth in the Bible have the nerve not only to glean the wheat in Boaz's field but the gall to lie down at the end of his blanket? And how about that strange woman named Jael in the book of Judges who had the gumption to drive a stake through wicked old Sisera's head in behalf of her people? God would give her strength. Why, only last spring hadn't she blasted a huge snake to smithereens? Blasted it right out of the oak tree with the double-barreled shotgun while it was crawling up to swallow the baby robins. She could even kill a Leghorn rooster with a rock if they only gave her a moment to aim. Guess she could splash a little water on a German woman's feet, even if it had to be done here in church.

By now there were murmurings, the thudding sounds of bare heels upon bare boards, the splashing of water as the ceremonial ritual was carried out.

Ted finished washing the foot of the athletic young farmer. He patted it dry with the towel. Was he hurrying too fast? Did he grip the brother's ankle too tightly? Lessening the pressure of his hand and fingers, he noted no marks. He was sure Jesus would wash his disciples' feet with the utmost tenderness. He must try to emulate the Master. Setting down the foot he'd tried to thoroughly dry, he brought the other one, calloused and bronzed over the water.

Was the farmer brother's leg getting tired, holding it in that manner suspended as it was? Should Ted support it more? Perspiration broke out on his forehead. He was never so aware of the joints of the body, calf, and thigh, hinged at the knee, the relaxed foot which could swivel and turn. His mind caught and hung on the words of some old Negro spiritual, "Ankle bone connected to the-hip bone connected to the ...." Concentrate, Ted! Concentrate! Dip the water over the arch of the foot where the veins rise, pulsing like thick cords or roots ready to bind the young farmer to his earth. Ted's breath moved over the glistening foot as beads of water ran to the side. Ezekiel and the bones, the sinews, the flesh ....

The foot twitched. Brother Hartzler's leg tired in the suspended position. "And behold a shaking and the bones came together, bone to his bone, and when I beheld, the sinews and the flesh came upon them and the skin covered them above."

It was a sensual, earthy task of ritual love Ted was performing. He was near exhaustion. *And do not grow weary of well-doing .... When I said my foot slippeth; thy mercy, O Lord held me up.* Ted prayed silently, remembering words long before committed to memory.

He was almost through. God had been with him, like David, he understood, "He will not suffer thy foot to be moved; he that keepeth thee will not slumber."

His hand dipped the water up, around, over. Then the towel. He was finished. They exchanged places. Control. That's what it took. Control of oneself. Look for the meaning in this ordinance of the washing of the saints' feet. He must ponder the meaning of servanthood, the meanings of the towel and the basin, true symbols of service.

The smell of feet, clean washed and prepared, farmer feet of the brothers and sisters of the meetinghouse, rose up like the earthy smell of newly dug potatoes. How perfectly they were reminded that they too belonged to the earth, received their sustenance from the fields and depended upon the services of one another within the community, then one day they would all return to the earth. Then came the clasping of the hands and the kiss. Smack. Ted felt the hard jaw and angular side of the farmer's face meeting his. He'd almost missed Ted's lips though. The whiskers scratched Ted's tender adolescent face. "The Lord bless," he murmured sincerely, relieved that he had made it through this second and most difficult part of his first holy communion day.

21.

The Teacher

There are two role models for isolated rural children eager to open themselves to the fabulous world beyond their limited horizons. These models are their teachers first of all, and secondly, the ministers of the churches, if they are at all privileged enough to be related to a church.

Without exception, Ted and Alden Yoder's country teachers had been loving, generous, and skillful in teaching. Often they taught the eight-month school year in bleak, darkened rooms by isolated, rural mud roads. Theirs was the challenge to lighten the souls and open the minds of these eager children who in later times and more urban places, might even have been labeled underprivileged.

A mystery and natural beauty surrounded their lives as they trudged along the country lanes toward these small one-room schools. Lunch pails in their hands, they carried with them the fruit of their family's labors; homemade sausage between slices of freshly baked bread, a jelly sandwich rich in the savory aroma of the wild blackberries or gooseberries, boiled down to make jam or jelly on a wood-burning kitchen range.

Frequently their mothers included a slice of apple or mince pie, and usually, had there not been too serious a dry season, a homegrown Bartlett pear or Jonathan apple.

Through the seasons of the year, they bounced along, close to

186

nature-feeling the rain and fog in their faces, their feet contending with the heavy mud of the rainy season and the soft velvet dust of the dry.

They knew the seasons intimately, the scorching heat of summer, the drenching rain of an April downpour, the glazed or drifted snow enchanted by a million reflections of golden light from the morning sun, and the heady goldenrod and yellow brightness of fall, with its backdrop of wood smoke, gray fog, and mist. There were, however, abundant times and episodes in the tiny one-room schools and even in the modest county seat high school at Harrisonville for Ted and Alden to express themselves in creative ways: Ted in art, writing, and drama; and Alden through his music.

But these were conservative and pious days in the community of Sycamore Grove. There were even some young people who were not allowed to continue their education beyond the eighth grade. Among these conservative families, higher education was considered worldly and even possibly connected with an unequal yoke. Ted felt a sorrow and a sense of loss for these four or five young persons whose formal education was cut off when they were handed their eighth grade diplomas.

Both Alden and Ted boldly and without question claimed by this time that their identities lay in the church at Sycamore Grove--these were their people whom they had personally chosen, their family.

However, there was an inner struggle. Ted was elected vice-president of his senior class and took a leading role in the senior play. Alden purchased a wonderful second hand trombone, donned a blue and gold uniform and joined the spirited high school band. Ted, however, suffered mild pangs of guilt, as the practice for the senior play, "Melissa, My Western Miss," conflicted with prayer meeting at Sycamore Grove. The exhibitionistic and dramatic side of his nature, however, won this battle.

Now, at age seventeen and in his last semester of high school, Ted had already registered to take the Missouri State Teacher's Examinations at the county superintendent of schools' office in the courthouse on the square.

Granted permission to miss a day of high school by the principal, Ted presented himself in the courtroom for the Friday and Saturday examinations. There was apprehension and nervousness, but Ted believed in himself and had no doubts that he would pass. He fully intended to be a teacher.

Within three weeks, his teaching certificate arrived. Ted had passed. One more month remained and he would graduate from high school, then commute to Central Missouri State College at Warrensburg, Missouri, for summer term, as many rural young people of the 1940s did to prepare to become teachers.

Now only one task remained: find a school within driving distance which would hire him.

Now Miss Bowlin, county superintendent, had nice schools reserved for experienced teachers. But there were other schools more isolated, floating in the sea of the perpetual Missouri mud. These, according to Miss Bowlin, were for the beginners like Ted.

One late April Saturday morning in 1947, Ted accompanied by his father, Aaron, set out on a bold adventure to find a school.

"Look out, watch it!" cried Aaron as he lurched against the door of the Ford with the two missing teeth in the grill, "Gonna get us in that ditch yet."

Ted snaked the Ford along in mud ruts and water, doing the best he could. He'd dressed well for this occasion, and had his application letters neatly addressed and by his side on the worn seat.

The sky grew dark, osage orange shadowed both sides of the dismal road, the mud was barely passable and another spring rain was on its way. Their consternation rose.

"Must be down that lane." Ted's voice quaked a little under the strain of it all. They were looking for the farmer Hiram Hobbs' place northwest of East Lynn.

Miss Bowlin had given Ted a lead for a small school in this isolated sea of mud. They'd passed it a mile back. In fact, even stopped. Ted had gotten out, in spite of the mud and his Sunday shoes, to walk up and look in the windows of the tiny building, hunching under black rain clouds and in need of paint. It looked cold and forlorn. Ted felt a chill sweep through him. This was so far away (seven or eight miles) outside of the Mennonite community-his loneliness increased. Oh well, there was enough of his Arkansas mother Opel's blood in his veins to persevere in spite of hardship and obstacles. He buried his fears, tried not to be discouraged by the shabby room beyond the window glass. He saw lanterns hanging from a peeling ceiling and below, the blackened oil floor.

Ted got back into the Ford, put it in low gear and on they crept toward board member Hiram Hobbs's farm.

Aaron got out to unhook the barbed-wire gap at the lane. Driving through, Ted hoped they would not get buried in the barnyard ahead. Smoke ascended from the house, squatting in a stand of locust trees. Cows mooed.

Lurching and sliding, they came to a stop. This was it. Make it or break it. Ted cleared his throat, selected one of his application letters, tried to quiet his thudding heart and started through the yard gate. It squeaked and sagged as it fell open. Two large yellow hound dogs yelped and bounded forward, smelling at his pant legs.

Ted held his application letter tightly in one hand and knocked on the screen door with the other. He knocked again, noting the stale odor of the morning breakfast cooking lingering over the screened porch.

An inner door opened and heavy feet sounded; boards quivered.

The screen door opened. There stood a squat farmer's wife, wisps dislodged from her knotted hair fell over the side of her face. Surprised at seeing a lad of tender years standing on her limestone threshold, dressed like a dandy to boot, her fat face broke into a wide spread as she smiled, "Yes?"

"I would like to see Mr. Hobbs, please," said Ted, courage rising.

"I understand your school district has an opening for a teacher."

"Why yes! Yes, wait right there a spell an I'll get Hiram." She turned, lifted a fat hand to her mouth and called "Hir-ram!"

Hiram came out. Ted swallowed as the strange farmer emerged through the house door and onto the porch. Mr. Hobbs adjusted his overall galluses as he pushed open the screen door and stepped out in front of the seventeen-year-old applicant-dressed in his Sunday best. Shoes polished in all of this sea of mud too!

Hiram swiped a hairy paw across his white-stubbled face, caught his cud of tobacco in his cupped hand and tossed it toward the forsythia bushes across the yard.

"How do you do?" said Ted, trying to hide his nervousness, and look straight into the eyes in the stubbled, tobacco-stained face. He extended his hand to the one that had just held the tobacco cud. "I'm Ted Yoder. Miss Bowlin informed me you have an opening for a teacher at Dodder School, I'd like to be considered as an applicant."

There, he'd said it. The earth had not shaken and the April shower had not commenced. He shifted his feet.

"This is my letter of application."

Suddenly the atmosphere was torn by high-pitched yelping sounds as the two yellow hounds bounded under the forsythia bushes in pursuit of a rabbit. The piercing screams of the rabbit rose up before they tore it to pieces.

It's a matter of survival, thought Ted, life or death. He felt his precariousness on the limestone step, his youth and inexperience struggling with his belief and faith in himself.

"And what, may I ask is the salary for the eight-month term?"

"Wall, now," allowed farmer Hobbs, "Miz Nickentucker had her pay riz plumb up ta ninety dollars a month. Guess we'd oughta raise it a bit for next year. Board thought a hundred would do."

"A hundred dollars a month? That would be satisfactory."

Ted didn't know from whence the words came, but he actually heard them coming out of his own mouth. He must watch his step, or he'd lose his balance and sink his Sunday shoe in the ooze.

They shook hands, these two strangers, worlds apart, yet meeting for a moment because a sensitive lad dared to gird himself and risk for a cause he considered important.

The farmer had taken his letter, thanked him, and allowed as how they'd "get in touch."

In exactly two days, Ted received a telephone call from Farmer Hobbs of Dodder School, saying that he'd brought Ted's application to the board and that Ted could have the teaching position if he desired ..

Mixed emotions swept over Ted. He felt excitement and the joy of accomplishment, yet at the same time an apprehensiveness and loneliness crept over him. This job would take him outside the Mennonite community, and this threatened his sense of security. His mind focused for a moment on the drab little Dodder School squatting in the mud.

God, however, intervened. On that very afternoon the grinding sounds of a Chevrolet in low gear could be heard, reverberating up the Yoder lane. Driving the car was none other than that wonderful loving and humorous Mennonite Elias King, board member of Clearfork School just a mile-and-a-half down the road. Would wonders never cease?

Now, having grown up so rural and isolated, Ted was often apprehensive around rural farm men. His parents had socialized only most sparsely with the people they'd joined at Sycamore Grove. Ted had been exposed to Aaron's acquaintances from over at Gunn City and East Lynn, Burris Tyatt, for instance, who could shame the very devil himself with his endless storehouse of invectives and swear words. Or Tar Harris, a middle-aged bachelor, who, squatting by the stock tank with Aaron and the two. lanky adolescent boys, leered at the insecure pubescent boys, grinned, and let fly from his mouth such off-color, unrepeatable sexual innuendoes, that Ted had been frozen and stunned.

But, Mennonite Elias King was a kind and warm man, generous and even fun-loving.

There had been only one episode where Ted, as a child, always believing everybody, accepting everyone's yeah and nay, wherein Elias King had nearly frightened Ted to death. It had happened this way.

When Ted was ten years old, he and Alden had walked from the Barb Yoder place centered in the woods to the Smith School, their very own grade school. There they stood among the growing sour dock and wild oats of spring, waiting for Esther Yoder to come by in her Model-A and take them on to Sycamore Grove for Bible school.

Another car, however, rolled jauntily along Highway Number Two ahead of Miss Esther, driven by none other than Elias King himself, elbow hanging out the driver's side window, breeze blowing his gray-streaked hair. The car sped past. Suddenly it stopped. Elias changed gears and backed up to the school yard he'd zipped past, to the two waiting boys.

"Well, what are you boys doing here?" queried Elias, a tease of a smile at the corner of his mouth.

"Why-uh-we're waiting for Miss Esther to come by and take us to Bible school," chorused the two boys simultaneously.

Ted lifted his foot unconsciously checking to see if the ground was under his feet. He wanted to make no mistake (this was in the days when they were outsiders).

"Well, now," said the smiling Elias, "You boys can't stand there!" Fear gripped their souls. Now what had they done? They'd tried to do this all just right, and here a Mennonite authority had spoken.

"Why not?" cried the panic-stricken boys, eyes big as saucers. "Why," said the chuckling Elias, "Don't you boys know you're standing on government property?"

Alden had handled it better than Ted did, being thicker skinned, and less gullible. Ted's day however was ruined, his foundation jarred, his security shattered.

Now coming up the sidewalk this April of 1947 was this very same Elias King, and he wanted to see Ted Yoder.

"Heard you were applying for schools, Ted," said Elias, encouragingly.

"Yes, well, yes-I am, or was," replied the startled Ted. "I've just received an offer at Dodder School for next year." Ted felt proud, accomplished, desired, and having something to offer.

"Well now," continued Elias King, "We have an opening right here in the community at Clearfork. Our board wondered if you would apply?"

Oh, heavenly bliss. Ted was transported. Already an offer in hand and a man (Mennonite, to boot) on his doorstep asking for his application. Blessed was he among men, for this truly was his day.

So Ted fetched one of his neatly done application letters, and the business of formally becoming a teacher continued.

By Friday of that week, Ted received a letter (handwritten, of course) from the school board of Clearfork School, a school smack-dab in the middle of the Mennonite community.

The letter allowed as how he'd been" excepted." Never mind the misspelled word. Ted knew he was accepted with a salary of $125 per month. Oh, hallelujah! Clearfork School was on a graveled road. Redeemed from the mud again!

Ted taught for five consecutive and wonderful years at Clearfork School with its bright, eager, and energetic children. Alden became a teacher the very next year accepting a job at Number Nine (without the engine). Number Nine School was less than three miles from Clearfork School. The Yoder boys had the world in their hand.

Following the five years at Clearfork School, Ted resigned to continue his education at Goshen College and Goshen Biblical Seminary in Indiana.

Alden who married nineteen-year-old Naomi Hershberger, the bishop's daughter, eventually changed from Number Nine School to none other than the Gunn City School two blocks down the trail from where old Aunt Louella lived. Oh, the flux and change of time and circumstance.

My days are like a shadow that declineth; and I am withered like grass. But thou, 0 Lord, shalt endure for ever; and thy remembrance unto all generations.

-Psalm 102: II, 12

22.

The Matriarch of Gunn City

Louella, bent as a shepherd's staff by the years, laid down her can opener, grabbed the can of salmon and shook it out, raking it with a fork as it spread into the cracked dish that had once been her mother's. She was reaching in the ancient pie safe for the crackers when she suddenly changed her mind. She decided to eat later. The smell of the salmon, her acrid fat flesh, and the moldy smell of old things mixed together in the small two-room house, a staleness she did not notice. Hand on her hip, which often pained her, she trudged over to the dusty parlor organ which was loaded with assorted papers, sheet music, and torn hymnals. Here and there family pictures had been displayed, as through the years she'd received them, stuck in the nooks and crannies of the ornate carved woodwork rising to the ceiling.

Staring straight ahead she surveyed her pictures. In a moment her tired and filmy eyes found the one she was looking for. Dora. Poor Dora. She reached for the faded picture as her elbow struck the Methodist Hymnal on the rack, toppling it to the floor. She sagged into the wooden sewing rocker that her mother had brought from West Liberty, Ohio, years and years ago. Staring at her sister's picture, she could hardly believe the news that she'd received. Dora was dead.

How the family had scattered. How devastating had been the

awful blows their family had received-her mother's death when Aaron and Ollie were so little and the added blighting and separation that occurred to thousands of families as a result of the Great War.

Tears began to flow through the creases and lines of her face, coursing down the dark skin. She could easily pass for an ancient Indian woman. Dora was dead. She'd known that, since widowed, Dora had grown more feeble. But not this! She'd noticed too that Dora had seemed so frightened of almost everything lately, so strained and fearful. When she and Aaron and Opel had driven over to Holden to visit her three months back, they had all been shocked at how Dora talked about her church. She'd leaned forward in her chair with a stark and frightened face, her hand tensely drawn against her cheek as she told them.

"And when I put my money into the offering plate, I heard the women around me snicker and whisper that it wasn't enough." The pain and hurt leaped from her eyes.

They hadn't known then how sick Dora really was, how distorted her feelings and perceptions were. The hardening of the arteries in her brain finally became so severe that the doctor had called her son in Iowa to come down and get his mother. She could no longer live alone. So poor, frightened, and troubled Dora who had once, years ago, almost stopped a revival with her giggling spell and through all her years was known and loved as a faithful Christian and devout Methodist, was transported to Iowa by her son. Here on their farm they would care for her, try to soothe her troubled soul.

She had not understood. Her paranoia grew by the hour. She had not been there a week when her granddaughter Ellen, an eighth-grade school girl, got up one morning and went out to the barnyard to help her father bring in the cows for the milking.

Sauntering along in the breeze and the lovely dew of the morning, a bit of blue cloth caught her eye. What was that over there in the stock tank? Approaching closer she saw something that resembled a towel floating in the middle of the huge water tank. Had the hired man taken a bath in the stock tank, leaving his towel behind? Well, she'd mosey over and fish it out. If it was a towel, she'd throw it in the wash.

Her steps were soundless as she walked through the deep pulverized dirt of the barnyard. She reached the stock tank. Her screams could be heard in the kitchen 700 yards away. A flock of blackbirds in the locust grove over by the pond stopped their morning songs and rose raucously into the air, a great black cloud, scattering in fright from the piercing cries.

In the water, Ellen found her grandmother's body, face down, bobbing and floating in the middle of the tank. Dora had found a tragic and final solace from the awful fear and terrors that had gripped her mind.

Louella wiped her eyes with the edge of her apron. She'd eat her salmon and crackers now. In the morning Aaron and Opel would come for her to take her to Dora's funeral.

The huge red sun was slipping down the western horizon as she forked away the salmon. Her mind wandered, thinking about Aaron's family. They'd surprised her, all of them joining the Mennonites that way. She could understand Ted and Alden, being surrounded by all those Mennonite young folks, but Opel and Aaron? That was a horse of a different color.

Oh well, she'd once been a Mennonite herself. Funny, she hadn't thought about them for ages, her Amish Mennonite forebears. Her mind wandered to a scene of her childhood, near Kalona, Iowa, where the wild roses grew along the fences, deep pink, blowing in the wind. She dozed off to sleep just as she began to hear the words of an old German song her father was singing: "I will sing with exultation, all my heart delights."

She was a child among the Amish. How strange it was that in her waking hours she was scarcely ever aware of the long forgotten land of her dreams. Iowa came to her in the night and with it the Sleeping Preacher, a plainsong, the Amish service, and, of course, wild roses on the fence.

A truck lumbered by, its wheels thundering in the chuckholes.

Louella awakened. She refocused her glazed old eyes as she looked through the dusty pane into the growing shadows. Was there time yet to go after the mail? Had she gotten it already, or hadn't she?

"Goodness, how time flies and how forgetful a body gets," she thought as she struggled to her feet. She waddled over to the organ and stuck Dora's picture back in a crack in the carving, rubbing away some dust as she pondered. "What'll happen to this organ when I'm gone? Hm-m!"

Somewhere deep within, she felt a twinge, not quite a pain

perhaps, but a twinge anyway. This organ was associated in her train of memories with a whole entourage of feelings. She knew that if she pondered long enough and dug deeply enough within them she would find the scars. Well now, how about Dora's grandson in Iowa? Hadn't she gotten a card from him once telling about his organ lessons at the university?

On the other hand, Aaron's oldest boy Alden was a gifted musician, could sing well, and played the piano exquisitely. The word and feel of *Mennonite* loomed into her being. "Oh yes, wasn't Ted, Aaron's youngest son off to Goshen, Indiana, attending seminary there? Yes, guess they'd have another preacher in the family," she thought. When Ted joined the Mennonites he bit hook, line, and sinker. Her mind continued. Oh well, nothing wrong with commitment. She'd had a lot of it too. Maybe, it was a Yoder trait. She'd liked it that Ted had remembered her, had written her about his girlfriend, Lydia. Maybe they'd come to see her if Ted ever got back to Missouri. But who knew? Young folks of these days scattered to the ends of the earth.

No. The organ and Mennonitism hadn't mixed well in her day.

Learned that lesson long, long ago. Yes. She rubbed more dust off the music rack. "Maybe I'll leave it for Dave, my great-nephew in Iowa. Didn't he write that he sometimes played the organ in the Methodist church?" She smiled, thinking about how nice it was if one pondered a bit how one resolved things.

After Dora's funeral, old Louella's bent body sagged even more closely to the earth, but her spirit was yet unwilling to relinquish her body. No longer able to tend to her daily needs, she'd tried a rest home which she experienced as a disaster. She needed her village and its friendly, warm, and caring people. She needed the sound of wind in the cedars and the sight of the tiny white frame Methodist church. She yearned for the touch and voice of her friend, Celia Carpenter, who like her, was alone in the world. They could minister to each other.

So Celia hired a car to take her to the rest home to get Miss Eller.

It'd taken them almost an hour to get the obese old woman down all the stairways and out to the car. By the time they'd managed to get her in the back seat, poor old Louella didn't have enough strength to sit up. She just lay on her side and smiled, feeling the bumps and curves of the road as the car took her home to her beloved Gunn City. She was warmed by Celia's caring and love. Together they'd make a respectable couple in their last days upon the earth. The death angel wasn't circling yet. Sounds of snoring rose up from her tired old body on the back seat.

The months passed. Alden and Naomi moved to the Ozarks to teach school and help build a Mennonite mission there. Ted, with his poetic and metaphysical bent had chosen to study at Goshen Biblical Seminary. One thing Louella did have to admit to herself was that her nephews certainly did take their church seriously.

With the aid of a walker, Louella eased herself back and forth through Celia's house. She liked it here where she could look out the front window or sit on the porch and see people she'd known through the years drive by. And better yet, there across the dusty graveled street stood the austere, little, white chapel where her father, Daniel Yoder, had preached. Over to the north about a block away rose gigantic cedars, still bowing low in the wind as if to protect an old and weathered building long gone. Celia Carpenter herself still trudged over to the pear trees with the broken branches in the back and filled her baskets with the fruit the trees faithfully offered, year after year.

During the Easter vacation of the spring of 1955, Ted Yoder and his fiancee, Lydia Zehr, drove back to Garden City. This was new country to Lydia, who had been born and raised in Mennonite communities in northern New York state. One of Lydia's first experiences outside of meeting Aaron and Opel, was the visit to see Aunt Louella in the funny sounding little town of Gunn City.

Ted and Lydia, standing on the narrow, wooden porch of Celia's house tried to prepare themselves for the visit. Ted knocked rapidly on the door. They heard rustling sounds, then the thudding of heavy feet crossing the floor toward the door.

"Howdy-do! Come right in!" Mrs. Carpenter greeted them, not giving Ted a chance to introduce Lydia. She held the screen door open with one arm while scratching her back with the other. The heavy fat quivered. Ted noticed the closeness of the air in the room as they entered. Against the wall stood an antique organ. Opposite it on the other side of the room was a dark-stained desk, top down, exposing small cubicles. "Two ancient pieces from the Yoder family," he thought.

"Mrs. Carpenter, I'd like you to meet Lydia Zehr, my fiancee," said Ted, bowing slightly and smiling.

"Why, how do, Liddie," smiled Mrs. Carpenter. Lydia extended her hand. "How do you do."

Old Arkansas-born Celia, rolling her bulbous fat from side to side, waddled through the room, words hemorrhaging from her mouth. They'd come to visit Aunt Louella, but Celia let the words fly like a sailor heaving bilge water from a sinking ship.

"Me an' Miss Eller jest been sayin' 'tis might nigh time fer you to be stoppin' in."

"How's Aunt Louella?" He felt that he needed to get that out first, otherwise there might not be a break in the wall of words.

"We been gettin' 'long jest fine, Miss Eller an' me. Sit a spell whilst I rid up a bit. Miss Eller's jest finishin' her breakfus."

"Eating pretty well, is she?" inquired Ted.

"Lan' sakes." Her face split into a broad grin. "Why, I thought I'd have to call in Nora Swish to get ' er stopped. She's done et two eggs, couple pieces of toast, three slices of bacon an' jest now finishin' it off with her second cup of coffee."

"Fine, glad she has an appetite," said Ted encouragingly. Maybe that was about all they had to live for, one wrinkled and broken down, the other a kind, but ignorant Arkansas widow. Eat and sleep. Sleep and eat, and Aunt Louella patiently awaiting death between the sleeping and the eating.

They heard grunting and straining sounds, squeaking of bed springs, and pounding of pillows. "We're all rid up now, ya come right on in and visit yer Aunt Eller."

"Thanks," Ted said, lifting himself from the rocking chair. Lydia followed as he entered the tiny bedroom with the sagging floor and the torn wallpaper. There lay Aunt Louella, white headed and stony faced, dark and wrinkled as an ancient Indian awaiting entry into the happy hunting ground.

Ted introduced his fiancee. Lydia extended a slender white hand, reaching out for the walnut-colored, wrinkled one wobbling up off the bed. Louella's face wreathed suddenly in smiles, truly glad for company.

"Did you folks have a nice Easter?" said Ted, hardly knowing where to begin. Before Louella could clear her throat for a reply, Celia had already begun.

"Why the neighbors brung in so much me an Miss Eller et 'till we might nigh foundered!" exclaimed nurse Carpenter. "The Aid brung in a chicken, Miz Hershberger an' Miz Pruitt brung in salads; pies and cakes come walkin' in here so fast me an' Miss Eller couldn't keep up!" Rolling against the woodwork, her face reflected heavenly bliss from the bounty "brung in."

"That was wonderful of your friends and neighbors," said Lydia, who'd hoped to get a chance to visit with Ted's interesting old aunt.

Heaving back the covers over Aunt Louella's feet, Celia continued. "Jest look 'ere. Look at them limbs. Your poor 0l' aunt didn't look like that, dyin' in that rest home. No siree! She's gained twelve pounds since I been feedin' her. Miss Eller ain't a' gonna' starve while Celia Carpenter does the cookin.' "

Ted looked at the heavy old leg and foot aimed at his face by nurse Carpenter. Wanting to gag, but getting hold of himself, he managed to say, "I'm glad you're taking care of her, Mrs. Carpenter."

"Look at them toenails." She heaved the foot higher. "Why, when I brung her home them toenails had growed so long they turned under her toes."

"They must have been rushed and crowded at the rest home."

Ted shifted his eyes. Lydia, however, stared straight at the foot. She had a stronger constitution.

"Why, I worked on them toenails for two days with a hacksaw.

Toughest toenails I ever seen. Started out with a paring knife and scissors. Had to give that up. Yes-ser! Worked on 'em fer two days with sandpaper and the hacksaw."

"You did a fine job." Ted appreciated the good work, but the details were getting him down. They'd be coming to the bedpan next.

"Ain't no bedsores either. When I brung Miss Eller here she had sores and scabs all over her poor limbs."

Ted was glad the window was open, letting in a breath of air, even if the window did frame the leaning outhouse, door ajar, a few steps beyond the porch.

"Mercee-eeeee!" exclaimed nurse Carpenter, dropping Miss Eller's foot. "Plumb forgot my beans!" Out to the kitchen she lumbered.

Aunt Louella, staring at Lydia, cleared her throat. She raised her shoulders to a better position in the bed. "You ever been to Iowa?" she said, still staring at Lydia.

"Why, no. No, I haven't been to Iowa. I do know quite a few people from Kalona and Wellman, though," replied Lydia in her soft voice.

"Used to live in Iowa," said the old woman, her eyes seeming to focus far of in some distant land.

"You were born in Iowa, weren't you?" said Ted, trying to get into the conversation.

"Born in West Liberty, Ohio. Came to Iowa when I was a tiny child, two, three or so." She pointed to the next room. "Those pieces came along. No, not the organ, but the secretary and the desk. Made by Amish hands in West Liberty, Ohio." She swallowed, her mind hung on some particle of the past.

Ted didn't know much about his family. Strange, wasn't it. He hadn't known his family had furniture made by Amish hands. Interesting though. He mused. Then turning, he looked at his pretty, blond Mennonite bride-to-be.

"Get that big box from under the bed," Aunt Louella began again. "I beg your pardon," Ted replied, not sure he heard correctly. "Get the box from under the bed," she said firmly.

Down on his knees, Ted beheld a lot of cobwebs and dust. Sure enough, there was a pasteboard coat box, the sides splitting with paper or trash. He began pulling it from under the bed.

"Well, what have we here, Aunt Louella?" He smiled as he placed it on the chair by her bed, just within her reach.

Her hand, wrinkled and brown, eased down, lifted the lid and dug through the contents. She seemed not to look at what her hand was selecting, as if her spirit guided her, or she could find what she needed through touch. "Here 'tis." She smiled and held up a faded picture. It was the picture of the "Red John D." Yoder farm home in West Liberty, Ohio. Lydia and Ted stared at the picture. Louella continued: "Your grandfather had thirteen brothers and sisters, all born there."

Wasn't it strange, thought Ted, that she wanted to talk about this past, all unknown to him, especially now, with Lydia here.

Aunt Louella raked through the box again. This time her fingers caught on a large piece of cardboard at the bottom. She fished it out. It was a picture that had been removed from a frame, obviously long, long ago. The portrait was of a plainly dressed, middle-aged woman, wearing small, old-fashioned, wire-rimmed glasses. Her black hair was parted in the middle. She smiled faintly, traces of Aunt Dora's smile.

" That' s your Grandmother Fannie Yoder," Louella said, eyeing Lydia who sat, prim and proper, but smiling, golden hair glistening through her net covering. "Your grandmother used to wear a covering," she said, pondering.

"Wasn't it strange?" thought Ted, "all of this coming out now."

These were topics he had never heard discussed among the Yoders. It was news to him. He never even thought about a grandmother who died so long ago. Why folks said it was when his father was only five years old.

"You can have the picture.'" Louella looked pleased. "The picture of your mother?" replied the surprised Ted.

"The picture of your grandmother," she corrected. "And the desk too."

"You mean that desk in the other room?" Ted was almost startled. "It's got secret drawers, false bottoms in some of 'em, though I don't remember which ones." Growing tired, she flattened herself down on the pillow.

"Why thanks! Thanks, Aunt Louella! Whenever we move into our own home, we'll hang the picture above the desk." Ted looked at Lydia. Both were smiling with pleasure. The desk would have to be scraped, sanded, and refinished. The picture could be matted and placed in an antique frame. It would fit the old desk perfectly. "Wonder if I can begin to get the feel of Grandmother Fannie Yoder," Ted thought.

Mennonitism was something he'd adopted with his brother Alden. If there was any trace of it here with Aunt Louella, he knew little about it, only that old Granddad Daniel Yoder had been silenced as a minister among the Mennonites. Aunt Louella never shared that at one time even she herself had been a Mennonite, baptized in the bend of the Clearfork Creek.

"Wish I could go back to Iowa." Louella looked off into the distance. "Would like to see where they lived," she added.

"Where who lived?" queried Ted.

"Uncle Chris and Aunt Mary. Uncle Noah, too. Did you know about Uncle Noah?" Her bleary eyes looked at Ted.

"Can't say that I do. Tell me about them." He settled back. This was interesting.

"Well, they were your great uncles and great aunt. Yes. Lived near Kalona. We all went to church together. Uncle Noah was called the Sleeping Preacher. He was your grandmother's brother." She swallowed.

Now Ted knew. One of his church history teachers had mentioned the strange phenomenon of a celebrated Amishman or the Sleeping Preacher, how even a doctor had stuck a silver pin deep into his leg and he hadn't even awakened. Somewhere there was a booklet of his sermons. Wonder whatever happened to him?

"Uncle Noah," she'd said. Did that mean that he was related to such a bizarre and unusual Amishman from the past? "That'd make this Noah Troyer my great uncle," thought Ted, as he pondered this new information. Oh, the fascination of family secrets.

"Look in the box again," croaked Louella, obviously growing tired, but intent upon the unfinished business.

"You want to look for something else?" Ted asked, staring at the old woman.

"There otta' be a little book. Yes, a little book of sermons. Sure I kept it. Published by the *Iowa Republican.*" She lifted her head, moistening her thick Yoder lips with her tongue.

So, Ted dug through the contents-old postcards with funny looking one-cent stamps on them, brown tintypes, small two-by-three-inch pictures of two young men in uniform. That would be Uncle Ollie and Aaron, his father. Ted was aware that he'd like to take more time with the contents of this box. Then he found it. A thin paperbacked volume, yellowed and tattered at the edges. The title was clear, however, as he lifted it through the collections from the years, *Sermons Delivered by Noah Troyer, the Noted Amishman, While in an Unconscious State.*

"Here it is, Aunt Louella." Ted handed it to her, hoping it wouldn't fall to pieces being transferred from hand to hand.

Old Louella lifted herself back up on her pillow again and beamed. "Why, yes. Heard him preach his sermon at our house in Iowa." Looking out the window at the countryside as if she were in Iowa, she began to reconstruct the scene. Lydia sat fascinated. Aunt Louella rambled on and on about how they were Amish then, the wild roses on the fences, the strange trances of Uncle Noah, his preaching in the language of the outsiders, and his moving prayers.

"Yes, your grandpa Daniel Yoder and Uncle Chris Warey

carried him into the house when he'd finished the service."

She lay down, silent for a moment, then turned to Ted and Lydia, smiling.

"Whatever happened to Uncle Noah, Aunt Louella? Do you. know?"

Silence continued. Then her aged, glassy eyes focused intently upon his. She licked her lips, preparing to proceed.

"Why, yes! Let's see-how did it happen? Only a few weeks after he preached in our locust grove between the barn and the house ... March 1886. Why, yes. Oh! It was sad." She looked out the window, obviously moved by some almost forgotten tragic event of the past. She turned her face back to them as she continued. "Uncle Noah was out in the backyard near the barn. Gonna shoot a chicken. Yes. Guess they had wild chickens, and company coming for dinner. Needed a chicken. I remember they raised big old fat Domineckers, spotted ones, good for roasting. Johnny, his youngest boy carried the gun. 'Twas loaded and ready. Uncle Noah wanted to teach Johnny how to shoot, but Johnny wasn't feeling well, or got afraid. Said he didn't want to do it and handed the gun over to his father. Uncle Noah said, 'Here, son. I'll show you how.'

"So he took the gun and aimed at the Dominecker by the fence.

Got aim and pulled the trigger. Old gun or sumpthin'. The blast blew out the breech screw, striking Uncle Noah just below the left eye. Drove so far into his head that the back of his skull was fractured. Lived only two or three hours after that."

There was silence at the end of the tragic story. They needed to go, but knew they would come again to touch roots with such an interesting past. Old Aunt Louella lay back on her pillow, obviously finished storytelling for the day. They bade her good-bye, then started for the door.

Celia followed Ted and Lydia out the door and down the crumbling walk toward the car.

"Why me an' Miss Eller's jest like sisters." Her tongue and fat rolled at every step. "When we took that trip to Arkansas, Miss Eller an' me had our pitchers took together. Jest like sisters." Tears were gleaming in her eyes.

She obviously needed a stroke of appreciation from Ted. How could he show his gratitude to this simple old Arkansas woman?

"I'm glad you had that experience together. You certainly do a fine job with Aunt Louella." Ted said, looking at her with the kindness he felt.

"She wants beige," Celia said, suddenly. She pronounced it as though it rhymed with *rage*.

"Beige? Beige what?" asked Ted, puzzled.

"When she dies, Miss Eller wants to be buried in beige. Jest like her sister Dora."

"Oh, a beige dress? Well that can certainly be arranged," said Ted, feeling slightly uncomfortable.

" An' a casket with innersprings," she continued. "Yes-ser, a body needs to be jest as comfortable dead as alive," said Celia with a serious, childish finality, not sensing any contradiction in what she'd just said.

"Those details can all be taken care of when the time comes," said Ted with careful reassurance.

Driving home to her parents' farm, he could still hear her words:

"Why I druther be buried in gunny sack myself an' see Miss Eller get took care of right, and buried proper. Yes siree! Celia's doin' all they is to do," she'd reassured them.

Indeed, Aunt Louella had a loyal friend and nurse in her last days upon earth. It was obvious that she was "doing more than necessary."

Likewise, give heed unto thyself, walk circumspectly, read the word, meditate upon its precious precepts, pray without ceasing, and in all things seek to be a faithful laborer in the vineyard of the Lord.

- Exhortation to a newly ordained minister

23.

The Ordination

It was inevitable that a sensitive, metaphysically bent youth like Ted would be ordained. Had he been born and reared as a Catholic or Episcopalian, he would have grown into the priesthood. Among the Jews, he'd have been a rabbi.

These people he'd grown to love were dedicated, committed to simple styles of living. The spirit of Christ was among them. Sins of the flesh were few and far between and when they were known, they were promptly attended to, though sometimes, perhaps a bit too harshly.

Though Ted would grow and change as he found his way through life, these kindly people and principles from this church would always guide him: nonresistance, love, and Brother Manasseh's "We ought to simplify our wants so that we might have more to give.

The autumn day of Ted's ordination was matchless in beauty. The great sycamores swept the deep blue sky, as if their topmost branches brushed the clouds. Ted loved country roads, the more undergrowth along the sides of them, the prettier he thought they were. On his drive to the church, wild asters, sunflowers, marigolds, and goldenrod interspersed with the shade of the osage oranges. It was as if nature itself made up for the austerity of the solemn service within the plain meetinghouse.

Most surprising of all, who should be present, sitting there smiling upon the front bench of the women's side, but Aunt Louella herself. With care and patience, the Zooks had loaded her into their car and brought her. Nursed back to creeping across the room in her walker, she'd insisted upon coming for the ordination of her nephew Ted. Even if he would not grace a Methodist pulpit, she'd honor him by her presence.

The ritual service of ordination began. There was the reading of the familiar passage from St. Luke, chapter ten, about the Lord anointing the seventy, sending them out by twos, "before his face into every city and place, hither he himself would come." Ted did not know that the old song he had requested had been a favorite of his grandfather, back in Iowa in the 1880s, and again was sung at Aunt Louella's baptism, long ago, down the road a ways where the creek bends.

I will sing with exultation. All my heart delights in God who brings salvation, frees from death's dread might. I praise thee, Christ of heaven, who ever shall endure. Who takes away my sorrow, keeps me safe, secure.

Ted, always touched in his inner being by sacrament and ritual, as well as soul-moving liturgy and music, opened himself to receive the blessings of the hour of his ordination.

Brothers Buckwalter, Troyer, Yoder, and Hershberger encircled him as he knelt before the congregation. He felt their warm hands upon his head. His spirit opened even wider to receive grace from the ordinance.

"Upon this confession and these promises which thou hast now made before God and these witnesses, I herewith, in the name of Jesus Christ and his church, charge and ordain thee to go and preach the gospel in its purity," intoned the full-timbered voice of Bishop Buckwalter.

"Continue thou in these things, for in so doing thou shalt save both thyself and those that hear thee. Amen."

Ted raised himself up from his kneeling position as the bishop extended to him his right hand and gave him the kiss of peace.

In April, following Ted's ordination, Aunt Louella died in her sleep one windy, dark night. Celia had to give up the friend and sister she'd loved. The village folk of the tiny church prepared for the funeral.

It fell upon Opel and Lydia to meet with the funeral director as family to make the necessary arrangements that related to Miss Eller's burial plan.

Ted had reminded them both of the importance of beige for her funeral dress.

When the proprietor of the funeral home paraded out the shrouds in beige, the choices did not seem at all appropriate to grace Aunt Louella's withered frame. The only one that was even slightly suited for the corpse of the matriarchal woman was the long-sleeved, beige lace. It was beautiful and expensive, but it was not Aunt Louella.

If old Louella could have risen from the cold slab that braced her body, she'd have shaken her head no at the elaborate beige lace. Never in all of her days upon the face of the earth had she worn anything faintly resembling it.

Opel, who was concerned about the money stretching and Lydia, who followed Anabaptist principles of simplicity, both cast their votes in favor of a simple, yet graceful dress for Aunt Louella. It was a navy blue, long-sleeved nylon, quite in keeping with the old woman's simple ways.

The next evening when Miss Eller's body lay in state, Ted, Lydia, and Opel were the first to arrive. The apprehensive proprietor met them in the vestibule of the funeral home. "I've got to talk to you, would you folks slip over here please." She looked ambivalent and afraid. Ted wondered.

"We had to change her dress."

"I beg your pardon," said Ted, not fully understanding. "Well," said the nervous woman, glancing down, "Miss Celia Carpenter arrived this morning. She said it would have to be beige." She looked up, as if she expected a scolding.

"Oh, the beige dress! Well that's all right, don't worry." Ted knew that Lydia and his mother had selected the blue. It had concerned him. Lydia though, had not fully understood its meaning and value to Celia who intended to see that Miss Eller was buried fit and proper, innerspring mattress, beige dress, flowers, and all.

"But that's not all," said the woman, "we had to switch caskets too." Lydia and Ted grinned. Opel stared straight ahead. What next?

"The beige didn't go with the other casket. I won't charge you any extra." She looked relieved. She'd given account of shady deals of stripping corpses and swapping caskets, and that some other poor cold body would get a slightly used coffin and shroud.

So Miss Eller was buried in state, the funeral at the village Methodist church. A Mennonite young couple, man and wife, sang one of her old favorites, "Lead Kindly Light," a song from her times and moods.

Lead, kindly Light, amid the encircling gloom, lead thou me on. The night is dark, and I am far from home, lead thou me on. Keep thou my feet; I do not ask to see the distant scene-one step enough for me.

Yes, God had led her, once a little Amish girl, now old and broken and in the pale of death, loved by the villagers as Miss Eller. The hymn continued, underscoring the hardness of life, its crags and rocky places, the lonely moors where one seems all alone, the torrents of accident, war, chance, fire, drought, and death. Yet it spoke of that eternal faith in union again with God and angelic faces that, once lost, now await on the farther shore.

Virgie Allen, one of Miss Eller's piano students from decades back, sat with hands outstretched above the keys of the first piano Ted had ever seen, back when he was seven years old. Softy, slowly, she played "One Sweetly Solemn Thought" as they sat in silence.

Aunt Louella, her beige wrinkled face and arms, her beige casket and her fabulous beige lace dress were highlighted only by wisps of her snow-white hair. Her body sank worn and wasted, like last years' wheat straw thrown on a haystack. The beige only confirmed that her remains lay in the dust of death. But she was buried in beige, nevertheless.

When they lowered the casket into the opened earth, Ted glanced at the names on the double tombstone nearby, "Daniel F. and Fannie Yoder." The dates were so long ago. What had this family passed on to him?

Glancing up at the dark green cedar at the foot of the grave, he saw a stick-and-mud bird's nest wedged in the branches. Bluebirds? he wondered. Bluebirds, of course. Through the years, the wind, the silence, and the blowing grass, the songs of bluebirds blessed this place.

The voice of the minister began. "Man that is born of woman is of few days, and full of trouble; he cometh forth like a flower and is cut down; he fleeth also as a shadow and continueth not. For all flesh is as grass, and all the glory of man as the flower of grass. The grass withereth and the flower thereof falleth away; but the word of the Lord endureth forever."

Three decades later, a fifty-year-old man turned from his office desk to the green beyond the window. He was still a Mennonite. He had ministered to the little flock at Sycamore Grove for four years in his youth. He had earned a doctorate and taught at two Midwestern universities. He had lectured on logotherapy at the University of Regensberg, Germany. Yet, he belonged here, here among those of the little flock as described by one of his mentors, Saint Augustine. *But as to us Lord, see, we are your little flock. Keep us in your possession. Stretch out your wings so that we may take refuge beneath them.*

Ted knew that no events would ever surpass those holy moments spent in that white meetinghouse nestled among the sycamores in the little glen by the creek. Aunt Louella had knelt there and received its baptismal waters. They still flowed, these waters. They coursed down over his soul and brought healing.

Acknowledgments

I express my gratitude and thanks to the following: To Neva White for her encouragement and assistance through her work on the Byler-Yoder genealogies, to Dr. Henry Troyer for his help with the ethnic language, to Alma Jantzi Steckley for her narration of the hysterics at church included in chapter 6, to John and Mary Gingerich for their assistance and help at the Kalona, Iowa, Mennonite Historical Society and Library, to Mary Katheryn Yoder for her help with some of the song lyrics, to Paul Schrock at Herald Press, Scottdale, Pennsylvania, for permission to quote both texts and lyrics, to Christie Dailey of the Iowa State Historical Society for permission to quote, to my wife, Lona Yoder, for her encouragement, to my typist, Jerry Marlin, and to my editor, Maynard Shelly.

James D. Yoder

Credits

Chapter 1. The sermons and prayers of Noah Troyer are from *Sermons Delivered by Noah Troyer, the Noted Amishman, While Sleeping in an Unconscious State. Daily Republican* Job Print, Iowa City, Iowa, 1879. The Felix Manz hymn, "I Sing with Exultation," translated by Marion Wenger, 1966, *Mennonite Hymnal,* Herald Press, Scottdale, Pa., and Faith and Life Press, Newton, Kans.

Chapter 2. Stanza from the 131st hymn of the *Ausbund,* translated by Henry Troyer. Bishop Conrad's table grace is from *Amish Society* by John A. Hostetler, 3rd edition, pp. 165-66. The story of Strong Jacob Yoder from C. Z. Yoder's *Genealogical Records,* pp. 97-99.

Chapter 3. Dordrecht Confession, 1632, from *Confession of Faith and Minister's Manual* by J. F. Coffman and J. F. Funk, Mennonite Publishing House, Scottdale, Pa., 1890. Texts for baptismal, funeral, communion, and foot-washing services are also from this book. The material about the Sharon church and the congregation and Sunday school in the Prairie Dale schoolhouse is from *The Mennonites in Iowa* by Melvin Gingerich, Iowa City, 1939, pp. 136, 137.

Chapter 5. The Daniel F. Yoder quote is from the *Herald of Truth,* August 1, 1896, p. 115. Reference to Cotton Mather's view on instrumental music in worship is from *Separated Unto God* by J. C. Wenger, Mennonite Publishing House, Scottdale, Pa., 1952, p. 205.

Chapter 6. Anabaptist hymn reworded in Dordrecht in 1570 concerning the martyrdom of two loyal Anabaptists is from *The Bloody Theatre or Martyrs Mirror* by T. J. Van Braght, Mennonite Publishing House, Scottdale, Pa., 1950, p. 900.

Chapter 7. Information about the World War I Draft is from *War, Peace and Non-Resistance* by Guy F. Hershberger, Herald Press, Scottdale, Pa., 1946, p. 230.

Chapter 11. Freiburg martyrdom of 1529 from *The Bloody Theatre or Martyrs Mirror,* p. 399.

Chapter 12. Letter from Maeyken Wins, Antwerp, 1573, from *The Bloody Theatre or Martyrs Mirror,* p. 982.

Chapter 13. Words of "Come, Ye Disconsolate" by Thomas Moore, 1816.

Chapter 14. Words of "Lord, Speak to Me" by Frances R. Havergai, 1872.

Chapter 15. Words of "0 Weary Wanderer" by John F. Coffman, 1883.

Chapter 16. Introductory poem written by the author at age sixteen, (1945). Story of Strong Jacob Yoder from C. Z. Yoder's *Genealogical Records,* pp. 9799.

Chapter 17. Opening quote from *The Shorter Catechism,* adopted at a peace convention held at Dordrecht, April 21, 1632.

Chapter 18. Words of "I Know Whom I Have Believed" by Daniel W. Whittle, 1883.

Chapter 19. Words of "My Sins, My Sins" by John S. B. Monsell, 1863. Words of "Wash Me, O Lamb of God" by H. B. Beegle.

Chapter 20. Words of "When I Survey the Wondrous Cross," second verse, by Isaac Watts, 1707. Words of "Christ in the Night He Was Betrayed" by Lowell Mason, 1830.

Chapter 23. Exhortation to a newly ordained minister from *Confession of Faith and Minister's Manual,* p. 80. Words of "Lead Kindly Light" by J. H. Newman, 1832.